THE GRAND SEA

Dedicated to my parents, David and Patricia,
for being the wind in my sails.
~G

Dedicated to my parents, Miriam and Michael.
Thank you for being a lighthouse during my
darkest storms.
~K

www.thegrandsea.com

TABLE OF CONTENTS

LIFE OF A *Pressman*

There was a young pressman, to Amrestir he
Did flee to avoid one more second at sea
By the edge of the blade did the pressman make rent
By the grace of the graves, and the sailors he sent
From the town, town, shipped out of town

In time, the poor pressman chased countless pursuits
But even bad seeds feel a need to make roots
T'weren't long til his hook snagged a catch, and beguiled
In the pressman's arms, soon enough pressed was a child
Settled down, down, merrily down

Well, his lass e'er fickle, she drifted away
Leaving pressman and babe, on their own now to stay
So those years dripped along, down the point of a knife
Too aware, for a child, this was no kind of life
Of renown, 'nown, little renown

When the pressmen of Amrestir flipped to the Press
The man found a talent for words and finesse
So caught in his writing, he never did think
As he lived by the pen, he would die by the ink
In the ground, ground, returned to the ground

The Merry Bower floated across clear skies and seas, heavy with the weight of her good fortune.

Captain Stan Lowry sucked in a fresh, briny breath from his position behind the wheel. Even with the new wealth of clams now packed in his cargo hold and his celebrating crew below, all the old sailor could think of was the rocking chair waiting for him by the fireplace back home.

"What'd I say about Ol' Brother Ron? The recycling business is hotter than ever!"

He didn't need to wait for home to feel the heat. Brother Fred was more smug than ever, strutting about the deck with a relit flame of holy righteousness. The Kei cleric swung his scrapper's pliers playfully in the breeze, rattish ears twitching with pride. Captain Lowry sighed, and pulled down his hat brim.

"Yeah, yeah, I can admit when I'm off the mark. Glad that detour by Warrack Isle didn't end up being a total wash for your sake. Had no idea the trade rates on spare Feo parts went so high these days."

"It hasn't been easy, lately," Brother Fred scoffed from behind his whiskers. "World's gone screwy, coddling the things like babes. We made them to work with no backtalk but a 'thank you', and now? Heard the governor of New Amrestir made one of 'em a blasted general! First the armor's running the armies, next the naval vessels are gonna run the navy! Probably give shipwrecks their own medals of honor soo—"

"Captain!" called Quartermaster Sandra. "There's some kind of… shipwreck, off the starboard bow!"

Dread filled the captain's head. He trusted his crew

with his life, more times than he'd care to admit, but they were like kids in a sweet shop when it came to picking out detours. Rolling his eyes, Lowry added an extra tally to his time left until landfall and blew a signal whistle for all ears present.

"Alright, then! At least it's not a government ship this time. Lads, do we really need to pick about in the detritus? We just got—"

"Plun-der!" the crew chanted. "Plun-der! Plun-der!"

Lowry sighed once again, and lifted his cutlass of authority above his captain's cap.

"Message taken, loud and clear. Never let it be said *The Merry Bower* passed on a chance to take scrap from everyone."

The junk ship drifted low in the water, coasting gradually within range of the supposed wreckage. Lowry was already flexing his doubts about a ship being left for lagan in an open stretch of ocean, and they doubled as he caught sight of it with his own eyes. Dismal and decrepit, the brig ship lay careened against a jagged islet, utterly packed to the gills with an unmistakable rainbow of rot.

"T-The Stagnance..." Brother Fred murmured, wringing a woven prayer shawl in his claws. "This is a grave omen. We should leave it be, sir."

The captain was more than ready to oblige, but a noise stayed his hand. Straining his senses, Lowry focused through the multicolored mush.

"Help me! Oh please, help me!"

The voice was that of a maiden's, tinged with hysteria and no small amount of terror. It caused every sailor on deck to pause and consider just how much further they could push their straining luck.

Jay, a young rigsman with but a sparse stubble of hair across his chin, whinged from the shrouds above.

"*Oughhh,* this sucks eggs. Can we go?"

Lowry shot the lad a look dirty enough to match the fetid ship. He'd gone along with quite a few morally questionable choices throughout their tour, but leaving a poor soul to decay away did not sit with him one bit.

"Everyone's been put off their plundering, then? Cold feet when you've got to put your own skin in the game?"

Brother Fred grimaced, turning to the captain with a spark.

"Stan, it's not worth it. She's already been forsaken by Mother Flame, we should just—"

"We can do one better than the blasted bint in this case," snapped Lowry. "If she can't lend a hand to someone in need, what's the point of all the praying then? Just torch anything that gets too clingy, Mr. Smoulder. Bring 'er in, I've a conscience to clean."

The Merry Bower reluctantly crept through the still sea until it could practically rub hulls with the lost dross. Captain Lowry stood by the edge, tapping the railing anxiously as he scanned the derelict deck for the mystery woman.

There she was.

She was beautiful, save for the horror distorting her features. Even amid the gaudy graveyard, the maiden glowed with an almost ethereal grace. She was like a warm harbor in a storm, a gift that Fred's Mother Flame herself could've laid before him. It might've also just been that she was the first lady he'd seen in ages that wasn't as salt-flecked and scabby as anyone else in his crew.

Captain Lowry unsheathed his speaking trumpet, and tried to push the terror in his voice under a sheet of bravado as it came through the horn.

"Ahoy, miss! Can you hear me? What happened to your vessel that you're out all on your lonesome?"

After months out on sea, the sight of a woman abandoned to evil in desperate need of a brave rescue felt downright fable-worthy to Stan. He could've sworn he even heard the soft melody of a flute on the wind as he called to her, but a good sailor knew to never put too much stock in lonely delusions.

"It–it happened all so fast!" she wailed. "One

moment, we were sailing to Amrestir, next the cargo hold is bursting with rot! Some of the crew and passengers escaped, b-but the rest of us—"

The woman could not finish her story, bringing a hand to her mouth to stifle a sob of despair. They were close enough that the captain could see faint tears pricking the corners of her eyes, dark as obsidian.

"Th-Those cowards left us to die! I had my husband with me, but he was—*hic*—lost as well. I've been waiting for someone to save me ever since this ship crashed. My prayers must've finally been answered, because here you are!"

Lowry looked across the faces of his crewmates to find a mosaic of fear, disgust, and suspicion. Sandra had a look across her blonde brow that was more murderous than the mushrooms.

"This is complete tripe. You're not seriously considering this, are you?"

Against the captain's better judgement, he was. Lowry had made a career off of trusting his gut when it came to leadership decisions, and the bulk of the wreck was twisting up his guts in more ways than one.

"Are there any lifeboats left on your ship, m'am?" he called, pointedly ignoring the protests behind him. "If you can get off and row, we can get you someplace safe."

"I… I would, but I'm in no state to row! I haven't eaten in days, I've barely the strength to stand."

Lowry could hardly argue, seeing how she slumped against the mainmast's base like a sack of flour. Her face was now a mask of fresh fear at the prospect of being left alone to her fate. Something in the captain's heart fluttered, and his mouth moved on its own.

"Don't worry, we'll send a boarding party over to retrieve you."

"What?!" Brother Fred flared up from behind him, voice sharp with disbelief. "May I remind you, that plague ship is nothing but bad news! Even if she isn't afflicted, we have no idea if the pox lays dormant within her!"

4

Lowry's gaze hardened as he met Fred's eyes.

"Are we to leave her to die, then? Doesn't that scripture of yours talk about compassion, humility, and all that?"

"Yes, along familial lines and brotherhood, but—"

"Just convert her later," Lowry reasoned, already slinging a grappling hook over his shoulder like a classical swashbuckler. "Look, if the bravery of my crew can't be relied on, I'll just have to take the initiative myself."

The Merry Bower was awash with groans, but Lowry was getting sick of the captain always having to capitulate. The mood of the maiden was the only thing that eclipsed his mind now, and her face was beaming with gratitude.

"Bless your kindness! I owe you my life, and more..."

Despite their gripes, the crew still had enough respect for their captain to not leave him hanging out to dry. As Lowry pulled his line taut, he was relieved to hear the whistling of other hooks to follow, and a hot sigh behind his shoulder.

"I suppose one leap of faith should be matched by another," Brother Fred relented with a flick of his tail. "Let's reel in your blasted prize, then."

With renewed vigor, Captain Lowry dragged himself across the expanse of sea, lost in his daydreams. Each tug along the rope sent a tug at his heartstrings, stirring thoughts of what form the mysterious maiden's gratitude might take. Dangling over the open ocean below, Lowry let his instinct take command of his hands until they finally clasped around a solid wooden railing. Courage filling his chest with each heave, the captain bravely swung his legs over the side, ready to be the hero of the day.

"Ahoy! We've come to—"

CRASH!

The timbers below crumbled like a soggy biscuit. Lowry collapsed with his legs caught between mouldering decks, now eye-level with the piles of rotting fungus littering the ship. He strained to pull himself upright, but something soft yet strong had snagged him from below. Even through stinging eyes and nostrils, he could see the caps wriggling of their own accord.

Lowry had heard his share of ghost stories over a pint, usually cooked up by Brother Fred. The Kei spun legends of sailors cursed to sail eternally, abandoned by the relief of Flame. He always took them as attempts by the Smoulder smelter to put the old drunks into funks, but the ghastly things now rising to engulf his loyal crew were far from imaginary. Worryingly, as he listened beyond the shrieks of his fellows, the music he had heard didn't seem to be imaginary either.

The girl was gone. Whether she'd been consumed by the monsters, a part of them, or some bizarre hallucination, there was no sign of that desperate damsel. Where she had once stood was a fetid mass of fungus and pitted iron, puffing away at an old tin flute. It warped and twisted above the deck into the rough form of a man, its broken helmet looming before Lowry like the ghost of their scrapped Feo profits made manifest.

"Avast, matey," it growled, gnashing the split tines of its visor like fangs. "Another fool, roused by the siren's call. Ye be too trustin', lad."

Lowry flinched, and readied to call for a retreat, when an iron grip clamped across his chin like a vise.

"Nah, yer not gonna be doin' that," the metal monster chattered. "While ye was busy oglin' our bait, we got some of our mates t'deal with that pesky rudder o' yers. Y'ain't gettin' out that breezy."

From his meager position, Lowry could glimpse the grotesque forms closing in on his collective crew. Brother Fred was preparing a ball of fire in his palms, but two tendrils across his ankles knocked the Kei down to Lowry's level. The Feo—the monster—scooped Fred's scattered pliers up from the deck, and waved them dramatically in its one distended arm. A judgemental hiss radiated from the surrounding abominations, gurgling in support of their

6

ringmaster as it shoved the captain back.

"Well I'll be, ain't even Snuffer's Day, and here be a gift! Usually me plunders are nothin' personal, but I can make an exception fer a crew o' scrap scalpers."

"*Anathema!*" Brother Fred shouted, straining against one of the brutish boogeymen. "You are a walking atrocity, not even worth the frame you've—"

Lowry heard something heavy whiz through the air, punctuated with a shrill squeak. Brother Fred laid crumpled on the timbers, clutching his gut as the tossed cannonball rolled across the deck.

The living nightmare laughed loudly, a harsh and guttural sound that scraped Lowry's ears like rusted chains over stone, as it patted what passed for a burly cohort's shoulder.

"Well lobbed, Rufus. There be some scrap fer ye, eh? Courtesy of The Rot Admiral!"

The color drained from Captain Lowry's face as the colors before him finally clicked into place. The Rot Admiral was a name that had haunted sailors in taverns across every shore. A harbinger of death and decay, it was said that his mere existence was the blame for all of the Grand Sea's woes.

"Now then," the Rot Admiral grinned. "We didn't just invite ye over fer some drinks. 'Tis the time fer gab, Cap'n to Captain. We've trade t'discuss."

Captain Lowry snapped to attention, finally finding solid footing on a topic he knew.

"Trade? What do dead men even need?"

"Lucky fer ye, not much. Ye get t'keep yer sorry hides, a gen-ro-city considerin' what yer usual trade be. We be wantin' yer vessel n' half yer rations fer ye to slag off. And because I be the better man here, I be lettin' ye scurry off with yer poachin' prizes. Savvy?"

There was a stillness across the shipwrecked deck as all present considered the offer.

"Even the booze?"

"...Half the booze."

Lowry felt the weight of the world across his back. The prospect of making a deal with the abomination felt equal parts comedy and tragedy. He'd dragged his long-suffering comrades right to the chopping block, and was now having to trust in the butcher's mercy. With a deep, foul sigh, the Captain deigned to meet the Rot Admiral eye-to-visor.

"Very well. We accept your… generous offer."

The thing tilted its head, and Lowry caught a glimpse beyond its maw.

"Aren't ye forgettin' something, chum?"

"…Thank you."

Stan, plundered of even his captain-hood, watched the ropes lowering their little lifeboats to the waves below. It was an ugly sight, but it beat having to look at the faces of his fellows. The wraith up top set them down next to the rest of his ramshackle fleet with a *sploosh* and a cackle.

"Quick tip: next time yer usin' yer head, pick the right one!"

8

Brother Fred, still wheezing into his robes, had murder in his eyes. Sandra was picking through the stacks of clams and cargo piling the dinghy, having patience for nothing else. Squirming for space between the shoulders of Jay and *The Merry Bower*'s former bosun, Stan wondered if the Rot Admiral had granted him mercy after all.

"...Well then. Still made a profit off this. Could've been worse, right?"

Pshhhhhhhhh.

They certainly had made a profit, and the boats hadn't been made to handle it. It was beginning to list, heavy with the weight of their own good fortune. There was ballast to be cast off if they were to make it ashore without sinking, and as Stan watched the eyes of the crew flip his way, he was beginning to get a sinking feeling already.

I should've gotten a better job.

9

CHAPTER 1
BEGINNERS

Eliza supposed, all things considered, that she was doing a pretty good job.

Being a waitress at the little Bouncin' Bean coffee shop made for a fairly unremarkable living in the vast scope of the whole ocean, but the young woman could think about ten thousand worse careers in the island city of New Amrestir. It might've played host to some of the rudest customers in a city already composed of scoundrels and entrepreneurs, and her boss Toni wouldn't give up a free drink if you wrung it out of him, but it still beat working at a tavern. Marginally.

Coffee, though not as vital to a sailor's diet as the stronger options on tap, still brought countless movers and shakers in for their rations of black gold. The first few months of Eliza's employment had been enjoyable at times, doling out eye-openers to stray sailors suffering from their decisions the previous night. Yet New Amrestir did, as it had always done best, grew far beyond its means. While the city festered beyond its natural borders, the docks poured forth with new cargo and commerce and Eliza now found her mornings swamped with the thirst of tourists, sailors, and merchants alike.

The kettle whistled by the back wall, the ever-present chatter of the Amrestir Audience rising around it like a chorus. Eliza watched the myriad flocks of life from behind the Bouncin' Bean's counter and company apron, both barriers between herself and the public in their own ways. The shop's door chime rang through the early-shift air, snapping Eliza's gaze upwards. Her attention rose, and her eyebrows followed suit as she spotted exactly who, or rather what, was walking in.

A Feo had entered the Bouncin' Bean, all on its own. Eliza peered over to check if it was bringing in fresh supplies, but there was none to be had. The tall figure forged of brass carried nothing but a tattered old coat, contrasted by a brand new tricorn hat perched on its round head. Someone had even punctuated the fashion statement with a gaudy feather shocking from the brim, a combination that Eliza couldn't imagine to be anything but a bizarre practical joke. She looked around to see if any of the other patrons were having a laugh at the poor thing's expense, but none of them seemed to be in on it either.

It said nothing. It stood rigid as a fireplace by her counter, flame crackling away with its visor staring straight ahead. Eliza tracked its line of sight to the brass kettle screeching on the flame, and wondered if the Feo felt like it was looking into a mirror. The silence was curdling, and it was starting to turn the air sour.

"...Can I help you?"

The Feo creaked for another silent beat before finally breaking its stillness.

"Is this a 'coffee shop'? Thank you."

It spoke with the croak of a horn with pops of embers at the edges. Eliza had to choke back on a laugh at the question despite herself, seeing as how the shop's sign illustrated with beans hopping into a pot was still in line of sight from the window. The intense brewing aroma that filled the air should've been enough of a hint on its own, at least for someone with a nose, but she supposed the Feo didn't have much sense in that category either.

Eliza rattled her tangle of a hairdo and reined herself back to the Employee Mindset, as Toni had drilled into her head.

"Yyyyyyeah. Welcome to the Bouncin' Bean, just like it says on the sign."

"...I can't read. Thank you."

11

A wave of snickering washed across the customers, catching Eliza in a riptide of guilt. Like all Feo, there was a baked-in expectation that any response was to be answered with a hearty 'thank you', but there was no genuine gratitude to the voice that Eliza could hear. She gave the metal construct her best customer service smile and a welcoming hand wave, doing her best to salvage her sale.

"Well, I'll be glad to share the menu with you, pictures for the less-than-literate. Are you... looking for anything specific?"

The Feo tilted its bulbous head to the chalkboard menu above the counter, as though it could understand any of the day's specials. Eliza tracked its gaze across the options until leveling on an illustration of a frothing white mug beside a bottle of booze. It pointed, like a child picking out a new toy.

"Does that have alcohol?"

"Yeah, that's a 'Milk Punch'." Eliza nodded. "It's a mix of coffee, cream, sugar, and rum. I can add spices to it too, but that's an extra charge."

"I'll take that then. Thank you."

Eliza was grateful for the chance to break what could charitably be called eye contact with its visor as she jotted down the order on a scrap of paper.

"Will that be to stay, or to go?"

Toni, industrious as he was hygienic, had come up with the brilliant idea to serve coffee in paper cups coated in wax for clients on the go. Eliza stood by her position that the temperature of the beverage would simply melt the outer coating of wax, to which Toni retorted to shut up and get back to wiping down the tables. The problem went double for someone whose core temperature alone could probably ignite the cups themselves, but it was clear that she wasn't the authority in this case.

The Feo swayed like a mainmast at rest, giving serious thought to such a simple question. Eliza wondered if she would have to snap it back to reality again when its visor lit up with inspiration.

"To go!"

"Great, great!" Eliza sighed, with a breath that could've filled a sail. "That'll be five shellings."

With mechanical precision, it produced a collection of finely patterned shells out of its coat, placing them one by one on the counter as though they were made of glass. When all five were accounted for, Eliza handed the Feo its cup of hot bean juice.

Eliza smiled. "Have a nice day."

"Thank you," it said, genuine gratitude finally making its way into the words.

With that, Eliza turned around, prepared to forget about the customer as quickly as any other she'd dealt with.

"...You have nice hair."

The compliment hit her like a brick to the stomach. Eliza had patrons croon honeyed words to her before, usually terrible attempts at flirting only tolerated because of the tips they gave her. Out of all of her years working at the Bouncin' Bean, this was the very first customer to

13

compliment the rat's nest that was her hair with sincerity, all the more galling considering its own sorry baldness.

Eliza spun back around, feeling an inexplicable need to attach a compliment to the Feo's order.

"Um, thanks... I like your hat."

If a Feo could look excited, this one certainly did. It reached up to tug at the rim of its tricone, going out of its way to show off.

"You do? I bought it yesterday, thank you!"

Eliza didn't mean to lie, but she nodded all the same. With a newly-wound spring in its step, the Feo clattered back outside with its order in hand. Only when the bell jingled did Eliza breathe again, the rest of the world rushing back to full clarity. She stared at the door, wondering what in the Grand Sea had just happened.

"Ey, stay sharp, Liz!"

Eliza startled from her sink at the sound of Toni's shout. She'd been too lost in her washing to watch the door, but the Bouncin' Bean's freshest customer was impossible to miss.

The Feo had entered their establishment again, this time with two fresh feathers flapping from its cap. As it clomped across the coffee shop floor, Toni's brows raised with the volume of its footsteps.

"*Hrmm...* gonna assume that's the one you meant?" he whispered, not quite quietly enough.

Eliza nodded mutely, eyes locked on the accessorized automaton with a mixture of fascination and apprehension. She gave Toni a lingering glance, then built up her strongest serving smile to face the faceless fellow.

"Welcome back."

"Ahoy again!" the Feo rumbled, crackling with cheer. "I really liked your coffee. May I have another Milk Punch, to stay this time? Thank you."

Eliza was still loading her reply when Toni beat her

14

to the shot with his signature flavor of charm.

"You even get anything outta drinkin' coffee? How's that s'pose'ta work?"

Eliza shot her boss a look that could've sliced limestone. Of all people, he was the last person she figured would make a fuss over a customer's purchase. If the Feo had felt any offense at the question, it didn't show.

"No, but the alcohol is still nice. Helps stoke our flames, and the coffee gives a nice smokiness. If there's trouble in any way, I can compensate for it. Thank you."

Pouring liquid coffee on a fire didn't sound like a smart idea to Eliza, no matter how liquored up it might be ahead of time. Before the words could travel from her thoughts to her throat, Toni's hand settled on her shoulder like an unwanted parrot.

"Makes sense to me! Liz, take care of its—"

"His," the Feo corrected.

"—His order, alright? I got beans to count."

The brass man stood breathless at the counter, as if he had any other option. Eliza tried to get a grasp on his expression, but the slotted visor was unreadable even with her lessons in letters. His metal was worn, pocked with sea spray and rust. It didn't take the salt of a sailor to know one, but Eliza wondered how much the ratty coat over his shoulders had actually helped in keeping him ship-shape.

"Soooo, you're new in town? Didn't think to ask last time, you seemed eager to order."

The two feathers swayed like Kei ears as the globe that counted for his head bobbed.

"Yes! The path was long and uncertain, but led to this place all the same. I didn't know what to expect, even with all the tales I'd heard the sailors spin."

"Well, is it everything you hoped it to be then?"

"It is!" he cheered with an ardent nod. "Thank you for asking!"

Eliza sighed. Tourists always brought the worst in from the waves, but this one had at least brought his manners.

15

"That's good to hear. I—"

"What do you think of it?"

While Toni tended to the percolators by the back wall, Eliza had to take a moment to filter the Feo's grounded question through her ears.

"...What?"

"You've been on this island for a long time, yes?" the Feo wondered. "How do you feel about it? Living in the city, creating these drinks, serving the public?"

Eliza crossed her arms over her apron in thought, wondering if it was kinder to tell Feo the truth or a happy lie.

"A job's a job," she settled on with a shrug. "Pays for the basic needs, keeps me free from being shuttled off to some lousy raft in the middle of the sea."

A beat passed, and Eliza remembered exactly where she lived.

"A smaller one, at least. In any case, it's fine. Working here takes up a lot of my time, but it's not my whole life, y'know?"

The Feo's glow dimmed, his unseen smile fading away.

"I don't know. My job was my life for as long as I've been... well, me. Now, I find myself here, with a new lease on life and a lifetime's worth of government IOU's I was apparently owed. I met plenty who'd sailed to the edges of the ocean to get what I've got now, but I don't know where my own tide is taking me..."

The Feo trailed off like the last notes of a dirge before a new spark popped up from within.

"Heh, well, suppose the tides pulled both of us here, didn't they?"

The morning rush was rolling in behind the metal man, which meant it was too early for Eliza to be digging into the weeds of her life's choices. Still, the timbre in the Feo's voice touched something in her, even if it might've just been the bass vibration. It was the gravity of the statement that deserved more than the blank stare she was

16

pinning him down with.

"...You mean in the world? The city? Or right here, right now, with me, on this shift?"

"You're not going to be right *here*, right *now*, on this shift much longer if you don't make his friggin' order and get back to work!"

Toni's shout snapped both of them back to the present. Eliza gathered herself again and scribbled out a quick receipt.

"Er, sorry about that. You can sit anywhere, I'll bring the coffee to you."

Eliza rushed off to get down to business once more, balancing the brews and prepping the pours. With a new Milk Punch ready, Eliza turned back to find that the Feo hadn't budged from his spot.

"I said you could sit anywhere."

"...I couldn't decide which seat I wanted."

Eliza was starting to feel more like a nanny than a waitress. However, she was in the customer service business, and he was in more need than most of the customers stewing in the queue. Picking up the tray with one hand, she used the other to motion for the Feo to follow her. She led him towards the back of the shop to a little table tucked away in the corner, right by the window overlooking the streets.

"Here, this is where I sit during my breaks. Best spot in the house."

"Oh!" he startled, hands running across the tabletop. "Thank you!"

Eliza set the pot and cup down and left the Feo to his drink, scuttling away to her waiting tickets before he could pry any deeper into her psyche. As she half-listened to the orders coming in, she couldn't help but glance back to that odd galvanized gentleman staring into the steam of his cup. At one point, he caught Eliza's trailing eye and gave her a little wave of his hand, coaxing a smile out of the waitress.

How cute, she thought, giving him a wave back.

17

The next time she turned around, the only remaining sign of the metal customer was the five shellings he'd left on the table. There wasn't much of a question in Eliza's mind on whether he'd be back; it was just a matter of when. If he stayed consistent with having a new feather every visit, she wondered if he'd arrive with the whole bird in tow one day.

Amazingly, Eliza only had to wait one more day for her prediction to come true.

As though the Feo hadn't made himself obvious enough already, he was now being trailed by a tall-tailed peacock. Unlike the Feo, who trodded as though afraid he'd break the floor with every step, the Ave strode in with an air of confidence as if he had been here a hundred times before.

Eliza would've remembered if he did. Ever since Amrestir's official SpritFlit branch had abandoned the roost years ago, the only Ave that usually stuck around the city were those too grubby or plain to make it in Aveila. The sight of a proud peacock like this, feathers trailing like a regal robe, would've made a note in her memory, if not her paycheck.

With pad and quill in hand, Eliza approached the Feo and Ave at their chosen table, walking in on the tail end of a conversation.

"...all this money to waste on coffee, and you're still wearing that rotten coat? Smells like you washed it in chum and sea cabbage!"

Whatever smells the Feo was lugging about with him, Eliza was thankful for the Bouncin' Bean's natural armor of aroma. As she stepped into their personal bubble, the Feo's helmeted head snapped around, a triad of feathers now flowing from his cap.

"Welcome back, I see you brought a friend this time."

18

The peacock turned his attention towards her, a smile spreading across his beak.

"So, this is the reason why you've been plucking me bald," he sniffed, extending his pinion feathers in greeting. "My name is Pauvus: Pauvus Julius Arlecchino III in full, but to friends it's just Paul. For the time being, he still qualifies."

Eliza reached out and took her best shot at shaking the wing. Something about the Feo seemed to be attracting customers with actual manners to the shop for once, and she was planning to relish it.

"It's nice to meet you. Mine's Eliza."

A realization dawned on the waitress when her eyes flickered towards the Feo, who was watching the interaction with rapt attention.

"You know, I don't think I ever got your name. Er, do you have a one, or—"

Pauvus let out a dramatic gasp at Eliza's question. She cringed, thinking the bird was offended on his friend's behalf, before noticing that it was directed at the brass construct himself.

"You daft brute! You've never introduced yourself to this young lady?!"

The still-unknown Feo did an impressive job at looking ashamed of himself, sinking into his armored body.

"It's Nemo," he muttered into his collar.

"I apologize for my friend," Pauvus said with such an air of sincerity that Eliza got the feeling he had done this before. "As you can tell, he doesn't get out of his shell very often."

Eliza hoped that she didn't look as embarrassed as she felt. She had to admit that Nemo was growing on her like barnacles on a ship, and it didn't feel right to start poking fun at him. Lifting the quill once more, she trained her attention on her work.

"It's fine, really, he's one of my more pleasant customers. Speaking of, what can I get you, boys?"

"I'll have a latte," Pauvus chirped. "Plasmotic

blend, with light Lefanti cream and a Tephra spice topper."

Eliza may have been literate by New Amrestir standards, but trying to track Pauvus' leviathan of an order was an ordeal. She scribbled out her shorthand, and pulled her eyes back up to the Feo.

"Uh-huh, got it. And I'm guessing the usual for you, Nemo?"

Calling the Feo by his true name felt like a spark on Eliza's tongue. Nemo's visor glowed hot at the words escaping her lips, and Pauvus croaked out a chuckle.

"Oh my! Looks like you've stoked his fires quite a bit!"

Eliza heard a crack, then the sound of Pauvus swallowing a squawk. Nemo did his best to pretend he hadn't nearly snapped the bird's leg in half, while the waitress hid a laugh behind her notepad.

Somewhat reluctantly, Eliza went on with her business. Bringing orders, cleaning up trays, wiping down tables, all things she was well equipped for. It pulled her back into the comfortable monotony of the working chump, at least for a little. While attending to a spill from an uncoordinated Ibi fellow with pincers not built for holding a mug, she couldn't help but pick up on the continued complaints of Nemo's feathered friend.

"And the nerve of my parents to just... cut me off like that! Practically clipped my wings! Don't they care for my wellbeing?! I can barely pay rent as it is!"

"It must be nice having parents. I wonder if she has nice parents."

Eliza looked up at the Feo's baffling thought, in time to see the Ave slump in his seat.

"Bud, you've gotta simmer down. I get it, you just got out of a floating coffin for the first time, but you're not gonna get anywhere bearing down like that. There's more important things to worry about... like me!"

A bell from the counter signaled the next order. Eliza had to admit that Pauvus did have the taste of a very important person, even if she was starting to doubt he had the finances of one. The tall flagon glistened with fresh spice, making Nemo's Milk Punch look like swill in comparison.

"Here you go, lads, made to order. Trust all is well?"

Pauvus made a valiant show of twisting his startled jolt into a cough, smiling with practiced poise.

"Perfect! Much appreciated, friend. Of course Nemo's good for payment, he was kind enough to offer. Quite well-to-do with all those government kickbacks. Isn't that right, hot shot?"

Eliza expected to hear another sickening crack following that statement, but it never came. Instead, she saw Nemo enthusiastically nod in agreement, his three donated feathers bouncing along. Pauvus returned the nod with a sage one of his own.

"Hard-working and flush with clams. It's a wonder you can make it out the door without women tailing your tassets."

Eliza covered her mouth in time to stifle another laugh. Was he being sarcastic or—

No, he's not trying to—

"Let me know if you guys need anything else!"

She made for a hasty exit, but not hasty enough to miss Pauvus' closing remarks.

"Not bad, eh? Dad always said I'd make a good salesman."

Eliza made sure not to go near their table again until it was time to give them the check. Thankfully, it sounded like they were on a branch of conversation completely separate from her own roots.

"You know, I heard someone yelling outside that tailoring shop in the Khuloct District. Sounds like they're trying to get their hands on some new workers, if you're still looking."

"Oh yes, what a splendid idea!" Pauvus hissed, leaning across the table until his beak was nearly touching Nemo's brass head. "Only, there's one teensy, little problem: no hands!"

Eliza put an end to their bickering with the slap of a bill on the tabletop.

"Aaaand here's your check. Have a fine rest of your day."

Nemo took a gulp that caused his visor to sputter, while Pauvus lapped up the remnants of his special order. As Eliza drifted off to deal with the backlog piling up behind her, her ear perked up to another fresh squawk from their table.

"Cripes, Nemo, leave the girl a tip! It's common courtesy, have some class."

"Oh, thank you. I suppose I do have class, now."

Clink. Nemo dug into the crook of his coat and smacked a stack of shellings onto the table. Eliza counted ten little patterned shells, which even for Pauvus' exotic tastes was going a bit overboard.

"Nemo, you don't need to tip that—"

"Nonsense!" Pauvus stepped in, waving a wing

dramatically as the two rose from their spots. "You've given us excellent customer service, and this hollowhead hasn't even made good on one order! Least a couple'a gentlemen could do."

"Mmmhm. And is that the *gentleman's* cut?"

Pauvus' wing returned to his side, pockets now two shellings heavier. Eliza smirked at the bird while Nemo obliviously busied himself with tidying the cups.

"Payment for my feathers," the Ave whispered conspiratorially. "Man's gotta make a living, right?"

Eliza didn't even bother. From what she'd managed to eavesdrop on, in spite of his confidence, the bird needed all the help he could get. Completely ignorant to their exchange, Nemo pivoted on a heel to face her.

"Guess we'll be heading out! Thank you."

"You two come back anytime now." Eliza's eyes drifted over to Pauvus with a knowing look. "If you can afford it, that is."

Pauvus' head backed away from atop his neck, and the rest himself eventually scuttled off towards the door. Eliza waited for the two to pass the doorway before allowing the smile to creep back to her cheeks.

She'd been sucked into the whirlpool conversation between that Feo and Ave, and for a moment, she'd gotten a peek between the cracks in Nemo's armor. There was something beyond the hollow shell on the other side, and every glimpse she'd managed to catch just drew her in more.

Even in his brief absence, Eliza felt a draft in the shop, and wished he'd return to keep it warm.

CHAPTER 2
REHEARSAL

Life outside the Bouncin' Bean, as little of it as Eliza got to enjoy, was burning hot.

The Proxima Port, New Amrestir's primary hub of culture and commerce since its earliest days, cooked along in the usual stew of consumerist chaos under the shadow of the great Kindling Lighthouse. It was a place for sailors, salesmen and scammers alike, all the sharpest that the Grand Sea had to offer. It was also about the last place that Eliza wanted to spend her time on a rare day off, but the mid-day bargains right off the barges were enough to risk an accidental keelhauling.

She remembered a time, back before Amrestir had become 'New', when the port's boardwalk traffic was dominated by fishmongers and tavern keepers. As a girl, watching the incoming harvest of the Grand Sea had been the closest she'd ever gotten to stepping beyond her own shores. With pop-up shops now caking the port like barnacles with their international wares, Eliza felt less of an urge than ever to venture out into a world already throwing itself at her feet.

Advertisements promising solutions to life's woes dazzled above exotic storefronts, tacky and impersonal as a fish hook. There was fresh food being hocked on all sides, though in New Amrestir you had to take 'fresh' with as many grains of salt as the food was packaged in. Even so, Eliza could never be thankful enough that actual meat and produce was available to buy, considering how much of her childhood diet had been green only thanks to creeping mold.

Drifting past stalls of beets, urns, and entrepreneurs waging psychological warfare for her well-earned wages,

Eliza noticed a commotion coming from under a decorated tent. Amid the bustle was a trio of familiar feathers waving from atop a brassy dome, and a few dozen copies flicking impatiently beside them.

"Nemo, look at that, wouldja? I think those are—"

"Gold? Why yes it is, my good *oiseaux!* Miracle gold, freshly harvested from Fríasa! Each and every piece is artisan-set with unparalleled craftsmanship!"

New Amrestir, as a rule, was not the sort of city where people greeted each other with open arms. It was a rare thing for Eliza to step out of her bubble of solitude and spark a conversation. She spent enough of her time dealing with crabby customers all day, and even the forced pleasantries of an above-average outing were enough to make her wish she had a shell of her own to scuttle into. Yet as she stood among a rushing crowd, unable to tear her attention away from the Feo and Ave, a stray thought popped into her head.

Go say hi.

The peculiar duo was growing larger, and it took a moment for Eliza to realize her feet were on the same page as her brain. They'd already taken her to the edge of the curb by the time she could put her second thoughts into action, until she was close enough to read the shop's sign promising *'World Claff Kraftsmanship'*.

Pauvus, growing bored with being part of the Audience, had spotted Eliza first. She caught what looked like a smirk from the Ave before he patted Nemo's back with a wing.

"Well, this is a bit rich for my blood, at least for now," he squawked, wiping something regretful back onto the Feo's coat. "I'm off for some'a those tephra-roasted nuts. Don't wait up!"

"Wh— Hey! Wait!"

Nemo spun to follow Pauvus skittering through the crowd, and Eliza watched him lock up in real time as his swivel reached her. The Feo was clearly looking for his words, but the huckster behind the counter was already winding back his pitch.

"*Salut, mademoiselle!* May I interest you in a ring, or perhaps a barrette?"

The shopkeeper got a good look at Eliza's frizz and quickly retreated from that front. He scooped up a delicate chain from the table without missing a beat, letting the large blue sapphire dangling off its end glitter.

"Better yet, how about a necklace? This would look beautiful on you!"

Eliza nearly scoffed. She didn't need to be a scholar to get a read on a grift, and this one was bolder than most. There was more gold on display than in all the dreams of New Amrestir's sailors, a metal known to be so scarce it may as well have been more legend than history. Among all the tempting trinkets and baubles dazzling in the daylight, the greatest temptation she'd felt to make a purchase had been from the roasted nuts Pauvus was haggling over on the next block.

"Sorry, but I don't think I could afford any of that. I'd be surprised if anyone here could, honestly."

"It's not even real."

Nemo had finally chimed in, ringing with a fresh tone of confidence. Ignoring the salesman's sputters, he gestured towards óne of the many rings littering the table. It had the same rough color as the rest, though it wasn't particularly shiny in the sun.

"See that tarnish? Pure gold doesn't do that. It's probably just polished brass."

The gathered Audience was already spewing gossip like a fountain; if you couldn't trust a Feo on metals, what could you trust it for? Eliza leaned in to inspect, and the salesman pulled the ring away in turn. Muttering what she assumed was a swear, the man meaningfully scraped a set of his pliers across the counter.

"How about I test that little theory, and make that head of yours into a cauldron?"

The Feo didn't have a comeback for that, too fixated on the pliers and their implication. Normally, Eliza would've done all she could to put as much distance between herself and the spectacle as possible, but something in the vendor's smug snarl brought her own head to a boiling point. Planting her feet firm, she braced herself for the national pastime of New Amrestir: arguing.

"Hey, don't take it out on him because your bluff got called!" Eliza shot back, making sure her voice was loud enough for other customers to hear. "As if someone who had all that treasure would be hocking it out of a dump like this. Sign's written like your kid did it for a school project. Here's a quick lesson, 'craftsmanship' has a 'C' in it. Like 'con', hm?"

Eliza may not have been the window shopping type, but the indignity in the jeweler's face made the whole trip worth it. She left him to be devoured by the questions of a ravenous Audience, and pulled Nemo by the sleeve away from the encroaching mob.

"…You didn't have to do that for me. Thank you."

"Oh, no 'thank you's are necessary," Eliza insisted, wiping her hand off on a torchpole. "My dad was with the Press as part of the advertising committee. That sorry display was an insult to his legacy."

A memory of her father hunched over various bottles and shades of *'Kindling Credible Inks'* sparked in Eliza's mind, but she snuffed it before it could burn her again. Shaking off the cobwebs of nostalgia, she gave Nemo's shoulder a firm shake.

"But hey, you put that chump in his place too! Fooled just about everyone, but couldn't fool you. How did you know about the gold and brass?"

"Well!" Nemo brightened, a new gleam rippling on his visor. "It's not a surprise, considering how few have seen the real deal, but I have first-hand experience with both. I was on… Apologies, I don't mean to ramble."

Bobbing along to a less hectic stretch of shops, Eliza could see another layer through the Feo's rigid exterior. There was a fire in there roaring like no common stove, and she would hate to snuff it out now.

"No, I'd love to hear the story behind that. What, you and your crew plundered some booty?"

"Not that time, no. It was an escort tour, bringing one of the high-rank Smoulder clerics up by the Lunemar Skerry. Brother… Doug, I think it was. A spiritual retreat, and it called for fashion in full force."

Nemo was weaving his tale with both hands, drawing the eye of more than just Eliza. Scattered shoppers from around the port were beginning to take notice of the odd conversation, yet Eliza found herself too curious to feel self-conscious.

"Part of the ceremony included transporting a relic, wide as a dinner plate and bright as the sun. Wore it around his neck the whole time like nothing could touch him. Not that anyone dared, what with those paladins crowding around all the time, but it had the crew in conniptions for weeks after. All arguing over what they'd do with that kind of wealth, and what they'd be willing to do to get it."

"I feel for them," Eliza snorted. "But, what about you?"

"Me?"

"I mean, aside from coal and fancy coffees, what does the man who doesn't need anything buy? You're in the shopping hub of New Amrestir, what're you looking for?"

Nemo drifted closer to a stand cluttered with knick-knacks, plucking a little ceramic crab from a shelf. It was clearly designed to hold something in its upraised pincers, but for the life of her Eliza didn't know who would buy such a thing.

"Paul's trying to get me used to 'civilized life'. Apparently, shopping is a big part of it, but I don't know what's so civil about people tearing at each other's throats like animals over it. Still, this is 'the best spot in the western seas', according to my fellows, so I figured that's what I'm meant to be wanting."

"Well that's them. What do *you* want?"

Nemo shuffled in place, gaze now directed to the bustling throng of frantic customers passing them by.

"...I'm looking for fashion. I know, that sounds like a joke, but it's true. I heard clothes can make the man. The feeling of being just another person in the crowd, while still being your own person... It's why I got this hat! First thing I ever bought with my own wages!"

As the Feo tipped the brim forward, Eliza found she couldn't take her eyes off of him. The idea of Nemo, standing in a shop and picking out a simple hat, painted a somber picture for her. She saw someone struggling to carve out an identity in a world where the majority demanded his kind fade into the background. Something in her chest tightened, as though compensating for the metal man's unfelt pain.

"Paul thinks it was a good pick, said it made my head look less round. He hasn't given up on bugging me to swap out my coat, though."

Eliza took a sniff she regretted. "Yeah, I gathered."

Nemo's hand dropped to his lapel, fiddling with one of its many loose threads.

"I got history with this thing. Picked it up off a schooner in Vorvaň and haven't dropped it ever since."

Eliza's gaze travelled up and down Nemo's precious jacket. It certainly looked historical, and now outside the protective atmosphere of the Bouncin' Bean, it smelled like it too.

"Well, if you ever need a good deal on some new duds, I can hook you up with my neighbor Margaret," Eliza offered. "She's a seamstress, runs a business right outside our apartment building."

She elbowed his arm with a hollow resonance and a wink. "You'd be doing me a favor if you hit her up. Maybe it'll keep her too busy to play matchmaker for a bit."

"Ah, I see." Nemo nodded thoughtfully. "Our ship's seamstress was also the needling type. Who's her pincushion of choice?"

"Me," sighed Eliza. "She tried setting me up with her son a few years ago, but that went nowhere. The woman's sweet, but she's convinced I need someone to 'take care of me', as if I haven't been doing just fine on my own. I don't think she'll rest until I walk down the aisle."

She'd meant it as idle conversation, but Eliza watched the Feo tug at his shabby collar like he had a throat to clear.

"Oh! Like, uh, matelotage! You've heard of those before, right? It's, er, a sailors' marriage, in a way. I-I attended one, back on the *SF Rapaci*... Well, not *attended* exactly, more like hung out by the back of the ship while they—"

"Nemo, get your brass over here! I found something you can buy me—I mean—us! It'll help brighten up the place!"

The two of them spun their heads towards the peacock's cawing, watching him wave his wings over a stall hung with suncatchers in every color of the rainbow. Eliza rolled her eyes, but her lips curled into a smile all the same.

"I'll let you get back to your birdy buddy, I need to do some more shopping anyway. Don't let him spend all you've got, you hear me?"

The Feo chuckled. "I won't. Thank you."

"I said no 'thank you's are necessary."

"Oh, um, alright... Goodbye, then."

Eliza watched Nemo clatter away to the next leg of his little shopping adventure. She didn't bother asking when she'd see him again at the Bouncin' Bean, knowing that he'd be right back around her workplace before long.

With the un-covered aura of his keepsake jacket fresh in mind, and a new lightness to her feet, Eliza knew it wouldn't be soon enough.

As the weeks rolled across New Amrestir and Eliza's shifts blurred by, Nemo grew to be something of a feature within the little shop. He'd given up on adding more feathers to his fashion, but the Feo made up for it by hauling Pauvus along with him whenever possible, enough that Eliza had graduated to "Paul" status in his eyes. They grew comfortable in both orders and conversation, to the point that she didn't even mind dealing with the peacock's elaborate and expensive requests.

For the first time in what felt like forever, the Bouncin' Bean had a regular that Eliza enjoyed seeing. Nemo, as it turned out, made for an ideal customer. Sadly, that set a bar of quality that might as well have been as tall as the lighthouse for everyone else.

"I want a refund!"

The ragged pelican at the counter was still flapping his beak, and Eliza had to wrangle her eyes away from rolling. Refunds were akin to a death sentence for Toni, the only exception involving an unfortunate swordfish finding a cockroach in their cup. Sadly, the man was busy in the back with a recent shipment, leaving Eliza to repeat herself for the third monotone time.

"I'm sorry, sir. Unless there's something wrong with your coffee, we don't offer refunds."

"There *is* something wrong with my coffee!" the pelican insisted. "It's molten! Practically roasted my tongue off!"

Eliza had figured it was common sense to wait for a hot drink to cool, but she should have known that was giving her clientele too much credit. It made her wish he'd been telling the truth, if it meant not having a tongue to complain with. She sighed despite herself, and immediately knew that she'd just dripped blood in the water.

"How dare you!" the Ave gasped, face flushing behind his feathers. "I want to speak with the owner!"

"He's going to say the exact same thing I told you," deflated Eliza.

"Well, on top of the coffee, now I want to address how useless his staff is! Are you even qualified for this job?!"

Eliza had a strategy when customers teetered on the edge of feeling shouty and stabby: zone out, focus on a knot in the wood or a smudge on the counter, and wait. Either Toni would come along to deal with them with extreme prejudice, or they'd burn themselves out on her impassive defense and fume off to somewhere with stronger drinks. Feeling the squall of the Ave's squawks wash against her, Eliza soon entered into a world of swirling patterns, a skill that she'd sharpened over the years into an art form. Lost in her smokescreen of ignorance, she didn't even notice the sound of clanging metal under the din of complaints.

"You should stop yelling at her."

A hush fell over the shop. The irate customer spun around to be met with the full towering height of Nemo. Nearly a head and a half below the Feo's visor, the Ave's attempt at a brave face was betrayed by the quiver of his gular pouch.

"I don't see how any of this is your concern,

32

tinman!"

"You've made it my concern," Nemo rumbled from somewhere deep within his shell. "You're disturbing my coffee time. Thank you."

Such a simple statement hung heavy in the air. Eliza looked over Nemo's ragged old coat, and it occurred to her that each stain and tear across its length had unspoken, visceral stories to tell. The only types who'd be comfortable walking around like that would be the truly dangerous or the truly mad, and the Ave didn't seem like he wanted to find out the answer.

"Wh–I– F-fine! Standards are in the trenches these days, swear'ta... You're not gettin' any business from me or mine, y'hear?"

The Ave pulled his beak into a tight line, and bristled to the doorway in a huff. Eliza had just enough time to stew over a comeback when Toni finally emerged from the back, a streak of spilled tephra spice dusting his shirtfront.

"What was all that about? Liz, what'd you—"

"Just some featherbrain," Eliza replied. "I'll be taking my break now."

"What? I didn't say you could take a break!"

Unfortunately for Toni, Eliza had already re-raised her complaint defenses. She slung her apron on its hook and left both it and her boss hanging. Stamping out and around, Eliza found Nemo still doing his best figurehead impression by the counter.

"Mind if I join you at your table? It is my favorite spot in the shop, after all."

Even in the roasting atmosphere of the Bouncin' Bean, Eliza could feel the temperature next to her crank up a few degrees at the question.

"Oh, right! Of course!"

Nemo chugged along back to his window seat and Eliza coasted on in his wake. She settled into the seat she'd spent countless breaks in, feeling an odd sense of comfort in being able to share it for once.

"I am sorry about that," Nemo murmured, dropping down onto his stool. "It looked like you had things under control, but something about screeching birds puts my rivets on edge."

"It's fine, I've dealt with worse. Been dealing with customers like that since I was thirteen. At least here I don't need to carry a gun during my shift."

Nemo's Milk Punch froze on its path up to his visor. "Thirteen? Isn't that young?"

Eliza shrugged. "You do what you gotta do when your parents are gone."

As she watched the lights flutter behind Nemo's visor, Eliza let the question roll over in her brain. It seemed rude to ask, but on its surface, she really had no way of knowing exactly how long Nemo had been kicking around for. She considered that the Feo had always been exactly as he had been built, never growing or having a proper childhood, and felt as though she'd taken a cannonball to the chest. Eliza wondered how much Nemo even knew about the concept of parents, and hoped that not all of his lessons had come from Pauvus.

A stray ember snapped from Nemo's visor as if in protest.

"I'm... sorry for your loss. But just because you're used to it, people still shouldn't treat you like that. Barking orders at you, demeaning you just for doing your job, treating you like you're a..."

Nemo trailed off, but Eliza knew what he was going to say. The treatment of 'artificial life' in New Amrestir might've seen a great deal of progress as of late, but out beyond the edges of their artificial shores she knew things hadn't exactly been rosy for his fellow Feo. From the amount of corrosion fighting for space across his brassy shell, she had the feeling the world hadn't gone out of its way to show Nemo that same kindness.

"I guess it's been worth it for you then," Eliza said softly, "settling down in the city. You can say a lot about how things are run around here, but if New Amrestir stands

34

for one thing, it's for living your life on your own terms."

Nemo looked out of the window, an almost wistful look on his visor as rays of sunlight danced off it.

"It's certainly an interesting place, there's nowhere else in the Grand Sea I could imagine the first Feo captain coming from. Sure, it's noisy, and rude, and crowded, but I'm used to all that. Every day I see something I've never known before, feel something I've never felt. Endless chances to meet new people, good ones. Patient, reasonable, open-minded... like you."

A surprised chuckle jumped up from Eliza's throat.

"Y'know, I never really thought of myself like that. I mean, I think people should do whatever they want as long as it doesn't hurt anyone, but I don't know if that counts as open-minded."

"You'd be surprised how rare that can be," Nemo retorted. "Most of the old crews I toured with certainly weren't, most of them treated me like I was just an object. Good ol' Paul was one of the few who would actually talk to me, even if it was mostly about himself. Still went out of his way to stand by me, despite everything."

A rattling sound came out of Nemo's visor, and Eliza realized that it was the Feo's version of a cough.

"Not all Ave can be as reliable as Paul. You don't deserve having to brave a blustering bird like that on your own. Someone like you deserves all the respect in the sea."

"There you go again, you charmer!" Eliza laughed. "If I didn't know better, I'd say you're doing this to get free coffee out of me."

"It's true, though! You treat me like anyone else, and odd as it may seem, that's the most special I've ever felt." Nemo fiddled with the brim of his ridiculous headwear. "Plus, you like my hat, so that must mean you have good taste."

A wicked grin spread across Eliza's face. "Want me to let you in on a little secret?"

Nemo leaned in closely, flames behind his visor burning low in anticipation of Eliza's revelation.

35

"Yes?"

"...I actually hate your hat."

Nemo pulled back. Eliza braced herself for the consequences of her own personal tastes, when the sound of a roaring fireplace came bursting out between his brass slots. The other patrons were spinning their heads around in alarm, most likely fearful that a fire had broken out.

"Don't let Paul hear, or he'll try to douse me for plucking him!"

Eliza could feel the heat across the table, but she picked up on his lamplight laughter. Without the lines of customer service or roommate judgment tying him down, Nemo seemed to be settling into life beyond the sea. He had a glow about him beyond the ordinary kind, and it was infectious in its own way.

"He's got plenty to spare, and I'm sure there's plenty out there that would be suckered in with a flashy feather. You don't need to ride his coattails to make a statement, believe me."

"I still think it's nice," Nemo shrugged under the lapel of his dishrag coat. "Bits and pieces earned and gifted... it's mine."

Before he could add anything beyond that, the brass kettle on the fire piped up for attention once again.

"Guess that means my break is over. See you around, right?"

As she stood, Eliza seized the moment, and leaned in to give the forehead of Nemo's helmet a kiss. In that same second, a spark of connection flared up in her mind and the sizzle to follow confirmed it. Eliza's lips stung like the first sip of an overcooked brew as she yanked away into a defensive crab-scuttle. The two stood frozen in abject bewilderment, caught between the passing seconds and the tangled lines of rigging that bound their possibilities.

Nemo creaked to motion first, doffing his cap to his chest.

"Aye, Eliza."

A collective 'ahem' from the untended patrons of

36

the Bouncin' Bean practically rattled the windows around them.

Eliza realized she'd pushed her luck far enough. Feeling like her cheeks were beginning to catch up with Nemo and the kettle, she scurried back to the impatient arms of customer service. She watched Nemo drift towards the door, and though the midday rush was threatening to rock the old Bouncin' Bean's foundations, Eliza held that brief touch in mind, and held it close.

The burn lingered for hours, and Eliza cherished it.

Other than that brief moment they shared, nothing much changed between her and Nemo as the days ticked along. He would float on in like driftwood across her shores, and she would take pains to ignore the flares her heart would shoot up to her brain. At each brush of Nemo's brass digits against hers, Eliza had to remind herself that he was still entering the paddle pool of society. It simply didn't feel right, pushing him into the deep end so soon.

The bell chimed, followed up by a drumroll of hard metal against creaky wood. Eliza's boot heels clicked the floorboards as she rushed out to greet the Feo, stopping to notice something was different today. He was sporting a silken scarf of fine greens and blues, still bafflingly draped over his same grotty coat. Eliza pictured the original seamstress of the garment blowing a blood vessel in disgrace, and couldn't help but smile at the absurdity of it all.

"Very fancy today Nemo, looking sharp! The usual?"

"Yes, thank you!" the Feo blazed, fiddling with the edges of the new accessory's hem. "Actually, on top of that, I was wondering if you could... come stop by the table again, during your break?"

Eliza rubbed her hands on her apron and glanced back to the back room door.

"Heh, if I can get a break today, absolutely."

"Why wouldn't you get one?" Nemo piped, tilting his head with a shine across the edge of the helmet.

Keeping her voice below the morning bustle din, Eliza leaned in below Nemo's hat brim.

"Toni's a big believer in the idea that 'time is money', and I think he's starting to get sick of me wasting mine."

Nemo sat, pondered, and considered the equation laid out before him.

"I have plenty of both to waste."

Steadying himself on a leg that Eliza couldn't believe she'd never noticed didn't match the other until now, Nemo thudded along to the door that Toni had just spilled out from. As he rapped at the oak surface with two sharp clacks, Eliza dearly hoped that her boss was having a pleasant morning so far.

"Hello, Toni. Pardon me, but can I buy Eliza a drink?"

Toni's bare head was already glistening from the morning's window glare. He squinted at Nemo, and took a good long look at the Feo's frame for the first time.

"Hello there, Mr... Nemo. Ey, you got gunpowder pocks 'round the wrists there. Have to ask, you a cannon man?"

Even from behind, Eliza saw a shift in how the Feo held himself. The awkward hunch to keep himself smaller ratcheted to attention, finding common ground he could stand on.

"Yessir! Thank you! Manned the linstock many a time. Caught the blastback occasionally, but better me than them. Gunner crews always were stand-up sailors."

"Yea, stand up with whatever they've got to work with. Had a hunch that'd be the root of that Bootlegger's Leg there," Toni tutted, nudging his nose in the direction of the wooden peg that stood in place of Nemo's right shin. "Knew a few lads who got rolled on by loose cannons, swept right off their feet."

38

Nemo ruffled his new scarf, the other fist defiantly cocked at his side.

"No sir, not quite. That foot's still lost up the backside of a scrap dealer we cornered outside Bellher Cay back in the day."

Eliza watched her boss, a man who could boil over quicker than any make of kettle, wheeze out a laugh that deflated his belly from within. He wiped a smudge from Nemo's hand with his counter rag, and gave a joking tug at his coat's collar.

"You've got some salt to you, lad. Just don't make another scene and you can have some time together. Long as you're still paying, a'course."

Nemo turned to Eliza, broiling with refueled cheer. "Any requests?"

It was funny. Eliza knew the Bouncin' Bean's menu by heart, but now given a blank check to any drink she could desire, her mind couldn't fill it. Despite her position, the waitress never had the budget for Toni's specialty blends, or any coffee that she couldn't sneak from the leftover dregs. It had left a bitter taste in her mouth, even if it did help to get through a rough shift. Watching the wall, Eliza propped an elbow up on the counter in deep performative thought.

"Wellll, there's that *Tlauillibrew* I've been looking at for ages. That Plasmotic Coast spice blend, with the cocoa beans and served with whipped cream up top. Of course, you'd have to spend an arm and a—"

"I'll order you that then."

Toni let out a long whistle, and Eliza was tempted to join him. That was an order beyond even Pauvus' standards, something only government officials or wealthy merchants would get if they'd ever gotten lost and stumbled in. She'd been joking, as she always thought her boss put it on the menu to make their little hole-in-the-wall coffee shop seem fancier than it actually was. Yet the ingredients Toni was already beginning to dig out didn't look like they were just for show.

"Comin' right up, 'boss'. I'll bring 'em over."

"Nemo, I wasn't being serious. If you have to get me something, order something more—"

"I insist," was Nemo's simple reply, already making his way back to his table before Eliza could beg him to reconsider further.

As Eliza made to trail behind Nemo's asymmetrical gait, she felt Toni give her shoulder a firm elbow nudge.

"Looks like you snagged yourself a rich fellow, eh Liz?"

Eliza responded with a harsh elbowing of her own, but Toni just laughed it off as she hurried her way to the table. Every second of her boss' good spirits was precious, and every moment she didn't have to work doubly so. The fact that it meant more time with the metal man was just a happy bonus, a fact that Eliza was almost able to believe herself.

Slipping in across from the living furnace, Eliza considered how quickly she had gotten used to seeing his face, let alone how quickly she had gotten used to thinking of the brass visor as a face at all.

"So, be honest. Did you buy that scarf of your own free will, or did Paul press you into getting it?"

"A little bit of both," Nemo admitted, idly rubbing the delicate folds between his fingers. "We were walking by the shops yesterday, checking out the new arrivals, when it caught my eye. Shipped plenty of silk bolts during my years in cargo, but I never imagined I'd get to own the final product for myself."

He unwrapped the scarf from his neck and held it out for Eliza to feel. She did just that, marveling at how the fabric slid easily across her fingers, soft and cool to the touch. It was a beautiful piece, one that any lord or lady would be proud to have in their wardrobe. The only shame was that it was an addition to Nemo's wardrobe, the fibers already starting to adopt some of its signature musk.

Nemo took the cloth back and re-bundled himself, oblivious to the senses he was missing out on.

"It was expensive, but I bought it as a compromise. One less day of Paul whining about finding a new coat."

"*Ha!*" Eliza called, slightly too loud for the morning crowd. "I swear, that bird is living through you! One of these days he'll have to get off his lazy tail feathers and find himself a real job."

A low, rumbling blaze came out of Nemo's visor as Toni set down their cups with all the care of a corsair. Eliza's order looked as decadent as it had sounded, to the point that she felt a bit embarrassed to be sitting behind the plume of frothed cream and sprinkles. The monolith looked like it should have been a display piece in a mainland boutique, not something to be guzzled down like a common porridge. Yet under the scrutiny of Nemo's expectant stare, Eliza braced herself for the most expensive sip of her life.

The moment the coffee and cream hit Eliza's tongue, her mind was blown wide open. The liquid gold pushed an involuntary moan from her throat as it went down, warm enough to wrap her insides like a blanket.

"I'm guessing it was worth the wait?"

Eliza leaned back into her chair, savoring the remnants of chocolate dancing on her tongue.

"If I died here right now, I'd die a happy woman."

"Perish the thought!" Nemo remarked, crackling behind a fresh Milk Punch-stache. "But yes, Paul's been looking. I think he found a gig as a bookkeeper for a warehouse by the docks... Actually, to be honest, he ran into a warehouse worker pitching open positions and I wouldn't let him leave without talking it over."

Nemo allowed Eliza to take a few more sips of her paradise in a cup before continuing, and she allowed him to take the helm of the conversation.

"Speaking of Paul... he's been talking about this opera that's going to be performed on the mainland, *The Ballad of Porphiose*. Supposed to be a show to remember, though I've never been to one before."

Through sheer willpower, Eliza managed to tear her lips away from her mug and look at Nemo straight-on. She knew where this was going, as the brass man was making an effort to look anywhere but in her direction. His confidence from earlier had drained as quickly as Eliza's drink, replaced again by that old timid stiffness.

"I was wondering if you'd like to... go see it... with me."

There it was. In a way, Eliza was proud Nemo was able to form the words for himself. The thought of being treated to a night on the town was rattling ship bells in her brain, but she pressed it all down into as casual a smile as she could manage.

"Well, I suppose I still owe you for saving me from that pelican."

Eliza tried to play it cool for the sake of her own excitement more than anything, but she felt Nemo's temperature take a notable dip.

"I don't want you to go out with me because you feel obliged to."

He sounded serious, more serious than Eliza

42

thought he could be, and she realized of all people, Nemo was the sort who wouldn't appreciate a subtle touch. Eliza reached her hand across the table and placed it on top of his, feeling brass fingers radiate faint warmth from between the joints and rivets.

"Nemo, I was joking. I would be more than happy to spend a night out with you."

The metal scorched against her palm, but she didn't dare pull away. Nemo tugged at his scarf to make himself presentable, steam hissing from the collar, and Eliza wondered if he'd planned this far along.

"I... Yes, perfect! There's the Mulligan Statue in town square. Meet me there at sunset, we'll cast off from there! T-Thank you!"

In a flurry of metal and fabric, he was swiftly gone, Milk Punch left half-empty in its mug. Eliza barely had time to blink, let alone call out his thanks, but she smiled all the same. With her own drink in hand, Eliza took advantage of the gap in Toni's attention, and truly savored every last sip.

CHAPTER 3
BLOCKING

New Amrestir was known across the Grand Sea since its inception for constant, shifting change, but it could always be relied on to be frustrating. It stretched far beyond what qualified as the mainland, stitched together with disparate gangways and bridges as stop-gaps for 'future developments'.

The trek from Eliza's apartment street to the mainland was a pain to make even without an anchorline of pleats weighing her down, grateful with each clomp across the half-built street that she had gone with her usual boots instead of slippers.

"It's... worth... it..."

Just as the lingering sunlight dripped into the horizon beyond, Eliza struck solid ground. She was accustomed to the ever-present ambient sway of the city's extensions, but even the sturdiest buildings cropped up around her neighborhood couldn't compare to the Boardwalk Boulevard. Freshly erected towers and shops loomed over the sky like Nemo at her counter, with the bright white shock of New Amrestir's great Kindling Lighthouse dominating it all.

The early-evening crowd was growing thick with activity, all puttering around the base of a large central fountain. Atop a base carved with patterns of writhing fungus was a statue of Mulligan, the Feo that'd struck out across the sea to the Garden of Life and come back unscathed. Eliza found it a bit morbid, considering the old stories, and she could almost feel the empty visor staring down at the people below in silent judgement.

Nemo's own visor was hovering beneath Mulligan's gaze, diligently standing guard by the stone edge of the fountain. His hat was now pruned down to just one feather, and his scarf still ruffled handsomely around his gorget, but what most surprised Eliza was the freshly pressed jacket of fine deep maroon draped across his shoulders.

"Nemo!"

Eliza grabbed a handful of skirts in one hand and burst into a jog, the other waving frantically at him. Nemo spun just in time to catch Eliza as she launched into his brass plating for a hug.

"Whoa! Hello, Eliza! I... well, Flame, you look—"

"Heh, you're looking great too. I like this new look on you. Hate to say it, but Paul was onto something."

The tailoring of the jacket glimmered under a growing night of stars and torchpoles, and rose under the thrust of his chest. It was leagues beyond his old ratty mainstay, and blessedly smelled like nothing but clean laundry.

"Thank you! I mean, it was a hard decision, but Paul narrowed the options when he tied my old one around a rock and lobbed it out the window. Probably sitting at the bottom of an Ibi's garden by now."

Eliza fought against letting a smile crack across her face, knowing how much that smelly vestige of his past meant to Nemo. The poor Feo must've mourned his loss for hours before arriving here under the watchful eye of the Mulligan fountain, and he didn't need her to rub salt in the wound.

"I'm sorry about that, but if it's any consolation, I think you look quite distinguished. Maroon suits you."

Nemo had gotten better at controlling his temperature around her, but Eliza could hear the beginnings of a low whistle escaping his visor.

"Thank you. I would say you look beautiful in your dress, but you always look beautiful."

"Thank *you*," Eliza snapped back, having to control her own temperature this time. "And that'll be the last 'thank you' of the night, okay? We're on even ground here, it's a proper date night."

For the love of Mother Flame, Eliza couldn't even recall the last time she'd been on a date. Digging through brief passes with the lads and lasses in the city, it dawned on her that in terms of proper courtship, she didn't think any of them could fully qualify. She buried and smoothed the dirt over her memories, patting down the hair that was already frizzing from her messy bun.

"So, then… Night's rolling in fast, we'd best get moving to make it in time. Do you have tickets already?"

Nemo's fingers fluttered to his new coat, already stomping on towards the west avenues of the mainland. A flash of freshly-printed tickets told Eliza that the show was going on at the old *SF Spettacolo*, a remnant of the town's original construction. Its history of high-flying sport and political intrigue still cast their long shadows on the galleon-turned-gallery, even if Eliza had only gotten to experience it from the outside. That outside had seen its share of inevitable storms and vandalism over the years, but Amrestir took great pains to cater to its hungry Audiences.

Even with tickets in hand, Eliza couldn't help but feel as though she were trespassing. The *SF Spettacolo*'s lobby made the public square look like her graveyard shift, with New Amrestir's visiting traders, dealers, influencers, and magnates preparing for a night of bumping expensively-tailored shoulders.

Eliza dragged her attention away from people-watching to catch Nemo by the former gunport wall, checking their seats with a squat Ave attendant in a ticket booth. He looked like one of the far-north Obrazheskian types, and he most certainly looked uncomfortable. It was hard to tell if it was due to personal biases, the temperature, or the fact that he'd been squeezed into a suit on top of his natural tuxedo and tail. Whatever was ruffling the penguin's dense feathers didn't stop him from giving the requisite marks, and soon Nemo was gesturing for Eliza to follow along once again.

"If that guy gave you any flack, I'm going to jump back there and give him some of my own."

"No need," soothed Nemo, with something of a smirk to his voice. "We're all square. When I came in earlier, that lad swore he'd have me barred by management. Now, by word from the higher-ups, I'm an 'honored guest'. Only in New Amrestir, eh?"

Being an "honored guest" apparently measured up to a spot in the upper galley, looking down upon the wide stretch of deck now acting as the stage for *The Ballad of Porphiose*. Considering Nemo's height and her indomitable locks, Eliza was grateful that nobody would have the misfortune of staring at the back of their heads for the whole show.

Bellowing Obra songs echoed around the curved hull, as the titular Porphiose mourned the loss of his beloved to the tendril of some nightmarish beast. His long journey following her whale fall to the depths of an Ibian trench had left the sea a new blossom of life, and himself nothing but heartache. It had also left the majority of the Audience downright miserable, a privilege that Eliza kept having to remind herself that they had paid good money to endure.

When the doors once again freed the Audience to the now blinding lights of the lobby, Eliza and Nemo stumbled out into civilized society without a word. She was busy clawing at the roots of her hair, and he was shuffling even more rigidly than usual. Taking a breath and jettisoning the sorrows through a mental blowhole, Eliza rapped twice on the Feo's shoulder in an attempt to knock them out of it.

"Well now, that was harrowing! I can imagine what Dad would've written about it for a Press review. You sure Paul wasn't trying to sabotage our date night?"

"No," Nemo admitted flatly. "He told me it was a classic affair for classy people, a tale of romance for the ages. I had just assumed that relationship would last beyond the first song."

The two of them stood quietly for a time, letting the current of fellow downcast aristocrats trickle around them. In the midst of their self-inflicted grief, no one even bothered to give either of them a second look. Nemo, who'd been getting the hang of quenching his dry silent spells, gave Eliza's shoulder a playful knock in return.

"What's say we stop by The Sick Fiddle?" he suggested, re-doffing his cap and straightening the remaining feather with care. "It's a little inn Paul and I've been staying at yonder by Calari Street. Might not be as fancy as all this, but it could help put the shine back on the night. Maybe give Paul our own review?"

The suggestion alone made Eliza brighten up. Strutting about with the upper crust may have sounded nice on paper, but sometimes it took cheap bread to fill an appetite.

"You know what? A few pints and shanties are just what tonight calls for. Lead the way, Cap'n."

The road from the *SF Spettacolo* to Calari Street was long, but thankfully well-paved. They walked and chatted into the darkening hours of the night, time slipping through their fingers as easily as his own digits laced between hers.

The exterior of The Sick Fiddle was hewn from the hull of a repurposed square-rigged ship, the keel of which had been carved to vaguely resemble the silhouette of its namesake fiddle. It was the sort of mindless marketing that Eliza had come to expect of New Amrestir's entrepreneurs. At least it lived up to the "sick" part of the name.

Passing a tavern doorman with all the friendliness the attendant at the *SF Spettacolo* hadn't shown, the unlikely couple seeped into the thickening mid-evening crowd, and knew they'd come to the right place. The patrons of The Sick Fiddle were the sorts that had already been fed enough real tragedy to spoil their appetites for fictional ones, and partied hard enough to even the scales. It was the kind of crowd that defined the "Amrestir Experience", and worked wonders to push the whale songs out of Eliza's mind.

Nemo fetched a set of flagons from a passing tray and whispered in the server's ear, slipping what Eliza assumed must've been a tip into the apron. He returned with drinks in hand, the closest thing to smugness chiseled onto his face.

"Now this is what tonight needed!" Eliza cheered, giving Nemo's mug a clink and a hearty quaff. It wasn't Fríasen champagne, but it tickled her brain in just the right way. As Eliza leveled the beverage again, her eye caught a fan of unmistakable feathers.

"Hey Nemo, your wingman's still milling about."

Eliza had a theory that Pauvus had pushed them towards the show so he'd have the apartment for himself, but that would've meant having no one to peacock for. The Ave was preening himself up with embellished sea stories for the unimpressed bartender, with the book he'd presumably brought to the counter sitting untouched.

Nemo tossed back the foamy dregs of his flagon and swept to Pauvus' side, joints already loosening from the fresh lubrication. Eliza watched the Feo land a heavy hand on the bird's shoulder, who looked like he was about to pop out an egg in shock.

"EEEeeyyyy, Nemo! You old crustacean, you're back! What, did she reject you already?"

That thought lasted about as long as it took for Nemo to point behind Pauvus, to where Eliza was waiting with a wink. She hunkered down on the stool across from the Ave's perch, sandwiching him into their date night.

"You really know how to pick 'em, Paul. Tell me, does your concept of romance involve wailing over your soulmate's corpse while it gets picked at by fish?"

"Hm, is that what it's about?" Pauvus trilled, swirling his glass on the tips of dexterous pinion feathers thoughtfully. "My folks always said it was the definitive text on relationships. Lays out a lot about their marriage, come to think of it."

From the counter behind him, Pauvus was repelled like a magnet from the scribbled tab now sneaking up on him. Despite his chumminess with the bartender, the peacock was quick to clam up now that the one laying out the clams for the tab was back on the scene.

"Well, I won't intrude on you lovebirds any longer," Pauvus hinted, giving Nemo's scarf a proper smooth and straighten. "I'll leave you with this: enjoy yourselves, make merry, don't do anything I wouldn't do!"

Tucking in his tail, conspicuously pocked with a few gaps in its pattern, Pauvus darted around to the upper apartment stairs under cover of rush hour. The titular fiddlers of the tavern were starting their sound test at the side stage, and the counter's crowd was beginning to thin.

"Pretty nice night, right Liz?"

Eliza groaned in tune with the rolling music. Even for him, this was getting a little too familiar for her tastes.

"I'm sorry, *Liz?*"

"Isn't that what Toni calls you?"

"You're under the assumption that Toni isn't doing that to try and get a rise out of me. I just put up with it on the chance it'll get me a raise out of him."

50

The night was going strong, and the drinks were a close match. As she took another gulp, Eliza realized the opera had given herself and Nemo precious little chance to actually get to that kind of familiar level. Eliza tapped the table along the drum check, and resolved to take the lead.

"You know, I never asked, but what made you come to the Bouncin' Bean in the first place? It's not really what I'd consider a tourist attraction compared to everything else around here."

Nemo didn't seem to have an answer for that question ready. He put his mug down, and placed a fist under what passed for his chin in thought.

"When Paul and I first got here, I was overwhelmed with too much, and too little," Nemo began. "There was so much to see that I didn't know what to do, just sat about the place sorting through memories. One day, Paul wouldn't have it any longer, told me to 'go get a coffee or something, like a normal person'. I guess I always worked best with proper directions, and you know what happened from there. Was worried that I'd overstepped my bounds, but I figure I ended up right where I needed to be."

Nemo rubbed the back of his neck, causing his scarf to slide back and forth under his fresh maroon coat.

"Honestly, when I saw you, my first thoughts had gone to those stories of sirens the boys would jaw about below-decks. Just... too radiant to be real."

In the name of Mother Flame, this Feo was determined to melt Eliza into a puddle by the end of the night. She took a hearty swig of ale, and the burn of the alcohol down her throat was great at cooling her down.

"A siren, huh?" Eliza repeated coyly. "You must be the first of my customers to ever think that. Running around all day in the heat and steam, I never really put in much extra elbow grease to keep up appearances. Caught me by surprise with what you said about my hair on your first visit; people usually tend to jump to complaints, not compliments."

"Well, those people are fools."

Eliza twisted a loose strand around her finger. Nemo's voice rang hollow from within his shell, yet there was nothing but genuine affection in the tone of it. Draining the rest of her mug, she decided that it was her turn to open up.

"My dad used to chase me around the house with this comb of his, an ivory one with fine needling teeth. He always pressed me on scraping it through my 'do before going out, but I think even he was afraid it'd snap on one of my knots. I keep it safe and sound under my bed, couldn't bear to risk ruining it with this tangle again... It's the last thing I've got left of him, now."

"It sounds like he really cared for you. Having parents must be a wonderful thing."

"Mmh, *parent*," Eliza scoffed, calling over a refill. "Don't know my mom, don't care to know any more either. I was barely off the teat when she skipped town."

The topic of family was something Eliza preferred to push out of mind with the longest bargepole she could imagine. It'd been years since she'd fished thoughts of her father to the surface, and even longer for that bottom feeder of a mother. The idea that at some point in her life she'd even bothered to ask around for word of her as a girl gave Eliza a headache, and the night was still young.

"Oh, I'm sorry," hushed Nemo. "I didn't mean to upset you. I should've—"

"It's fine," Eliza sighed, pushing a lock of hair out of her face. "Everyone's got their own share of sorrows, I don't have anything extraordinary there."

A thin curl of flame danced out of Nemo's visor. "You're extraordinary to me."

Eliza groaned and buried her face in her hands. From the time he'd walked through the Bouncin' Bean's doors, there had been a certain charming helplessness to the sailor that tugged at her heartstrings, but now he was digging in like a common rake.

Eliza pulled her face out of the safety of her palms, and brought them together in an authoritative clap.

52

"New rule! No more lines like that for the rest of the night, alright?"

Nemo pulled his drink in close, which the bartender knew to keep consistently topped up.

"Heh, fair play. Let's keep it even then. You hit me with some instead."

"Deal." Eliza leaned across the table on her elbows, digging deep to find a chink in his armor. "Hm, well you're probably the most polite fella to walk through the Bouncin' Bean's doors since it opened, for one."

"...Is that all?"

It was hard to tell, as usual, but Nemo didn't seem very impressed. Eliza realized a little too late that it may have not been the best compliment to give a Feo. She pulled her line in, looking for a new angle to cast from.

"Of course not! Hey, when you manage to get out of that shell of yours, you can be pretty suave. You're pretty bright, and I'm not just talking about the fire behind your visor. You know how to have a good time, despite Paul's advice, and I can tell that you got a heart of gold under all that brass."

Eliza felt Nemo soften within his shell as she went on. A fine sheen of sweat was starting to form on her forehead as the Feo heated up, but she smiled all the same. She had the old kettle from back at the shop on her mind, and the waitress was looking to turn up his burners.

"You're also adorable when you get all steamed up."

Before she could raise a mug to her lips once again, Nemo had swiped a grubby water glass from behind him, dunked it over his head with a harsh hiss, and slapped an extra shelling on the table. By the time Eliza stopped laughing, the boisterous voices of the Audience and stringed instruments were beginning to pick up, setting a ceasefire to their Flattery War for now.

The titular Sick Fiddlers were composed of local Kei, save for one. Slapping all across his own frame in the back was a stout iron drummer that Eliza recognized as

Jough, an old washtub of a Feo back from Old Amrestir's halcyon days. Between the hollow banging and the frantic sawing, the band was roiling the crowd up hotter than an overcooked kettle.

"Mmh, opportunities for Feo in all fields, eh?" Eliza quipped. "I prefer him to that little prancy jester I saw as a kid back in Ogden's, way too loud for me. Now you, I'd bet you know enough shanties to pack the Institute's library."

The winds of the conversation were finally blowing Nemo's way, and she watched him breathe a new gust of life into his core.

"That," he chuckled, "is something I've got some authority on. Never joined in much with the crews considering, but I've gotten an earful of just about every song from here to Norcroft."

The band of Kei fiddlers at the bar front was wound up tight now, striking the strings quick enough to send fingers of smoke into the air. They'd rolled onto a new tune just as quickly, and it prodded at the back of her skull like a well-meaning comb.

Little Liz, I love you, honey...
Little Liz, I love you...

"I thought you said you hated that name."

Eliza snapped back to a higher level of sobriety, and realized that the newest voice adding itself to the din was her own. The words had climbed up her tongue and out into the world of their own accord, the melody dredging up a sunken memory.

"I... yeah, I do, but I must've heard this song a thousand times as a kid. Dad always sang it right before bed."

"It's sounding great, keep it up!"

The thought of breaking out into song would've been mortifying, if Eliza had any more second thoughts to give. She puffed out her chest with a hand to her breast, catching along with the chorus' end.

I love you in the springtime and the fall
Little Liz, I love you, honey!
Little Liz, I love you
I love you best of all!

Opening her eyes after the last note, Eliza watched Nemo's visor sparkle, bobbing strangely in her vision.

"Wow, good show! Eh, are you alright though?"

Eliza caught her breath with a grip at the counter, realizing it was her own head that had been bobbing. She reached behind Nemo's back to push an empty mug for a refill, then tugged him close by the coat on the way back.

"Having the night of my life, sailor-boy!"

The moon hung low by the time Eliza stumbled out of the pub, giggling madly and dangling off Nemo's sturdy shoulders. Strands of hair had escaped from her bun and tumbled down to her shoulders, waving free in the wind. She must've looked like a mess, but it was far too late in the evening for her to care.

Lost in her own stumbling dance, Eliza failed to notice the rubbing strake curb until it caught her heel. She might've had mastery over the wooden pathways of Amrestir, but that had been when she was sober. Arms flailing, legs failing, she was going down.

"Careful there!"

An arm projected out and caught Eliza solidly around the waist, the stability of brass wrapped in fine fabric holding her firm. The rush of adrenaline from the failed fall washed across her as she twisted and looked up at Nemo, looking down on her in his vaguely vacant and concerned way.

"You okay?"

Another hysterical giggle escaped Eliza's lips. She reached her arms up to wrap them around Nemo's neck, like a pose from the cover of those cheap pamphlet romances sold in the boardwalk shops.

"My hero."

Nemo helped her back up on her feet after a moment worth savoring, and led her closer to the water.

"Here, let's go get some fresh air. I know a place."

The dock coasts of New Amrestir were, as a rule, some of the least fresh highlights of the city. Much of the waste, junk, and detritus of the day to day inevitably crusted along the edges for disposal, and even the open sea was starting to get a lot less open feeling.

Eliza zigged and zagged about piles of something-or-other under the whirling beacon of the great lighthouse's lantern, the beacon of Nemo's glow driving on through the dark. Nemo had a course in mind, pulling both of them along with mechanical precision. Past the private-owned ports and scattered bait shops on the fringes, twisting down to a lower level of boardwalk just skirting the sea's surface, Eliza fought to keep her footing and pace with him. There were no more embarrassing trips where she needed to be saved by a dashing Feo, though she wouldn't have complained about the opportunity.

She was just about ready to give the timbers a shine with The Sick Fiddle's liquor when they emerged to a long stretch of dock sprouting from the foundation's base, uncluttered and private. The sky was vast as the ocean, a thin glimmer of starlight slicing the horizon. Eliza gazed across the expanse, feeling as though they were standing on the world's edge.

Nemo guided her along the dock where the full moon shone in the water like cream frothing on a coffee, helping her to its lip with the care of a craftsman. Eliza's feet dangled off the edge, tips of her boots just shy of skimming the water.

"Here we are, best spot in New Amrestir," Nemo proclaimed. "I found this place when I got lost exploring on my first day here."

Eliza's eyes went wide as she gazed skyward to the

moon. Swirls of blue and purple were brush strokes across the canvas that was the black sky, the stars its ornaments. The tall tilted buildings and torchpoles usually kept them veiled from sight, along with the unspoken rule in New Amrestir of keeping your eyes on the road and your valuables. Now, each one glittered as brilliantly as a diamond, glimmering so bright that she wondered how people didn't go blind looking up at them. Amrestir was no stranger to fireworks that crackled and filled the skies with light and smoke, but the quiet modesty of the night in its purity outdazzled them all.

Eliza spun to find Nemo ignoring the spectacular view in favor of watching her awe-slackened face. The heat of his gaze caught her off guard, and she laughed to see him studying her like a scholar.

"What's so fascinating?"

"Nothing, just your eyes..." Nemo trailed off. "Never really got a chance to see anyone's eyes so close up. Prettiest stars I've ever seen."

"Hhhhhhey, I thought I told you no more sweet talk like that!" Eliza protested, leaning heavily into Nemo's side.

Nemo exhaled with the sound of a faint whistle and dipped his fake leg into the surf. The feather in his cap billowed in the breeze, but his natural warmth pushed away the night's chill.

"If you think this is special, you should see it when you're out in the middle of the water. New Amrestir is a fine place, but there is so much wonder out beyond the horizon. The spire-peak cliffs off the coast of Aveila, Bellher Cay's golden sands, the uncanny lights churning through Vorvaň's winter skies. I've gotten glimpses at what the world has in store, though never of my own accord. Now I do have that freedom, and the possibilities are... overwhelming."

"Sounds like you miss being out on the sea."

"Aye, I do," Nemo admitted with a sigh. "Sailing is back-breaking work, but I know I'll be bound for a ship before long. S'just the course I'm bound for."

If it wasn't death that pulled a person away from their sweetheart's side, it was the alluring, dangerous mistress that was the ocean. Eliza couldn't find it in her heart to get upset at the Feo though, despite the last she knew of someone who chose the water over their loved one. Nemo had more than earned the right to go where and when he pleased. She was just glad he had the time to share a night like this with her.

"You should come with me."

That suggestion tore Eliza's eyes right away from the night back to Nemo, looking into his visor for any hint of a joke.

"I'm sorry, *bwuh?*"

"You should come with me!" Nemo repeated with enthusiasm, resting his hand on top of hers. "You've never left the city before, right? It can be your chance to see the world."

Eliza would be lying if she said it wasn't a tempting offer. Like any kid raised among the comers and goers of Amrestir, she'd had her dreams of growing up to explore the distant lands that the pirates and sailors would wax on about as though they were kingdoms from some fairytale. Of course, having known countless sailors that'd never completed their round-trip, she knew the true cost of running out to the sea. It'd be a life at the mercy of nature and her fellow man, and she didn't have a high amount of trust in either.

Still, Eliza hummed as she buried herself deeper in the Feo's fine coat. What would the harm be in playing into Nemo's little fantasy for one night?

"You think I'd make a good sailor? Maybe even a pirate?"

"You'd be the fiercest scoundrel on the sea," the Feo replied, as his hand made its way to her loose ringlets. "You'd lead a fleet that would have the greatest of pirates shaking in their boots."

"I wouldn't be nearly as frightening as First Mate Nemo," Eliza added, starting to get into the scenario. "If I could shiver the timbers of those drunkards, seeing you would send them to an early grave."

"Aye, yer making me blush. Beware the Dread Siren Eliza. She steals your treasure, then she steals your breath away."

On their private pirate outcrop, the world fell away in the sea of potential before them. It wasn't the only thing falling into the sea either. A squawking tangle of cloth and feathers broke the surface's serenity. Eliza and Nemo leaned in tandem, squinting through the dim, until recognition nearly knocked Eliza in herself with laughter.

Pauvus was flailing in the drink, desperately working to unite himself from a patch of littered netting. Nemo joined in with her hysterics once he realized that his friend was safe from drowning, hot plumes of smoke whisping out of his visor. When the peacock finally got the leverage to free himself and cling to a dock piling, he shot a glare in the Feo's direction.

"Nemo?! What, I— What in blazes are you doing here? You two wandered off without paying the blasted tab!"

"What are *you* doing here?" called Eliza, catching her breath.

"Why were you on my tab?" pondered Nemo, doing likewise.

Managing to shake off enough seawater to free his feathers, Pauvus leapt and fluttered from atop his piling to the narrow dock with a fraction of a mailman's grace. It was his turn now to get his bearings, as he moved to slick back his plumage.

"Ugh, same answer for both. When orders were being wrapped they looked for someone to make it whole, and well, I couldn't deliver. That tavern manager had some nerve, stringin' me along and givin' me the old heave-ho! Hope you're good for it, Nemo, that swim's gonna be much worse for you than me."

Eliza looked up to the underside of the boardwalk, and wondered at how small the city could feel at times. While Nemo did his best to brush the salt out of Pauvus' coat, a trick tickled at her thoughts.

"Arghh, landlubber, welcome aboard! Will ye join our crew, or walk the plank? Again!"

The Ave's eyes inflated in bewilderment. Eliza couldn't look without cracking up further.

"What happened to her?" Pauvus boggled. "Did she catch something from you?"

"Let her be, you dropped in mid-conversation," Nemo soothed, choking back a chuckle himself. "We'll handle it, no worries, but you really should—"

"I know, I know, I'll haul my own weight soon once I get my paycheck. You owe me a new set of clothes, though. Mine are gonna end up smelling worse than your old rag at this rate."

Eliza recovered, and pushed off what felt like the beginnings of a migraine for Morning Her to deal with.

Imagining the worn board below her feet was the deck of an outbound ship, she playfully flicked at the feather in Nemo's cap.

"Guess it's only fair. We won't press you on it... yet."

Pauvus snorted and shook himself off over them. "As if I'm going be a sailor again any time soon. Leaving that up to you, nutcases."

The trio watched the sky begin to lighten in increments, stars fading from their posts bit by bit. The late hours under New Amrestir were rapidly shifting to early hours, and Eliza knew that the shuffling feet of partiers above would be replaced by the thundering of worker's boots soon enough.

Work. Work was something that existed, and something Eliza couldn't entirely drown with thoughts of high-seas adventure. She still had to consider herself lucky to be employed, as long as she'd be able to claw herself back through the Bouncin' Bean's door in the morning.

Yet, with Nemo's hand clasped around hers, and the twinkling of the waves stretching away from the one home she had known, Eliza's brain brewed on the tides that had brought them to the same place, and where they might drift together in the end.

CHAPTER 4
SPECTACLE

Throughout the countless moments that made up the patchwork of Nemo's life, very few of them could be described as truly happy.

He could pick out some pleasant sunrise, or a beautiful vista from the memories of toil, but much of his time rusting at sea all congealed into a salty slurry. Any peace that Nemo was granted by nature's indifference had sadly never willingly been offered by many of his fellow men. Now, every day he was with Eliza, he was making up for the years of doldrums and drudgery.

She was the ray of sunlight peeking through the clouds after a storm. She was the pearl grown around a speck of detritus. She was the fair wind on a warm—

She was kicking the cup off the counter.

At some point after the fourth round of drinks, Eliza had gotten it in her head to clamber across the loosest tabletop in The Sick Fiddle and dance away to the tune 'Streets of Amrestir'. Nemo was glad to see her letting loose, but that didn't mean he wanted her to risk breaking any bones in the process. While the Audience cheered her on, the bartender shot him a sidelong look that told the Feo that he'd be responsible for covering any broken merchandise.

"Eliza, please get down!"

"Why should I? I'm having fun!"

Nemo watched Eliza sway on two wobbly feet atop equally wobbly furniture, and racked his core over how to pierce through the haze of her tipsy stupor.

"Because... I can't dance with you if you're up there!"

Thank the Flame, that seemed to do the trick. Eliza's wide, drunken grin softened as she let Nemo lead her by the hand to the safety of the floorboards. A few disgruntled murmurs rang from the crowd at the end of the show, but a majority of patrons were just glad to continue drinking without risk of getting a mug kicked in their mugs.

Eliza reeled Nemo through the river of cavorting customers, swimming along to the Kei fiddler's mad rhythm. The two of them whirled across the deck, right in line of sight with the one-eyed frontman. With what Nemo had to assume was a sly wink, the Kei cued up the band, and slipped their staccato screeches down towards a smoother tune.

It was slow enough for Nemo to get his bearings, and for Eliza to lose some of her wild momentum. The two stood in the midst of an Audience that had already caught the new current, sweeping them in with the rhythm. Nemo watched the hands of the lads around him and ratcheted to match, leading Eliza by the arm and waist through the unseen map of the dance. He was feeling rather proud of himself as he worked to keep in step, even if a few of them ended up being trampled by Eliza's stumbling boots.

"Whoa, watch out! You got two left feet or som'thing?"

Nemo wanted to retort that he only had the one left foot to his name, but wasn't looking to give her any ammo for a verbal barrage.

"No, still getting my land legs, is all. Hard to do when I got a pretty lady in my arms."

Instead of chastising him for the sappy compliment, Eliza giggled and rested her head on his cloth-covered pauldron, definitively proving that she was too far gone.

"*Heh*, aren't you the sweetest?"

They danced until Eliza was practically snoring into his shoulder, Nemo more dragging her across the floor than dancing. When the band rang out their final note, the Feo pulled her close to his chest, face inches from his visor. Thick curls framed the borders of her cheeks, with a sleepy smile plastered on her lips. He brushed a lock off Eliza's chin and set her back on ground level, only just realizing that her toes had barely been touching the floor.

"It's getting late. What's say we head upstairs to my place and sleep off tonight?"

"Ey, what sort of lass do you take me for?" Eliza teased. "I'm not one to be... wooed by just any swashbuckler, y'know."

Ah, so that was the angle. Nemo had caught onto the game Eliza was playing, and he was happy to play along.

"Well, would the Dread Siren make an exception for her First Mate?"

His metal hand caressed her cheek, the flame behind his visor fluttering when Eliza nuzzled further into his palm. In that moment, Nemo understood why the wealthy would go through the cost and effort of immortalizing their beloved in a painting.

"Aye, I can."

Nemo led Eliza past the remaining revelers to the back of the tavern, and eventually managed to wrangle her up the steps to the apartment floor's landing. They staggered and jagged down the hall until the music drifted out of hearing, and the door to his and Pauvus' shared apartment loomed ahead.

Slipping through the door frame with nary a creak of a floorboard, Nemo half-carried Eliza to the lip of the bed, where she near-instantly dropped like a fish on gravel. He considered going the extra mile to tuck her in properly, but barnacles had less bite than her grip on the covers.

"*Mmnh*, I wish e'ery night was like 'is," she mumbled into his pillow.

Nemo chuckled. "If every night was like this, you'd be seeing double for the rest of your life."

"Noooo, I m'n beingh wif you. Havring fun, laughin', just… enjoyin' today, wi'out… worrying 'out 'morrowww*wwhfhffs*."

For the first time tonight, Nemo found himself speechless. The only sounds that filled the room were the crackling of his core and Eliza's gentle breathing. Unable to come up with a witty response, he simply brushed his dearest's ringlets behind her ear and wished her goodnight. The Feo sat at the foot of the bed, content to watch her chest rise and fall in a rhythmic motion.

"Well, I'm awake now. Join me for a nightcap?"

Even the rattle of Nemo's visor wasn't enough to rouse Eliza. The Feo snapped his hands around his head, and focused his vision to spy a fan of feathers waiting in the dark. Pauvus was sitting at the edge of his downy bed, talons tapping on the hardwood floor.

"Paul!" he whispered. "Have you been there this whole time?"

"Yes," Pauvus groaned. "Anyways, nightcap?"

Nemo hesitated. It felt rude to leave your beloved alone in your room while you and your friend went drinking, but with the way Eliza was sawing logs into the pillow, he felt like she wouldn't be missing much. He relented, and stood as gently as his joints could lift him.

"I suppose so… Just a quick drink, okay?"

As they headed out, Nemo held a lingering look on Eliza before easing the door shut with a soft click. By the time he stepped into the hall, Pauvus was already fluttering down the tavern stairs.

Little of the night's revelry was still cooking this deep into the evening, with even the fiddlers checking their tips and tucking in. The bartender gave Nemo a nod as he clomped across the floor, having last seen each other about five minutes ago. Pauvus was nestled at an open booth seat, two spiced rums filled and ready.

"Soooo, you and Eliza, *hm?* Getting pretty serious there. Told you it's worth getting out in the world."

The Feo nodded, tipping back his liquor on the upturn.

"It would seem so. Every day, I'm still surprised she'd want to spend time with a rust bucket like me."

"Don't be modest!" Pauvus hissed from behind his draining glass. "You got a lot going for you! I've overheard some of the things you croon to her. Plus, it doesn't hurt to have that government treasure in the bank, does it?"

For a bird without eyebrows to speak of, Pauvus was waggling his up and down like two buoys. It was enough to reel a chuckle out of Nemo, knowing that the clams to his name wouldn't have been the right bait for Eliza even if he'd tried. Every pricey present and gesture he'd offered would always be met with a scolding, and a promise to keep themselves equal by going out of her way to gift him something in turn. Nemo thought about the delicate ship-in-a-bottle on the shelf in his room and whether Eliza's snores were vibrating the glass.

"Well, she did like the Incadessian chocolates I got her."

"Everyone likes a fancy present now and then," Pauvus nodded like a toy drinking bird. "Just be careful flaunting those clams around, hot stuff. You gotta be mindful in a city of conmen and cheats. I know you could handle a mugging, but the biggest thieves sit behind a counter."

The Feo took a dry sip, and decided not to bring up Pauvus' past raids on the Bank of Nemo.

"I get your meaning. Speaking of clams, how's the job going?"

"*Auuuughhhhh*," Pauvus groaned into the ceiling. "It's fine I suppose, but it's a job, not a joy. At least now I can pay rent and stop mooching off of you for drinks... Not to say I'd refuse an offer, eh?"

A series of crackles left Nemo's visor as Pauvus sipped slyly, watching The Sick Fiddle's stragglers fizzle out of the bar. The Feo sucked in a cold breath, and patted his chest in thought.

"It's funny, I have most things people search their entire lives for. Money, freedom, someone to share my love with. It's... more than I could've ever dreamed of, but... well, now I suppose I don't know what comes next."

A thoughtful hum left Pauvus' beak, and the Ave took a contemplative pull of his rum before answering.

"I remember you saying that you actually liked sailing, baffling as that is. Thinking of taking another tour sometime, one on your own terms? Plenty of captains would be happy to have you aboard."

Nemo cocked his head to the side, causing his hat to spin.

"Really? Even if they have to pay me now?"

"Why not?" Pauvus shrugged. "Even with a salary to pay, you've got years of sailing behind you. Not to mention a knack for the, well, rougher business on deck, n'all. I know there's still somethin' of 'The Brass Brute' in there, even if you're playing it soft these days."

Pauvus leaned over to give Nemo a nudge and a grin, neither of which the Feo felt he'd earned. The paces he'd been put through as a tool of his superiors came in blurred afterimages like a failed copy off the presses. He remembered commands, desperate pleas, a young scream plummeting into the cold sea below. The echo still vibrated in his head and rattled his core, enough for even Pauvus to notice.

"Ah, cripes Nemo, I shouldn't have—"

"No, no, you're right. I can't say I haven't thought about it," admitted Nemo, "but Eliza would never take to that kind of life. I think if I'm making decisions for myself now, I'd rather start a new chapter with her... even if it does mean one on dry land."

"As if Amrestir qualifies as 'dry land'," Pauvus scoffed with an amused caw. "But hey, you do you, kettle-man! Eliza's far from the worst person to tie the knot with."

The rim of Nemo's glass stopped short of his visor.

"What?"

"What'dya mean, what? You're talking about marriage, right? Matelotage?"

The Feo expected Pauvus to be dripping with sarcasm, but the Ave was dried of all cynicism. Nemo knew about the ceremonies, the great weight that the bonds they forged held, but the thought of anchoring down Eliza seemed unfair to her.

Shaking himself back to the conversation at hand, Nemo held his chin to keep the thoughts from ringing through his head like a ship's brass bell.

"I don't think The Church of Smouldering Ash would be, um, happy to recognize us like that."

Pauvus sneered, a skill he had a lifetime to practice, and waved a dismissive wing.

"Who cares what a bunch of fanatic firebrands have to say? Are they the ones running this island? No!"

Pauvus did have a point. The Smoulder's grip on common culture in New Amrestir had apparently been slipping since the island's change of management, to the point that Nemo hadn't had to deal with any accusations of blasphemy for walking around un-owned. Eliza had never made much of a fuss over the values of Mother Flame either, unless it came to lobbing a curse in her venerated name.

"True, but…" Nemo puttered. "If they're out of the question, we'd need a genuine captain to make it proper and legal. Ours skipped town weeks ago, and I've got no clue of anyone else who'd be willing to get on board with the idea."

Pauvus was staring at him as though his visor had sprouted a nose, utterly baffled.

"Do you really think *here*, out of anywhere on the Grand Sea, people would give a fig if your marriage is 'legal'?"

Pauvus once again made a good point. Yet as progressive as New Amrestir claimed to be, there were countless locals stuck deep in their old-fashioned, bitter ways. Nemo thought on the stares the two of them would get while out in public hand-in-hand, the whispers he would occasionally overhear about why some dolled-up Feo was hanging around a young woman like her. The comments and glares might not have bothered Eliza for the time being, but would that be the case in a few months? A few years?

"I know, it's just–she's–I'm a… Eliza deserves the world. Can someone like *me* give that to her?"

Pauvus sighed, and in a show of genuine affection, placed his wing on Nemo's shoulder.

"Listen, Nemo. I know you don't exactly have eyes, but anyone with them can see she's crazy about you. Just go with what your heart says… or your core, or whatever. Be bold, loverboy, life's for living to the fullest."

Nemo stared down into his cup of rum, watching his brassy reflection dance off the dark liquor. He was still unsure about exactly who it was that he was seeing, and who it would end up being in the end, but he knew it would be a happier scene with Eliza in it.

"I will."

Pauvus' words had taken up a permanent residency

in Nemo's head.

It tugged at his thoughts every time Eliza would pull herself close to his metal frame, every time she laid a kiss on his scorching helmet without fear of catching another burn on her lips. Nemo knew that she cared, she'd gone out of her way so many times to let him know it, but a lingering flicker of doubt remained. Despite her claims to the contrary, he couldn't help but think that Eliza deserved a real person to love, one with a heart of pumping blood instead of flame, one that could feel in the same way she did.

Yet even with skin of brass, each gentle smile and unalloyed comment shared between them sent an unknowable giddiness that had the Feo reeling. Pauvus had given him a sanding about being 'hopelessly in love', but Nemo didn't know what was so wrong with that.

"Nemo? You still there?"

Nemo sparked back to the present. He'd gotten lost in his own head again, but Eliza was still taking the lead on guiding them back to their secret dock below the boardwalk.

"Uh, yeah, just thinking."

As they twisted down the obscured path, Nemo felt for the bundled object resting heavily in his jacket pocket. The gravity of its meaning weighed each step, balancing the lightness in his chest like ballast on a balloon. There was a chance that he'd make a fool of himself, but Nemo had the feeling he was built to be one in the first place. It was the law of the ocean that no great reward came without great risk, and the Feo could not think of a single risk that would keep him from Eliza's side, except himself.

Nemo floated along to the edge of the dock where they'd capped off that first enchanted evening, and held Eliza's hand steady by the brink of the sea.

"Eliza, I… have a gift for you."

"Please don't tell me you got reeled in at the gift shop again!" Eliza chided, giving his shoulder a playful shove. "Your treasure's not bottomless y'know, you've

70

gotta think about the future!"

"I know, I know, but this one is important."

He watched Eliza's face shift as he slipped a small bundle from his jacket pocket, wrapped in bundles of fiery-red cloth. She had the patience to wait about half of a second before trying to snatch up the package, but Nemo's hands were quicker on the draw.

"Wait! Before you open it, I have to— Well, it's going to seem... strange at first. But, I promise you, it's something very significant."

Nemo handed the bundle over formally, and she took it this time with far greater care. Eliza's face continued its fall into confusion, just as he had expected it to, as she unraveled the layers of thin dyed sheets.

"It's a piece of coal?" asked Eliza, turning the black lump over on her palm. "I mean, I can take a guess as to– Oh wow, that is *hot!* What—"

Nemo chuckled as Eliza juggled the glowing stone between her hands like the eponymous Hot Potato. He inched back on the dock for the present to lose a portion of its pep, though he knew it would not cause her any real harm.

"That's a core coal!" he explained. "Its purpose is to find lost Feo. The closer you are to the one it's connected to, the more it glows, and the hotter it gets. Sorry, must've been a bit of a surprise."

Eliza flipped the ash-colored coal back into its flame-resistant wrapping, gaze flicking between it and Nemo's burning visage.

"Why would I need this?" Eliza grilled, raising a brow. "Are you going on the run? Look, if you're in trouble with the law, Toni's talked about some guys he served with who're still over in town. We could—"

"What?!" Nemo startled. "No, there's no price on my head... At least, I hope so."

Eliza laughed and marveled as the coal blistered from white to yellow to red in her protected hands. Her face fell from wonder to sincerity, as the gravity of Nemo's intent fell on her shoulders.

"Sorry, I was just pulling your leg. But... Nemo, this is the kind of thing that would mark you as mine. I'm not going to keep you on a leash every minute of the day, you're your own man to own."

This time, it was Nemo's turn to be shocked as Eliza passed the wrappings back into his hands.

"We're equals here, and to the trenches with anyone who says we aren't."

Nemo thought on the care and joy that he had felt in the time since knowing Eliza, the fresh sense of self and belonging without any strings of law or judgment to bind him. She had taken his roughness in stride, treated him with neither hostility nor pity from the very start.

Flame, I love this woman.

The Feo let the coal simmer into the air, a gentle orange glow illuminating the hair framing her face under a melting sky. Each strand he could see in the labyrinth looked like another new path ahead, another horizon.

"Eliza, I'm granting this to you in trust and dedication. I even had to squeeze Paul into helping get the coal sanctified by that Sister at the Smoulder smith shop. He... really got into the part."

"He must've gotten a kick outta that," Eliza scoffed.

"He certainly got the opportunity to play up his prestige for a bit. I got a kick out of it too: right to his tail feathers."

Nemo patiently waited for Eliza to work the humor out of her system before continuing in earnest.

"I don't mean for this to be about ownership... I'm asking for the honor of your partnership."

It suddenly became very difficult to meet Eliza's gaze. Nemo averted his visor to the moonlight dancing on the water, hand instinctively wringing at his scarf ends.

"From what I heard, you're supposed to give your significant other an expensive rock to prove that you're ready to commit. The coal wasn't that expensive, I swear, but it's the most valuable rock I could think of. I just wanted to..."

It was like a cup of water had been poured directly into his helmet. Nemo searched for the right words to explain exactly what he meant, what she meant to him, but all sense was escaping his head like steam. His searching gaze finally dared to dart back to Eliza and locked there.

Eliza was staring straight at him with eyes wide, shimmering like the sea at sunrise. The shifting of her face had fallen into a far-away flatness, still in its thoughtful beauty. Nemo allowed the night's silence to drift on until he simply couldn't take it any longer, doing what he could to fill in the empty space.

"...Eliza? Are you alright? I mean, this must be a really big shock to you, and maybe it's too soon so I understand. I-It's not like we can *really* get married anyway unless we find a very open-minded priest or, um, if my old Captain comes into port sometime soon, but I don't think he'd—"

Eliza threw herself at his torso with so much force

73

that Nemo nearly toppled off into the water. His sea legs managed to do him right, and kept him grounded while she clung to his maroon coat. With her face buried in his scarf, Nemo couldn't tell if she was smiling or crying, but all he needed to hear was a single word escaping from the depths of his chest.

"Yes."

A tidal wave of warmth flooded every crack and crook of Nemo's frame, feeling the coal and his own core cooking in tandem as he held Eliza tight. It took all his willpower to hold his tongue from whispering a "thank you", wishing to keep the moment as pure as possible.

Nemo embraced the connection between himself and the love in his arms, having never felt more hopeful in all his days.

If Nemo owned a mouth, his smile would be aching. He could barely keep track throughout the week after his brave proposal, present changing into past in a blur of plans, excitement, and unspoken anxiety.

Getting married had never seemed to be a prospect that would be in the cards for Eliza, let alone himself, but even without Pauvus' tales of grand ceremonies and wedding parties, they felt a need to lay their best hands on the table. Eliza had threatened to straighten her hair into something more "manageable" for the occasion, but Nemo stood firm that she kept her natural locks. In turn, he'd threatened to indulge her with a freshly imported dress from a boutique in town, and she'd shot down the offer in much the same way.

"Listen, Margaret's been bugging me about making me a wedding dress for ages," Eliza had told him. "She's gonna really, truly stick it to me if I don't take her up on the offer after all this time."

Sooner than he could have imagined, Nemo found himself again at the edge of their solitary aisle, gaze locked on the sight of his maiden in moonlight. Eliza stood resplendent in her pale gown infused with amethyst dye like the marbling of a clam, caringly tuned to fit just right. As proud as he stood in his gentleman's coat and newly-polished brass, Nemo felt like a beggar in the presence of a queen.

A queen she may have been, but neither of them were looking for a royal procession. Pauvus was their witness and only guest aside from Margaret, who couldn't have been stopped from attending by the entire New Amrestir Coast Guard combined, and Toni, who'd offered a hand at 'officiating' their marriage. Nothing about the hairy Aveilan man's demeanor spoke to being the mushy type, but he'd supposedly sat in at enough matelotages as a bosun to get the gist of the speeches. Besides, he was eager to actually put it into practice for once, and a happy boss for Eliza was a victory for everyone.

Beyond them, the secret dock remained as such, and would stay that way as long as they could help it. Their brief vows were spoken for their ears only, for there was little more that needed to be said between them. They both promised to provide for each other, care for each other and above all, stand by each other's side on even footing. Whether the world would have them or not, they knew that they would have each other.

At Toni's bequest, the Bouncin' Bean's doors were unlocked for the private reception, then promptly locked again afterwards. Nemo, Eliza, and Pauvus crowded around a table while he doled out Milk Punches, for once playing loose with the rum portions now that Margaret was breathing down his neck.

Pauvus raised his drink high, and managed to keep it upright even with five already behind him.

"A toast! To the—*hic*—gride 'n broom! Er, flip that."

The couple stifled their snickering, raising their glasses to join the salute.

"Nemo, Eliza, here's to your love! May it...

75

weather any storm that comes your way, and may fffoooortune follow you, wherever you go... And may it trickle down to the rest of us, eh?"

"I'll drink to that!" Eliza laughed, leading the quartet's flagons in toast with a clink. "Surprised with you, Paul, figured you'd make a bigger deal about your wing in all this."

Nemo watched Eliza knock the drink back as he felt the alcohol burning in his chest. Her teeth shone like pearls as she grinned, her eyes glinting like two onyx baubles in the dim firelight. Pauvus' own eyes were hazy with confusion, head swaying slightly atop his neck as they battled the drinks in his system.

"Whuh-huh? Why would I do that? Nemo's... the one who made the move. I'm just along for the ride."

Eliza leaned back in her chair, letting the night's booze wash over her like the tide.

"Hey, you're a swell fella. Might give you flak at times, but for some pampered kid you turned out alright."

"Pampered? *Hah!* I haven't even gotten a new set of clothes in months!" Pauvus groaned, waving broadly to Nemo. "He's the... high-class one now, see? Got th' shiny buttons n' the frilly trim n' all, like a proper noble there!"

"That's only because you kept bugging me to buy new clothes," Nemo shrugged.

"That was a public ssservice! Your coat was a hazard to every person with senses, you'll have'ta... take my word for it. Look, it'sh not about lookin' spiffy fer others, it's about *you* knowin' yer spiffy."

Pauvus punctuated his speech with a chatter of his beak, and swayed up to the counter to keep his tipsiness topped off. Nemo let the thought ring through his head, sinking into the peaceful moment with something close to relaxation, when he heard a wistful sigh from his side.

"I wish Dad was here to see this."

Nemo felt a sharp pang at his core. It was a fact of life that many sailors met their end before reaching their journey's end, whether by bullet, blade, or the simple wrath of nature taking its course. Even Feo ran the risk of shutting down for good, should fortune not fall their way. He had never bothered much with reflecting on his own mortality, not until he had something worth losing.

"If your father really was a Press man, I think he'd have loved the chance to write a story about this... and he would've loved to see how radiant you are tonight."

Eliza chuckled, letting her dark curls spread over Nemo's shoulder as she laid her head on it.

"I'm just glad the gossip hasn't spread outside the coffee shop. Could give less than a Kei's tail about what they'd think, but I don't need to give Toni's customers any more excuses to act like animals."

As if on cue, Toni's mug popped into the spot beside the couple, along with a fresh-filled one of his own.

"Ey, Liz! Look, I know you don't wanna talk about work on your Big Day, but I gotta get some air from Marge fer a sec. Besides, I got a business proposition ya might be interested in."

Nemo caught the roll of Eliza's eyes at the name, but even seven cups in she was still on stable enough footing to haggle.

"Shhhhure boss, what's the big idea?"

"Well, here's the deal," Toni began. "Remember that fancy *Tlauillibrew* you got, the Plasmotic blend? Yea, well you're the only person to order it, ever, and the beans aren't gonna last forever. Too good for the likes of this city, I tell ya!"

With a stiff pull, Toni drained his glass, and sent it sliding off to the very edge of the counter. He leaned between Nemo and Eliza, conspiratorially huddling with the happy couple.

"Now, I know a guy, Guy Chopin, out in Gémmisant. Fella sweet-talked his way into owning a sugar surplus, but doesn't have a lick o' sense in his head. He'd scoop this batch up like nobody's business on the premium, so if you... happened to be cruising about the coast, you could maybe... make a little business trip."

Nemo's head might've been vacant, but he wasn't ignorant. Toni was too proud to just give up a vacation, and visions of the beauty floating off of Fríasa's coast dazzled fresh in the Feo's mind. Eliza seemed to be tugging along the same line that he was, but she was still sampling the bait for any hidden barbs.

"That's quite the journey, could take weeks. You sure you'd manage that long without me here?"

"Ey, with all the time ya spend yammerin' with these two? Practically workin' solo as-is. Just get it secured and we'll be squared. Gotta pay off these drinks anyhow."

Eliza turned back to face Nemo, a smirk tugging the corner of her lips.

"Well, hon, what do you think? Would you be ready for another stint at sea?"

Nemo thought on all of Eliza's complaints about the horrors of sailing life, the nonsense of wannabe pirates throwing themselves to the sea. She always seemed perfectly content with never setting foot off the docks of New Amrestir, but now there was a gleam in her eye that Nemo had never seen before. He had to be sure that it wasn't just a reflection from his own spark.

"I'd be happy to sail away with you, but I would never want to force you into something you don't—"

A finger pressed itself to Nemo's visor, hissing him into silence.

"Hey, I've had my share of whining, but this isn't some press sentence. It's my choice... both of our choices. I can't think of anyone I'd rather see the world with."

"Hear, hear!" crowed Pauvus, who'd managed to pickle himself even further behind Toni's back. "What a guy, amirite?"

Nemo pulled Eliza into a warm embrace, allowing Toni and Pauvus to hash out their business without them. The world had opened itself to him, and she was ready to open herself up to the world. They chatted into the wee hours of the night under the Bouncin' Bean's roof, of the life they couldn't wait to share with each other.

CHAPTER 5
STRIKE

One week back on the open ocean ironically had Nemo feeling more grounded than he had since landing on New Amrestir's admittedly meager shores.

Ever since Toni's proposed plan, the Feo had been feeling the sailor's itch stronger than ever, an itch that no amount of city living or regular scrubbing could clear. Being out in the sea's rolling breezes, floating with the gentle ebb and flow of the water, was to witness the very breath of the world itself. And now he got to share it with the one he loved most.

Nemo rested on the deck of the *Marigold,* a schooner-rigged touring vessel bound for the western seas. They were already in the midst of their 'honeymoon', which by tradition called for a month of indulging in celebratory mead. He basked in the rise and fall of Eliza's restful breaths as he gazed across a skybound sea of constellations, tracing lines between the dots his past crewmates had once spun stories about.

"That one up there is called Lophina, an Ibi from the deepest trenches of the Empire. Never built to rise above her position in life, yet she had an insatiable desire to see the stars. They say the pressure did her in just before she reached the surface, but now she can swim through the night forever. Look, that line of stars there is her lure, signaling north for all on the sea."

Eliza hummed in interest as she nestled closer into Nemo's side. She was still training her sea legs, and sea stomach, but no minor discomfort would stop her from dragging him topside to watch the sky in its shining glory, or from quizzing him on all the constellations he could remember.

"Hm, real cheerful. How about... that one? The big swirl, that has to be something."

Nemo tracked the path of her questing finger, and a flicker of recognition flashed through his memories.

"Oh, that's the seahorse Achampos! Another proper Ibi legend, a common soldier that once outraced an entire Imperial chariot fleet by himself. All those little stars below are supposed to be his many children, carried along the sky in his rushing wake."

"Whew, big family," Eliza sighed. "Must've... been a stud."

Nemo chuckled, pulling the blanket tight around them both in the catching breeze.

"Sired and raised the lot of them all on his lonesome. Single father for the ages, immortalized in the minds of sailors. Sounds like quite the honor, right?"

Eliza's soft breaths grew longer, and her chest rose heavily against him. He turned to catch her eyelids drooping, dragged off to dreamland on Nemo's storytime line. Sweeping the blanket away, the Feo took her into his arms gently and left the watching stars a polite nod.

They crossed the threshold together, traipsing down to the warmth of the common deck. Nemo tip-toed past the room of his neighbor Oksana, a Bulwark guru who'd been offering spiritual meditation sessions for the extended cruise. Eliza might've been able to hibernate with the best of them, but he had no intention to risk any of the Obra woman's beauty sleep.

Nemo nudged open their suite door with his pegleg, and clicked it shut behind them. He tucked Eliza into their generous bed, placing his hat on the bedside table once his arms were free. After taking a brief peek in at the contents of an old leather bag he'd been waiting for the right opportunity to reveal, he eased his rigid frame in the bed with more care than really needed. As the Feo laid next to his wife, staring at the swaying timbers above, he was scarcely able to believe this was all real.

He was laying in a bed, a luxury he never thought

he'd get to enjoy, with a beautiful woman who genuinely cared for him, a luxury few of his past crewmates ever thought they'd enjoy. Once again, he was carried along by the whims of the waves, but swelled with pride in the knowledge that it was his decision, in his direction. Even in the dead of night, Nemo couldn't bring himself to nod off for one second, not wishing to miss out on any of his new life.

Ding-Ding! Ding-Ding!

That was odd. Nemo knew the skeleton crew must still be on-duty up above, even if they were killing time by rolling the bones, but it was far too late in the night for the ship's bells to be signaled. Perhaps it was a slip of the hand, or an ill-timed test, or—

Ding-Ding! Ding-Ding!

If there was one thing Nemo knew about his wife, it was that she slept like the dead. Eliza's dark curls were splayed across the pillows, arms stretched wide as she took full advantage of the sizable bed in their quarters. Not even a firm shake of her shoulder could rouse her, so he decided not to push the matter.

The Feo sighed, a bellow of steam escaping his brass slots. He reached over to the nightstand to put his hat back on, then allowed himself a moment to brush away a stray hair that had fallen into Eliza's mouth.

"I'll only be a minute," he hushed.

Nemo wasn't the only one concerned about the commotion, as most of the passengers couldn't hope to match Eliza's level of slumber. Many of his fellow travelers were standing outside their doors still in their nightwear, concerned murmurs drowned out by the bells. The Feo turned as Oksana peered out from her room, her sea-lion slickness caked with a nighttime mud mask.

"What's going on out here?"

"I have no clue," Oskana replied. "Sounds like something's going on up top."

The sea was still, as was the wind, neither of which was a good sign. At this time of night, in this part of the

81

sea, Nemo knew it would have to be trouble. A hoarse cry joining in with the bells confirmed his anxiety. His seafaring instinct flared up, and he charged ahead through the crowded hall to the upper-deck steps.

Whatever was happening topside, he would not allow it to reach his love.

Nemo burst out onto a deck in chaos. A swarm of unfamiliar sailors were sweeping across the meager active crew of the ship, draped in lush greens and blues under the moonlit sky. The rest of that sky was lit up with the sails of the *Marigold*, quietly crackling in full blaze. From between the collapsing lines and tackle, Nemo spotted a tall mast looming right beside their vessel, the Fríasen national standard proudly billowing from its peak.

Some of the other passengers were filtering up the decks with the same lack of self-preservation as Nemo, but he paid them no mind. There was a figure silhouetted at the bow, unmoved by the raging flames, and Nemo had the uncanny feeling that he was the focus of their uncanny stare. The slant-brimmed cap atop their head tilted, a single word drifting through the surrounding cacophony.

"...Feo?"

Something in Nemo's core ignited. He burst out from the gathering Audience in a sprint, coattails billowing in the chill of night. Even with only one proper leg at his disposal, Nemo dove and dashed across the deck, an irresistible burn driving him on through startled pirates.

"I am not having my honeymoon spoiled by you wretched bas—!"

CLANG!

Nemo's vision was engulfed in darkness, nearly driven right into his chest by the impact of a heavy bell clamping around his helmet. Staggering blind against the force tugging him across the deck, he felt the roar of his core suffocating within the great snuffer, sapping his stubborn strength. Nemo walked until his knees could carry him no longer, collapsing in a heap atop the timbers. Just as his flame fluttered near to failing him entirely, the world flooded back into view, along with the face of the assault's commander.

She towered before him, an air of superiority carrying her head and shoulders above even her taller cohorts. A mantle emblazoned with Fríasen colors billowed above her shoulder, her long hair waved with streaks of grey below a dirk-pinned cavalier hat. Her breastplate of composite colored glass gleamed in the firelight, scattering rainbow hues over Nemo's prostrate form.

She gripped his collar in a deceptively strong grip, yanking his visor in inches from the scar tracing over her nose.

"*Quel cadeau[1]!* A Feo delivered right to my feet, and a brass one. *Imagine ça[2]*. This one's got a spark to it, lads, and comes with its own accessories, too! Hm, it's missing a greave, and there's a bit of wear and tear, but not bad at all! Bring it along, Jean!"

---

[1] What a gift
[2] Imagine that

"I am not your plunder to pilfer!" Nemo raged, pulling against the calloused hands locking him into a submissive position. "My life belongs to another!"

"And it's loyal!" The Fríasen captain sniffed, letting a chuckle escape her lips. "That's a good sign. But I believe you forgot a certain level of gratitude for your new opportunity, *fantoche*[3]. We'll have to work on that, hm?"

The hands at his weary joints began to drag Nemo inexorably towards the boarding lines of the invading ship, unmoved by his pleas or well-placed kicks. The Feo railed against the vice-like hand at his neck, and managed to glance back to the captive Audience.

The passengers who weren't frozen in shock or being manhandled by marauders were struggling to hold back a woman straining to break through the crowd. She lunged in his direction, helpless as the planks were pulled up from the *Marigold*. Nemo noticed the cloud of dark hair flashing in the extinguishing light, and it set his core even colder than the snuffer's chill.

Eliza was howling like a wounded animal, clawing at the arms that held her at bay. Her cries echoed over to his kidnapper's ship, piercing the ears of all present. Nemo twisted and turned in his captor's grasp, trying to get an arm free to reach out to his beloved as though she would be able to save him from this fate.

"No! Please don't—!"

"Oh, *par pitié*, can you deal with that? This is really spoiling my good spirits."

Nemo gazed at the sea of stars, catching one more glimpse of Eliza's struggle before another clang shuttered the world, dragging him away from the owner of his heart.

Awareness filtered through Nemo's visor in waves, vague impressions of shoving hands and barked commands

---

[3] puppet

dragging him through the motions. It was a familiar apathy, the sort of dissociation he could really get into by getting out of himself. He couldn't forget the sight of Eliza's wild efforts to reach him, the terror in her far-away eyes. It tugged at his core like an anchor, grounding his thoughts despite his best efforts to drift back to nothing.

"Réveille-toi[4]!"

Someone shoved a handful of powder into Nemo's face, and the world exploded into view. Coughing up clouds of sawdust, the Feo had a chance to finally get a good look at where he'd been stolen off to.

What Nemo saw was a graveyard. Scrap and trinkets of brass cluttered the interior of an unfamiliar cargo hold, a not-insignificant amount of it looked to have been salvaged from lost Feo. Nemo's gaze flicked between heaps of metal from his kin and piled-up jewelry, and nearly learned how to vomit on the spot.

Before his imagination could leap off the deep end, a scarred face lowered itself to dominate the scope of Nemo's vision. The woman before him had the glee of an eager child finding a new toy, lips curling around teeth that looked too well-maintained for an average pirate. It backed far enough away from his visor for him to see that she was swirling his precious hat around a finger. He could do nothing but watch as she plucked Pauvus' feather from the brim.

"I may have had reservations about shooting for that target," his captor marveled, safely tucking the feather behind the lip of her own cap, "but I cannot deny the prize. Your old owner had taste, even if she didn't have dignity."

The woman allowed the tricorne to float to the ground, giving it a significant boot back over to Nemo. He pulled it close, then pulled himself together in order to face her properly.

"How would you know about either?"

A swift kick found itself right in the middle of his cuirass. Stars swam in Nemo's vision as he felt his chest

---

[4] Wake up

cave in for one terrifying moment, then bow out in a dent that gave him a nasty case of heartburn.

"You best show our captain some respect, tinman!" snarled the stout sailor hovering above Nemo, sporting an eyepatch and an extremely familiar jacket. "Let's see how much nerve you've got as fool's gold jewelry!"

A single hand was all it took to silence the man. There was a flavor of amusement in the woman's cocoa-brown eyes, and more than a little mania.

"No, I think I'll be keeping this one," the woman insisted. "Fully functional, in this sturdy of shape? We'd be the fools to pass up an opportunity like this, Antoine. Besides, it seems impolite to peel it to pieces, considering it brought such nice welcome gifts for us."

Something clicked in Nemo's head, and he thought to look down at himself. The crew must have stripped him down to his bare brass at some point in his transportation and apparently decided to treat themselves on his behalf. Nemo reached up to grab the hem of his coat when another boot stomped him into the timbers. The kidnapping captain kneeled above him, eyes glittering brighter than the stained glass encircling her heart.

"Pay attention. I don't know what that mewling *bambin*[5] let you get up to, but this is my ship. *Mes règles*[6]. You play nice, we play nice, it's wonderful for everyone. You can even keep the hat as a good-will gift, courtesy of the generous Madame Vitrail. If I can't have the fortune of having a Feo with its own plume, I'd prefer one to my name with at least a shred of dignity."

Madame Vitrail plucked a slender 'golden' chain from a crate by the wall, allowing the individual links to cascade before Nemo's sight.

"Let's get down to brass tacks, then. We've important business waiting in Faffton, and you can make the journey there in one piece or many." Now, if I have my way, which is hardly even a question, I would pick the

---

[5] toddler
[6] My rules

former, but we've got someone on board this vessel who could boil you down to price-gouged doorknobs. Do you understand, *laiton*[7]?"

Nemo wrung the tricorne in his hands, staring up and fuming beneath the surface. It went against every lick of instinct in his core, but an old, familiar hopelessness was soaking into his shell like the wood of a sinking ship.

"...Yes."

Madame Vitrail's heel dug deeper into the dent, a harsh slice of authority cutting through her former good cheer.

"Yes, and?"

"Yes... Thank you."

A grin found its way back to the captain's face as she let the pressure off from Nemo's chest. Madame Vitrail took a handkerchief from her pocket, making a show of superficially polishing the bootmark.

"*Merveilleux*[8]! Glad we understand each other," Madame Vitrail smarmed, turning to the cargo hold exit with a flip of her wavy hair. "Antoine, give it the itinerary, set it to work. Expecting great things ahead!"

The door slammed with a kick, and Nemo was left alone with his thoughts and Antoine the coat thief. He allowed a deluge of commands to wash over him, shifting back into his automatic obedience with shameful ease. As his frame straightened itself and prepared to do as asked once more, the Feo's mind drifted leagues away.

---

[7] brass
[8] Wonderful

CHAPTER 6

DIRECTOR

A glob of spit sizzled off the Feo's visor.

Nemo pinched a barnacle to pieces, looked down, and sighed a hot breath. He leaned back on the harness of ropes tethering him to the railing of *La Fille Patronne*, as was labeled on the old ship's hull, and craned his neck to catch what else might've been coming out of the sailor's mouths from above.

"Whatta sham! That ol' crone's a real coal crusher, I tell ya. Tried to get 'er to tell me where I might find my own real treasure in the future, 'n she tells me I'll find it as a corpse in the sand!"

"Well what'dya expect?" another voice spat. "It's her job to do that whole flame-seeing flim-flam for the Captain, not palm-tracin' to read your love life. As if you're ever gonna see gold, Remy."

Flicking shell residue off the side of the ship, Nemo's flame rose in curiosity. The sails of the *Marigold* fluttered through his thoughts, burning away with no trace of gunfire. He had a sinking feeling that he knew the sort of 'crone' they had meant, and he knew what it would take to see her personally.

Nemo angled a scraping chisel against the hinge on his left shoulder, taking a moment to keep Eliza's face in mind before he plunged the tool into his brass body. He pried and twisted at the joint unflinchingly until the arm hung limp, flapping in the breeze like a window shutter. It took a careful balance with only one working hand, but he managed to yank the ropeline at his side in a three-tug pattern. By the time he reached the topside of *La Fille Patronne,* Nemo found himself face-to-face with a very annoyed and out-of-breath Remy.

88

"Cripes, what happened to your arm?"

"...I slipped. Thank you."

A sigh escaped the bosun's beard. He hooked Nemo's anchoring line on the railing with a grunt, and hauled him over by the pauldron.

"Well shite, yer not gonna get any work done like that," the Fríasen man grunted, flexing his shoulder to point below deck. "Go head to the Sister's room, right next to the kitchen. Knows all that Feo stuff. Get sorted 'n get back, I'm not doin' this again."

"Thank you."

Nemo promptly spun on the one heel he had, not sticking around to get distracted by any other orders. Letting his shoulder sag as grotesquely as it could, the other workers on duty left the Feo alone as he trudged down the steps to the inner decks. He spotted the redwood door beside the galley entrance and shoved his way inside before he could consider offering a knock.

There were candles draped across nearly every surface, like stalagmites in a crimson cave. It was an unacceptable fire hazard for any ordinary ship's quarters, but this was the quarters of no ordinary sailor. A shape draped in thick red robes was squatting by the base of a great oven, flipping the firewood with her bare hands. Only when the door shut behind Nemo did the Sister stir from her tending, turning to gaze at him with eyes like milky glass. The silence dragged on as the holy woman stared into and through the Feo, allowing the fireplace to crackle in harmony with his own. When she finally spoke it was with the softness of an ember, a pop at the edges.

"What is required of me?"

"My left arm is in need of repair. Thank you."

No further explanation was asked for or needed. The priestess of the Smoulder gestured for him to come forward and after a moment of hesitation, he did. Lowering himself before the oven, Nemo watched her hands trace over his sabotaged shoulder, prodding along the loose rivets and hinges.

89

"This is nothing."

With a wave of the Sister's hand, a lick of flame stretched across from the open oven, reaching out like tendrils of a jellyfish into his metal creases. Nemo had the uncanny experience of seeing his shoulder melt without any feeling, watching as aged and trained fingers molded the joint back into working order.

Neither spoke as she went to work, kneading away at the shoulder like a masseuse. Only when the shape was set and brass left to cool did Nemo croak out again, if only to assert himself to his blacksmithing nurse.

"My name is Nemo."

"A fitting name for a Feo."

Nemo reminded himself of what he was here to really do, and let that comment float over his head for the time being.

"The sailors above spoke of your... sight."

"These eyes may have been dimmed a lifetime ago, but my vision remains vast," the woman hissed, a flicker of clarity flashing through her face. "I am Sister Ann, steward of this vessel. My fellows may see me as a teller of fortunes, or a spare stove, but my place is as envoy of the Mother Flame: She who guides all bonds, all connections. Even yours, Feo."

Nemo went quiet. His core burnt with questions, with possibilities, yet he had no idea what he could say to explain himself. The cleric turned back to the oven by the wall, but he felt the pierce of her sight in the light of every candle.

"Speak up, then," Sister Ann sighed. "In our own ways, we are tools of the Captain and the Flame both. But you have no thanks to give, and neither of us has the time to waste on pretense. You are longing for someone, hm?"

"I... I am," Nemo admitted, stunned at the woman's insight. "We were separated, and I am trying to return to her. I need to know that she's safe, if nothing else. Please... help me."

The silence that followed his request was deafening,

filled only by the sound of another red candle scraping across the tabletop, this one unlit. In an instant, Sister Ann's fingers had prodded directly into the slit of his visor and plucked from within it a singular ember. She guided the speck to the wick, where it sparked with new life.

"You hold a pact that spans across the Grand Sea, formally sanctified. A tethered existence, born not of obligation, but… partnership?"

Nemo backed away from the flame, watching it burn with an oddly nostalgic terror. The candles across the room had taken to the same scarlet of the candle, as though his own existence was being projected across the walls.

"Yes… My wife."

If Sister Ann had any heretical complaints about that, she kept them to herself. Her eyes were engulfed with the story sputtering before her, pupils like glowing coals framed with faint tears.

"Her sorrow weighs heavy, a grief that I… I cannot fathom. The bond forged of your coal, tinged with the aching of her heart, roars with a desire to join once more."

A sigh of relief Nemo didn't know he had been holding hissed from every vent in his frame. Eliza was alive.

"Is she okay? Where is she right now?"

Sister Ann leaned close to the crimsoned candle, nearly singeing her silvered eyebrows.

"She is– She is atop a floating abomination."

The Feo went rigid, chassis rattling in distress. Sister Ann tilted her head back until her face was parallel with the ceiling, itself beginning to crawl with scattered flames.

"There is a miasma, wicked of spirit, soaked into its sails." The priestess gasped, as if the very words burned her tongue. "I hear shouting, pleading. There is a man—no, not a man—a *monster* haunting her. H-He is decaying before me! By the Flame, he is *rotting!*"

"WHO?!"

Nemo stood abruptly, the fire inside flaring and the flames outside to meet it. Sister Ann screamed as she fell to her side, her hands clawing at her face. Whatever vision had engulfed the priestess deafened her to his question and the world. Even as the room burnt to a deep red, it was impossible for Nemo to calm himself now. He gripped Sister Ann's shoulders to prop her upright, too lost in swirling questions to notice the singeing of her robes.

"Where is this ship?! How can I find—?!"

Smoke clouded the Feo's vision, and Nemo joined the ranks of the blind. Every light in the quarters was snuffed as though caught in a great yawn, save for the single candle burning with his core's ember. Sister Ann fell limp in his arms, her weight sagging against his newly repaired shoulder.

"There is a whisper on the wind… *Please don't resent me.*"

The Feo leaned back, the room once again lit by the cool orange glow of *La Fille Patronne*'s oven. His mind raced as the holy woman before him caught her breath and folded herself back into a prophet-able condition.

"If you wish to see her again, conform to the Captain's will," Sister Ann's voice wavered, cutting through Nemo's despair. "It will buy you time, if little else. In many cases, time is more precious than any fortune I can see."

Whether another prediction or simple advice, Nemo did not care. All he wished now was to be alone, to stew in the longing that Mother Flame had seen fit to deepen even further. He pinched the candle's wick between his brass fingers, checked his shoulder joint with a click, and offered the Sister a vacant tip of the cap. The Feo staggered to re-enter the world above, leaving behind the only words expected of him.

"Thank you."

Nemo rowed with all his might, and watched the hull of *La Fille Patronne* shrink away.

It would have made for a far happier sight, had he been alone to enjoy it. He was forced to leer around the wide brim of Madame Vitrail's hat with each stroke of the small dory's oars, the captain making for better ballast than she did a rower. She simply sat back with her boots kicked up on his seat, luxuriating in her idleness.

"*Allez*[9], Feo!" Madame Vitrail commanded, topping off the powder pan of her pistol with primer. "Ahh, this is what I've been missing out on all this time! A little elbow grease goes a long way, doesn't it? Watch that shoulder, I'm not having you waste any more of Sister Ann's time with that."

As he tore the oars through the surf, Nemo watched a smug smirk spread across Madame Vitrail's face. They were alone, floating beyond the confines and regulations of

---

[9] Come on

the captain's crew. It would be so easy, he considered, to just crack her across the skull and flee, row off and take his chance on the greater Grand Sea.

The thought crystallized in Nemo's mind, and immediately shattered. Even if he could make a clean break of it, he'd be shot down by the other ships in an instant. Any hopes of seeing Eliza again would be up in smoke. Still, the Captain couldn't do anything to stop him from using his imagination, even as it started to reel up flashes of memories best left submerged. Nemo poured all of his nervous energy into his arms, free on the open sea yet with only one path open to him.

Before long, their little rowboat came upon the base of *Le Veinard*, a lesser vessel in Vitrail's Fríasen fleet, along with a ladder being lowered down to them. Nemo was left to tie their tether while the captain climbed ahead, having another brief moment of mutineering spirit until a new chorus of cheering from above doused it. As he climbed, Nemo picked up the tail end of Madame Vitrail's warm welcome.

"...*oui, merci, merci*. Now, Renaud, what could possibly be so important that you had to waste our collective time on calling for a personal visit?"

Nemo climbed over the railing to see a regiment of sailors and soldiers saluting the Madame with a blend of fear, respect, and awe. A gaunt man stood at attention before her, dripping down from his bicorne hat.

"*Désolé*[10], captain," murmured the man presumably named Renaud. "We would not have bothered if it was not serious. Word carried over from the north. It seems there is a flotilla en route with our line, incoming from the direction of New Amrestir."

Madame Vitrail lifted her hat to claw a hand through her hair, and snapped twice in Nemo's direction. Sensing his cue, the Feo rumbled up to stand at his current captain's side and watched Renaud's sagging face fall even further.

---

[10] Sorry

"What was it I had said during our conference again?" Vitrail sighed, orbiting around Nemo with the posture of a predator. "Ah, yes: dealing in any business with the gnats circling that wretched little island is nothing but an invitation to get bitten. It's bad enough we had to waste inventory on that terrible jewelry stand idea, but this is—"

"*Ngh-guh...*"

"...Right then. Thanks to the will of the people we've fired our shot, and now I have to handle the physical *and* political recoil. If the fight is coming to us, my will is law until further notice. Send word down the line, organize a full—"

"*Huhhngh...*"

A second grunt from somewhere in the assembled Audience shouldered Madame Vitrail right out of her momentum. Nemo recognized the fire behind her eyes, and wondered if she was about to start steaming from the ears too.

"Okay, where's the dead man that keeps doing that?"

A twiggy sailor with tall curls brought a hand to his mouth, muffling himself with a mixture of a cough and a spasm. Whether a nervous tic or a poor attempt to cover a laugh, Nemo could tell that the lad would have preferred to be anywhere else on the Grand Sea at that moment.

Stomping up under his nose, Vitrail shot the uncomfortable sailor a sneer that stretched her scar.

"Is something funny, *marin[11]*?"

Sensing an imminent flogging, Captain Renaud stepped forward and trained a placating smile at his superior.

"Oh, *pardonne-lui[12]*, Madame Vitrail. That's just something our good surgeon does from time to time."

"...Is that so?"

"Aye, 'tis ol' Twitch," the captain nodded.

[11] sailor
[12] forgive him

"Disregard the nickname, the lad does fine work. Aces as a barber to boot."

The surrounding crew exchanged knowing glances and nods, one even elbowing Twitch in a teasing nudge. Vitrail's gaze remained sharp as she beckoned for the boy to step out from his fellows, wearing a smile that Nemo could tell was feigned.

"Now, 'Twitch'," she drawled with deceptive cordiality, "I trust you understand why I might have some reservations about your... little habit, given the importance of your role here, let alone preventing you from showing proper courtesy."

Nemo watched as Twitch lived up to his name once more with no regard for the woman's threats. He swallowed his muttering and pulled himself into shape, trying to politely reflect Vitrail's sharkish smirk.

"I completely understand, Madame, but I never let it get in the way of my duties. I'm ab—*hrghnn*—able to keep it under control while focusing."

Vitrail's eyes narrowed. "Are my words not worth your focus, then?"

That sent the surgeon reeling. He sputtered and stumbled backwards as if the accusation had swept him from under his feet.

"Wha—No! I-I would never— I'm here to—"

Vitrail spun her attention back to Renaud, who looked as though he was about to melt through the ship's timbers.

"How am I supposed to believe you're able to keep your crew under control when you let this one get away with such childish outbursts?" Madame Vitrail spat. "Your surgeon is not only undermining my authority, but yours as well!"

"Madame, be reasonable!" beseeched Renaud. "Now is not the time to be picking through the ranks, we've a battle to be priming ourselves for!"

While the Fríasen bosses bickered, Nemo remained stock-still by the railing. He was grateful to not be the focus

96

of attention for the moment, until he felt Vitrail's sharp eyes slashing in his direction.

"*Mmh*, you are right. We've a battle ahead, one brought about by our own hands, and surely 'Twitch' will have his kept quite busy. Perhaps we can help him with washing them... *Laiton,* grab him."

Nemo had his hands on Twitch's shoulders in an instant. He hadn't thought to, or even intended to, but his body had obeyed the order nonetheless. The surgeon squirmed in his grip, straining against his brass digits in vain. None of Nemo's pity could loosen them.

"Throw him overboard," commanded Vitrail, with no pity of her own. "A quick dunk will clean up his act."

The deck of *Le Veinard* churned with chaos, the waters below the ship churned along with it. Nemo could do nothing but watch from within himself, frozen between his instincts and his shame, shouts ringing out a hollow roar through his head. As the Feo's core twisted in his shell, faces around him twisting in all flavors of emotion, Sister Ann's advice drifted and blended between past and present.

If you wish to see her again, conform to the Captain's will.

"Hey! Let me go!"

Capitānee, quid est illud?[13]

"Unhand my surgeon, Feo!"

Id est Feo. Nemo est.[14]

"AAUUGHH!"

A scream pierced through the cacophony, dragging Nemo back to the surface. He looked down to see that Twitch was still in his grasp, writhing and contorting in pain. Smoke was drifting up from the Feo's hands, his frame searing hot enough to burn straight through the lad's shirt and into his shoulders. Twitch dropped to his knees, the Feo responsible for his suffering unable to tear his visor away from the scraps of singed cloth stuck to his fingers.

---

[13] Captain, what is that thing?

[14] That is a Feo. It is nobody.

All hands on deck stood in stunned silence as the surgeon breathed heavily through his agony. Save for one.

"*Ghe-heh-HAH!*" Madame Vitrail barked, parking her thumbs on her belt. "Looks like *le petite bouilloire*[15] reached its boiling point!"

Nemo looked again at the faces surrounding him, alien in their organic horror. Renaud fumed up to Vitrail with nose-scrunching disgust, facing down his superior with newfound courage.

"How dare you! This is my ship and my crew to command by the letter of Fríasen law, Madame. You overstep your bounds, and with the spoils of a conquest you claim to condemn, no less!"

"You overstep *yours*," Vitrail hissed, placing a firm hand on Nemo's shoulder. "It was not by my word that your boy was burnt, the Feo did that of its own accord. It will be dealt with, but this still stands as a fair compromise: your surgeon's been taught a lasting lesson, and he's still in

_____

[15] the little kettle

98

proper enough shape to clean up our scrapes. *C'est juste, non?*[16]"

Turning from the hushed distress across *Le Veinard*, Madame Vitrail led Nemo along to the railing ladder once more. She pulled him down to her level by the gorget and whispered into what qualified as the Feo's ear.

"Bravo, bouilloire, you've made our point with brilliant brutality. Wait down below, allow them to simmer while I handle the rest. I see great potential in your service."

With a pat on the pauldron, Vitrail sent Nemo down the ladder. Before he dropped below the railing, the Feo watched Twitch being pulled up by his fellows, the lad wearing a mask of terror he had seen on his previous victims many times before. When the surgeon's eyes glimpsed over to Nemo, his fear only deepened.

Leaving his current captain to whip the crew into action, Nemo followed the path of his thoughts, sliding down the ladder into the depths of his own dejection.

From the depths of *La Fille Patronne*, Nemo could hear that it was a busy night up above.

The sounds of gunfire peppered the isolated cargo hold, along with the whoops and hollers of true naval warfare. Madame Vitrail had opted against letting Nemo take part in the festivities, both to keep her new toy in near-mint condition and to keep him from hopping into a new toybox. That would be a job left to the crew with blood to spill and loyalty to Fríasa in their hearts, a statement to any who would question her decisions going forward.

Left with a generous assortment of charcoal briquettes for his "good service" aboard their sister vessel, Nemo was grateful to be left out of the savagery above. The

---

[16] It is just, no?

sights and sounds of Twitch's agony were still burnt on the inside of his visor, and the last thing that Nemo wanted was to slip back into being nothing but a—

—The cabin boy's scream, raw and desperate, ripped through the air as he plummeted into the cold sea below—

An explosion of cannonfire outside blasted Nemo back to the present. His memories were beginning to cling to each other like crabs linking their claws in a chain, threatening to drag him down into the boiling pot with them. In the midst of the muffled carnage, a new sound thundered deeper into the ship's hull, far too close to have been an external attack. The Feo creaked his neck up to listen in, ignoring a new nightmare that had decided to tug at his collar, and caught a vague screech under the sound of incoming bootfalls.

Light from beyond the hold poured onto Nemo's brass, silhouetting two tall-capped sailors in full combat garb. Something blue blurred past his face, someone shouted something in Fríasen that he couldn't quite make out, and the temporary brig slammed into darkness once more. Even without eyes, Nemo's vision took time to focus in the changing light. His ambient glow eventually lit up a colorful pile of cloth and feathers at his feet.

Some poor Ave had been snatched up by Fríasen forces, just the same as—

—CRACK! The Ave stood with beak agape in horror, as chunks of it scattered across the—

—himself, caked with salt and sweat from the war still raging in the night. Two eyes like topaz earrings scanned the cramped supply room they now found themselves in, only to land squarely on the Feo. They glimmered in the dark, and the slender unbroken beak crowed out in a familiar tone.

"Nemo! You old crustacean, I knew it! Brew on that, Toni!"

100

For a moment, Nemo worried that he'd fallen even further into the spiral of his own memories. He smacked his head and popped a new briquette in, illuminating the battered mass of what was undeniably Pauvus. He looked about as awful as Nemo felt, but that didn't stop the waterlogged bird from pulling himself up on the Feo with grasping wings, pressing close to his cuirass like it was a warm oven.

"P-Paul! Where did you—?"

"*Shhhh*," Pauvus shushed, "shut up for a second. I'm having a reunion with my best mate. Don't spoil the moment by yammering."

Nemo chuckled in disbelief, and followed the only order he'd been happy to obey. He reached around to match the Ave's hug with a warm embrace, and listened to the exhaustion and relief seeping from Pauvus' shoulders hiss on the hot brass.

"*Whew*... I may have beaten you this time in pure boneheadedness. The *Marigold*'s skeleton crew came back to shore without you, said the ship got hit by a Fríasen raid of all things! Toni was going on and on about getting his lads together to strike out on a rescue, as if they're about to bust outta their easy chairs guns blazing. Nah, I knew it'd take wing power, and some government aid. Gotta say, it was easier than I thought to get those Coast Guard types in a bloodthirsty mood, once you bring some nationalism in the mix."

A fresh scream echoed in from above, followed by a wet squelch. Nemo had seen much in his time, maybe too much, but he was happy not to see it now. The senseless fighting, the wasted life, the—

—The iron helmet lay hollow and cold in the sand. He was staring at his future. A tool to be used, discarded when it was no longer—

Something bobbed up in the tempest of Nemo's mind. Listening to the Ave's thin whistling wheeze, a thought managed to wriggle its way through the storm and to the surface.

"Did you just say I'm your best mate?"

"Shut up, would ya?" Pauvus demanded, fluffing his feathers dry against a wine cask to hide his relief. "But yeah, they woulda come around to protect their 'honor' one way or another. Figured no matter who came out on top it'd get me in close, and here you are! Not ideal, but we can grab Eliza and get out once things calm down a bit. She sleeping down here too?"

Nemo slumped further down the wall at his back, his mood darkening along with the room.

"She wasn't on the lifeboats, then."

"No! You think she wouldn't have come along too? I thought she was with you, where else would she be?!"

Nemo's arms went limp, dangling at his sides like a marionette cut from its strings. He didn't know what was a more terrifying prospect: Sister Ann's vision being wrong, or right. The hope that had been re-sparked within his core was drowned out just as quickly, the words of the prophet spiraling through him like a whirlpool.

"...She's atop a floating abomination, with a monster haunting her."

–KNOCK KNOCK KNOCK–

The sound shook Nemo from his sorrows, and he realized that it wasn't just in his head. Pauvus was rapping his talon against the Feo, beak mere inches from his visor.

"Hey, hollowhead!" the bird squawked. "I don't know what kind of Fríasen tripe they're feeding you here, but you know Eliza! That Smoulder scammer who set up the core coal said you'd know if something happened to it, you've got that py-romantic connection and all. What's your heart tellin' ya, then?"

Pushing past what his head was screaming, Nemo looked deep inside himself, an act that was easier done than said in his case. The bonds that Sister Ann had peered through were still left intact. The lingering line of heat was tugging closer, however faintly.

"It's getting closer."

Nemo felt a rush of air across his visor as Pauvus put a wing on his back, patting the brass encouragingly.

"There ya go! She's probably got a whole fleet under her thumb by now, scorching the sea to catch up with you... and me, I suppose. Was kind of hoping I wouldn't end up stuck on another stinkin' ship this soon, so much for New Amrestir naval superiority. But hey, at least it's like the old days, eh? So brighten up a little, I can hardly see over here."

Even if it was through a beak that didn't believe its own words, Pauvus' positivity broke the surface tension. Nemo tossed back another briquette, glowing bright enough to take in the full state of the bird in front of him.

"What happened to your tail?"

Pauvus tucked in the shambles that was his fan-tail, doing a poor job of covering his shame with exhausted bravado.

"Oh, eh, cost of warfare, there. Caught a stray four-pounder when I tried to make the ship-swap, then that sea witch of a Captain up there plucked a few more feathers as a 'housing expense'. As if she could pull it off as well as the two of us!"

"Jealousy breeds mimicry, Paul. Can't hold a candle to the original."

The laugh that came out of Pauvus sounded forced, but Nemo appreciated the effort all the same.

"Speaking of fashion, what happened to yours? This might be the first time I've ever seen you *au naturel*, pardon my Fríasen."

"It's degrading," Nemo admitted. "Vitrial took everything, even gave her First Mate my coat."

Paul let out a scoff, and plopped down next to the convenient fireplace that was Nemo.

"Yea, thought that cyclops' style looked familiar. Savages, the whole lot of them."

Nemo settled in against the peacock's shivering side, prepared to weather the storm that was to come. A few moments passed before he heard a faint pluck and wince, followed up by a familiar weight being threaded into his cap.

"Here, gotta look stylish when you see your love dove again, right? Just you wait, we'll all be cooped up safe in New Amrestir again before you know it, sharing some fresh brews and wild tales."

The din was dying away, and Nemo imagined that Pauvus' rescue brigade wasn't about to risk the same of its crew. Even with the Smoulder Sister's warning, Nemo felt he was drowning in the possibilities of what was to come. He was barely holding his past back from flooding his present, much less what his future could hold.

Still, squatting in the warm glow, cozy in their current prison as the free world outside exploded, the two friends took solace that even with the burdens of the world to bear, they wouldn't have to do it alone.

Eliza was alone.

Being alone was something that Eliza had become used to over the years, even cherished at times, but memories of losing a loved one remained raw in her mind. The moment she had finally unlocked the door to her heart for the love of another, it had been cruelly torn from its hinges once more.

She sat at the edge of her bed in her nightgown, still as a statue, the cabin all the more empty without Nemo's hollow frame beside her. Against her thrashing efforts, the *Marigold* was whipping around on course back to New Amrestir, leaving the Fríasen privateers to flee with all but the poor cruising schooner's bare essentials. Any other news about the raid hadn't reached Eliza, but she already knew there was nothing she wanted to hear.

The proposal coal in her hand grew colder and colder with the passing days, mourning within her locked couple's cabin. Some of the other passengers had taken pity on Eliza, delivering meals and sympathy to her doorstep, but that dried up once news got around about what she did to the Quartermaster when he informed her of the "good news" on their insurance claim for her lost Feo. In the time since, Eliza had taken to wallowing in what she considered to be a well-earned sulk, letting the rest of the world go on churning along without her. It sounded like things were certainly churning about up top, if the clatter and shouted orders through the ceiling were anything to go by, but Eliza was in no mood to step out into another nightmare.

With our luck it'll be another pack of vultures looking to peck what's left of the carcass clean. Let them.

Even from within Eliza's cocoon of sorrows, the din

was starting to grow frantic enough to unravel her woes. She groaned and dragged herself on protesting feet to the doorway, if for nothing else than a way to kill a few more seconds of cursed travel time.

The *Marigold*'s passenger hall was still, hosting none of the confused panic that had fueled the Audience on their fateful assault. Eliza imagined the others wouldn't be jumping the gun to put themselves, or any remaining valuables, in harm's way again, and she was in no position to blame them. Creeping to the landing of the main deck's steps, Eliza managed to tune her ear to the wavelength of a shouting match above.

"...this be some sort of joke? What, that pod of wretches strip yer cargohold bare first?"

"Yes!"

A thoughtful pause split the conversation, along with a wet gurgle that Eliza couldn't quite place.

"Well, that be on ye, then! What an embarrassment. Truth be told, there do be pity in this ol' grotty shell, no mistake. We be havin' no desire for yer deaths, just yer vessel. Ye can flee to that city of lights in yer dinghies with yer lives, and the thought of them Friasen swine soon bein' brought to heel. Ought to keep ye warm along the way."

Friasen. Eliza closed her eyes and pictured the flag that had been strung up the mast of the ship that had swept Nemo away, along with the shadowy figure in command of it. The gears in her brain crunched into action, and she was already regretting the idea they were winding up.

"W-well, I—"

"Gooood lad. Let them vacation-types know, we be wasting light! And, t'state the plain 'n clear, we was never here, eh?"

The heart in Eliza's chest was threatening to burst, along with her lungs, as she raced back to her empty cabin. Whoever was making sloppy seconds of the *Marigold* shared a common enemy with her, and that was all the ammunition she needed to set a spark. As dangerous and foolish as it may have been, there was a glimmer of hope piercing her overcast thoughts, and she owed it to Nemo to grasp for every sunbeam.

Eliza scrambled about her sleeping space, weighing out potential options for stowaway spots like she had played with her father back in the day. She pictured the different ways she might end up losing the highest stakes game of hide-and-seek in her life, until her eyes landed upon the shadow of the Bouncin' Bean's barrels squatting in the corner.

A candle flicked on in her head. It would be a waste of good coffee, and Toni would probably never let her hear the end of it even into death, but it was something.

With a heave, the lid of the barrel popped from its seal under Eliza's savage pull. She got to work bailing enough beans out the porthole window to permanently ruin her salary and gathered whatever small trinkets could accompany her for the cramped trip. Vitally, Nemo's core coal remained tight in Eliza's fist as she shimmied herself down into the walls of the cask.

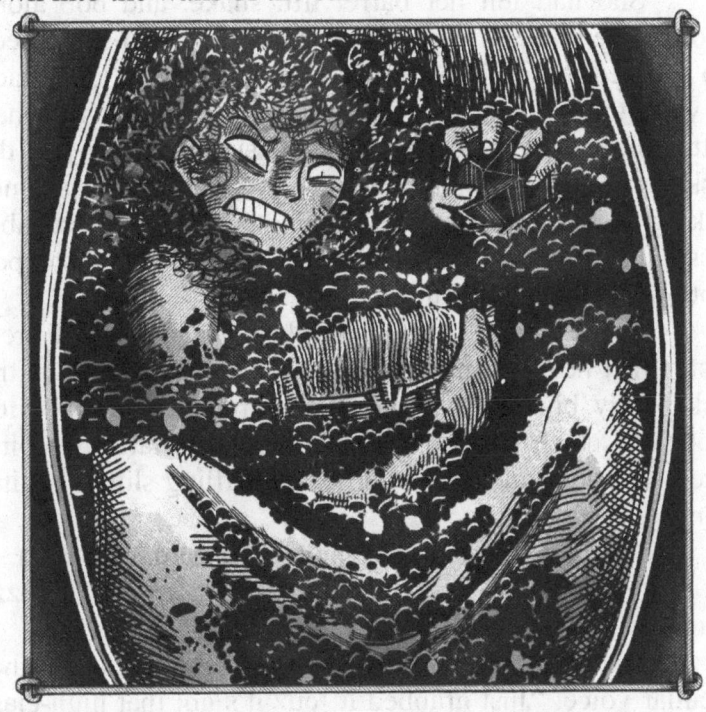

They could take all the clothes off her back if they wanted, so long as that gift was safe in her grasp.

Setting the lid back into place with a solid *thoonk*, she sucked shallow breaths of coffee-scented air through a crack in the oak surface and tried to imagine how mad she would have looked to her past self. As she took the plunge to bury herself in her work, Eliza felt for a brief moment a pang of longing heat from within the cold rock. With beans beading themselves into her locks and the sounds of footsteps on the outside, she steeled herself for whatever the world was prepared to throw her way.

For Nemo.

Eliza never expected that, out of all times and places, it would be her honeymoon where she would get most lost in her work.

She had felt her barrel lift, shake, and bob along through the noise of the outside evacuation, but she'd been too focused on her impression of loose beans to keep track of what the rest of the world had gotten up to. Toni had gotten his money's worth with his custom packing job: the cask remained unbroken and was neither burning to ash nor sinking in the ocean. In a way, it had been the most reliable vessel that Eliza had crawled onto since she'd first stepped foot off of New Amrestir.

In the midst of trying to clear her sinuses of brew dust, Eliza heard something new. There was a seam in the cask barely big enough to breathe through, and just wide enough to catch the sound of staggered footfalls clomping across the floor, along with an odd shuffling slither behind them.

The barrel shifted and spun. Eliza held her breath.

"*Hrmmmm...* Bou...ncin' Beeeaaan. Wuzza Bouncin' Bean, ya reckon?"

"Welp, looks foreign t'me," muttered another peculiar voice. "Just grabbed it 'cuz it's got that high-class

108

printing on it. Bet ye it's rosewood, that's fine stuff there."

As Eliza listened, something soft prodded at her foot from inside the barrel. She kicked out against her better judgment, shaking the whole sorry thing with a sloppy hop.

There was a long stretch of silence, one that Eliza dreaded to be around for the end of.

"...Maybe it's jumping beans?"

"Oh Rufus you dense prat, I swear to—"

A loud chunk hit the seal above Eliza's head, and she was forced to face the outside world once more.

Even neck-deep in coffee, the smell clocked her like a punch to the face. If the New Amrestir fishmongers had decided to start wrapping their leftovers in scraps of Nemo's old coat, it could've made for a nice change of pace. It was the stench of pain, pure and simple, and the whiff of it set her muscles twitching with a nostalgic terror.

The Stagnance.

Two hard-worn sailor's faces hovered in the opening, framed in quilts of blooming mushroom caps and sprouts. In between patches of flesh and fungus were the remnants of ruined sailors' garb, and what looked to be gardening tools forged from brass bizarrely wedged in their carcasses. It was the unmistakable mark of that great rotten plague that had swept across Amrestir when Eliza had been but a girl. Each growth's iridescent colors stung her eyes almost as much as her nose, sending off instinctual signal flares to flee as far and fast as her legs could carry her.

Though the sight of them rang every warning bell in Eliza's brain, the infected sailors looked more annoyed than mindlessly bloodthirsty.

"Check for stowaways, the Cap'n said!" the skinnier of the duo groaned. "Check the cargo, the Cap'n said!"

"I weren't even on luggin' duty, Edmund!" whined the bulkier of the two. "Nate's the quartermaster, lo-jis-ticks is his end!"

The one called Edmund snorted under a mustache

that writhed with mycelial tendrils, as Eliza felt a sharp kick slam into the edge of her barrel. Beans, trinkets, and woman alike spilled out into the open air and a waking nightmare.

Since the outbreak of the Stagnance in New Amrestir all those years ago, rumors had spread among sailors of a floating fortress of fungi on the open seas. Some claimed it was manned by the souls of Amrestir's past, cursed ever to roam, never to belong with the living again. Eliza had always found the ghost stories incredibly tasteless, considering the genuine suffering that had come from the terrible incident. Now, she wished she weren't able to taste at all.

Eliza was sprawled across a sheet of beans, the thinnest barrier between herself and slimy wood rotting in technicolor. She gagged on the stench, nearly thick enough to bite on without her rosewood-and-bean shelter. Scrambling back and over the fresh barrel, she gazed out from the stern of a ship caked port to starboard in writhing mushrooms, and onto a crew in much the same state. Bodies half-missing and half-patched with mold watched her in shock, all except her 'rescuers' remaining eerily silent.

"Oi, what are ye lads fussin' about?"

The rough voice had slashed through the air, like a town crier who'd fallen down a well and never managed to claw his way back out. Among the twisted and melted bodies on display was a tall, slender shape that stood above all, approaching her corner of the bizarre vessel with a crooked gait. It had one unnaturally distended arm and an overflowing colony in place of the other, yet the faint glint of metal below the caps marked it as far from an ordinary sailor as possible.

"Well now, quite the sneak in our midst, eh?"

The tainted Feo looked down upon her, gnashing metallic teeth that might've been parts of a visor at some point, stretching along a neck that drooped down its torso like a cobra poised to strike.

110

"If ye lookin' t'make Audience with the Rot Admiral that bad, could'a written ye a proper invitation."

Fear froze Eliza's throat like an Obrazheskian winter. As though it had stepped straight through the words of a midnight horror story, the Rot Admiral himself loomed over her. Nemo had told her about the legends, the tales of the decaying captain who ruled over the Stagnant crew with a literal iron fist. It took all the strength left in Eliza to resist diving overboard to take her chances in the open ocean, the image of Nemo being swept away into the night helping thaw her frigid nerves.

"Wait, listen to me!" she begged. "You–*augh,* you're chasing those Fríasen privateers, right? I need to catch up to them, t-they kidnapped someone very dear to me!"

Eliza held up her precious coal high for captain and crew alike to see, with the desperate faith of a holy relic.

"Here, look! This is his—"

"I be knowin' what a core coal is," the Rot Admiral

spat, voice chopping down on her words like an ax on the executioner's block. "Wot, yer toy Feo got swept up by them marauders and ye decided t'throw yerself on the rocks fer him? How d'ya figure he wasn't plannin' to take the leap o' his own accord, hm?"

Eliza hugged the coal tight to her chest, away from the roving metal digits that were clawing for it. If this monster wished to pry her connection to Nemo from her hands, it wouldn't be from living ones.

"No, he trusted me with this! He's not just a Feo, we... we're married."

The words hung in the air like an anchor, and crashed down just as quickly. An uncanny squeal of laughter chattered out from the Feo's improvised jaw along with a trail of slime, echoed by the chorus of its crew.

"Of all the yarns been spun aboard *The Bastion* t'save a sorry hide, that be the thinnest I ever heard! Ye think me senses be so far fettered t'swallow such scum?"

Eliza shook her head frantically, a few beans falling loose from her hair as the ghostly crew closed in on her. She could feel the line connecting herself to Nemo slipping through her grip, but she clung to it with all she had.

"Please, you don't understand! I love him! I would do anything for—!"

"Cap'n! We're nearly on them!"

Both heads swiveled in unison to port. Eliza had been so frazzled by the chain of world-shattering matters that she hadn't taken inventory of exactly what mess she had dumped herself into. The undistracted crewmembers of the rotting ship were driving her along with silent expertise, in active pursuit of a smaller sloop unable to build enough speed to flee. It was alone, and looked to be in no state to put up a proper fight with the monster Eliza was standing on, but the familiar flag rippling from its stern told her all she needed to know.

"We be dealin' with ye later," the Cap'n spat, pulling himself to his full height with a wet *schlop*. "Quartermaster Autumns! Fetch the horn, we've business t'tend to!"

Eliza could feel the Stagnant Audience's eyes drifting away from her, somehow disturbing her greater than having their full attention. A shorter man in an oversized coat of wool and even larger coat of moss was helping the Rot Admiral through his vocal warmup by the railing when something inside Eliza snapped.

"Avast, Fríasen slime! Word be that yer countrymen came into a surplus of gold, aye? Well, this be— *Hey!*"

Scrambling to her feet and weaving around piles of fuming sailors, Eliza had stormed right up to the Cap'n's side and swiped the corroded speaking trumpet out of his hand.

"Wait, hold off! Nobody is doing anything until I get some answers!"

Both ships' crews were thrown off their rhythm. The vessels had tacked to match speed along the water, allowing Eliza to get a good look at the aghast faces of the men crowding the comparatively puny decks. She heard the rotten cadre behind squelching to close in on her, but the Cap'n opted to halt them with a wave of his hand.

"Give'er a sec, lads, let's see what she be brewin'."

The stray privateer's ship had floated close enough for Eliza to catch the baffled expression on what she assumed to be the Fríasen captain, framed in a thick tangle of thatched black hair and beard. He put on a brave face as he called into his own horn, confusion quickly pouring in to replace his draining dread.

"*Qui es*[17]— Who in blazes are you?! What diabolical trick of the eye is this, a fresh dame amid the Stagnant mire? *Les amis*[18], that coast guardsman did not completely crack my head, right?"

Eliza risked a glance back at the decaying, colorful mess behind her while the opposing ship tried to get its bearings. The Cap'n was bending down to whisper in the ear of the supposed Quartermaster, who had migrated his

[17] Who are you
[18] Friends

113

way over to his shoulder at some point. Members of the crew were already in the process of sneaking, crawling, slithering, and chewing their way below decks. Eliza caught a slight nod of approval from the Cap'n.

"No, you haven't lost it," she continued undaunted. "Listen, I need—"

"Are you okay, *mademoiselle?* What have these vile beasts done to you?"

Eliza blinked. Did she really look that miserable? A fresh whiff on the air gave her a reminder of the company she now kept, and a speedy answer.

"What?! No! I mean—yes—wait, no— Yes, I need help, but not in the way you think! Just– Everyone, hold your fire and hear me out!"

"...You sure you don't need rescuing?"

Eliza aimed a groan directly into the trumpet. The floating dumpster she was currently stuck on was about the last vessel she would have picked for a daring rescue mission, but the wayward Fríasen runt somehow managed to outrank it on that list. The fact that the Cap'n had let her flounder on this long without comment spoke something for his confidence, at least.

"No, as stupid as it sounds, I am here of my own volition… for now. Listen, you were a part of a fleet, right? Raided the *Marigold* recently? Know where they're headed?"

"Look, lass, we just got through being trounced by those New Amrestirian meatheads! With the sorry state of this hull, *La Hareng* cannot keep pace for where they're bound without repairs, we've nothing left!"

Eliza had a feeling the Fríasen captain was losing his patience, and his voice. The crew of *La Hareng* was already scrambling to action behind their confused spokesman, and the Cap'n at her side was idly whistling.

"Well fine, if you're not gonna tell me, I'll just have to—"

BOOM!

The gun crew below decks had been busy. A salvo

114

of shots bloomed from *The Bastion*'s hull, a sampling of cannonballs, chainshots, and firebombs peppering the sky. A well-arced blast sent a payload of Red-Hot Fiery Plasmotic Grapeshot square into the base of the mainmast, and chaos erupted aboard the deck of *La Hareng*. A few projectiles from the other vessel's broadside clipped the edges of the ship's unnatural frame but in a game of pure firepower, the Fríasen vessel was sorely outmatched. The main shrouds folded over the deck like a dying man while the exhausted Fríasen ship sat dead in the water.

Eliza screamed and huddled behind the blocks at the railing as they absorbed a hefty load of shrapnel. The whole situation was starting to bring back some uncomfortable memories of her time working at Foolish Glory, where it was considered a good shift if the town guard didn't have to scoop bodies off the floor at the end of the night. Now there were no guards on their way to stop the madness, or to clean up the mess.

The Fríasen privateers had fed most of their ammo into the fungal bodies by now, and the Stagnant crew sounded eager to share the leftovers. Eliza clutched Nemo's coal in her hands like a Smoulder prayer, trying to ignore the sounds of towlines flying and sailors screaming beyond. From the midst of her terror, a hard, metallic slap struck her shoulder.

"Well blow me down, what a show! Ye shocked 'em so severe they can't even shoot straight. Congrats, lass, ye get yer livin' privileges back."

Eliza had been so busy stressing about dying to gunfire that she'd nearly forgotten about the mass of mushrooms, marauders, and murderers she was mucked in with.

"...Living privileges?"

"Never mind that!" the Cap'n barked, letting her go with a snap of his iron fingers. "Point is, ye had them failed farmers in the palms of yer hands! A silver tongue if I ever seen one, and you'd be amazed the tongues I seen."

A spark of hope ignited in Eliza, even as the shouts

115

and swears of both crews had her keeping her head down.

"Then can I stick around, at least for now? To hunt down those privateers?"

The Cap'n pulled back, a confused gurgle echoing from the back of his gnashing visor plates.

"Wot? Ye so eager to lose them privileges I just so graciously gave back?" the Feo barked, gesturing broadly to himself and the crew busy evicting blindsided Fríasen sailors out of their own ship. "In case ye didn't notice, ye be lookin' a bit fresh t'be one of The Rot Admiral's crew. If it be life and adventure on the sea you seek, ye might be better off joinin' them sorry sacks."

Now that the shooting had stopped, Eliza was able to find her footing again. Kicking away loose beans, the weary woman straightened to full height, which in this case came about level with the Cap'n's cuirass.

"What— No, I'm not doing this because I want to!" Eliza insisted, holding the distressingly cold coal to her chest. "I'm looking for someone!"

"Aye, aye, yer Feo problem," the Rot Admiral dismissed with a wave. "Well, we ain't a bleedin' courier ship here, even if ye did go through the trouble t'pack yerself up. Next port's in two day's sail, ye can float out fer some new sucker there."

The Cap'n was already skulking away, less interested in Eliza's protests than the new hauls being lugged across the towlines. She sputtered, trying to find words that could sway the heart of the Rot Admiral himself, but she wasn't sure if it existed. The adrenaline that had been keeping Eliza upright since she'd spilled onto the deck was completely spent. She lingered in place with knees locked in shock, aiming a thousand-league stare in the direction of the calamity that she inadvertently helped cause.

Something poked at Eliza's foot in the same way she'd felt from inside her barrel. She looked down to notice a searching mushroom sprout, following it up to the sailor it came from. It was the one she'd heard called Rufus, a

youngish-looking lad with broad sloped shoulders that
hung heavy with infectious flora. He had two dark bottles
in his hands and a lopsided grin on his face.

"Sorry 'bout the trouble, miss! I knows this is a bit
tricksome, but lookie here! We's gots just the cure fer
mopesome spirits: spirits!"

Alcohol was fine and well, but after however long
Eliza's barrel-bound trip had lasted, she was starving for
some genuine food.

Unfortunately, very little aboard *The Bastion* made
the grade. Eliza cracked open the lid on a package of
salvaged goods, and it took every ounce of her constitution
to not spill her stomach out on the floor. Fresh food was a
rarity among sailing ships, but even by nautical standards,
the options aboard *The Bastion* were vile.

She was no stranger to picking at food past its
prime, and for hard bricks of bread and cheese that tended
to be good enough. That strategy might have sufficed with
your average mold eating away at the perishables, but Eliza
was watching evolved strains of Stagnance chow down on
the available rations ravenously enough that she could
swear it had burped.

The crew had granted her free reign to wander the
ship while they patched their hull's holes, as though they
were treating her to the Grand Sea's least appealing tour.
The cargo hold remained the only spot on the ship with
some level of sanitation, which may have partially been out
of the Quartermaster's undying passion for proper
rationing.

Holding a half-empty bottle of *Soucian* wine in one
hand, Eliza dug the other through what meager belongings
she'd managed to squeeze with her into the beans. She
didn't have any real need to take stock, but anything to take
her mind off of the ambient smell sieging her nostrils was
welcomed. Her fingers brushed across an old leather strap

and froze when they hovered over a familiar bag.

Nemo had been oddly possessive over his satchel ever since they boarded the *Marigold,* stealing glances at times but unwilling to spill his own beans. He'd told her that he'd packed a gift inside, and was waiting to give it to her "at the right moment". Considering he wasn't exactly here to tell her when that might've been, Eliza figured she earned the right to decide when that moment would be herself.

Wrapped inside scraps of cloth was a small box of wood, polished to a gleam. It looked like an artisan-carved jewelry box of some kind, save for a small mechanical crank sticking out from its side. Eliza creaked the lid to be greeted by an odd collection of gears, plates, and rollers completely alien to her untrained eye. Whatever it was, she had the feeling that it must have cost Nemo more than her monthly rent.

As she tipped the box to check the bottom side, Eliza watched a note flutter down from the interior, and caught its corner before the hungry fungus could snatch another snack. It was sealed in an envelope, with 'ELIZA' scrawled across its surface in an unsteady hand.

The sight of the handwriting reeled Eliza right back to New Amrestir, back to when Nemo had asked her to help teach him his letters. He'd still held onto the embarrassment of not being able to read the signs at the Bouncin' Bean, and had the humility to ask her for private tutoring. Eliza thought on the beginner's books they'd borrowed from the Kindling Institute's learner's program, their nights tracing through letters in her apartment by the firelight's glow. Nemo was an eager student, a trait he attributed to his teacher, and the first thing he had wanted to learn was the spelling of his own name.

Hers, of course, had been the second.

Eliza ripped the envelope open, dropping the now-unimportant imported wine. There, inked on fresh parchment, was but a simple note:

TO MY LITTLE LIZ,
I LOVE YOU BEST OF ALL!

Eliza's fingers fluttered to the crank. She clicked the gears with a feather-touch, as though the lightest touch would shatter the machine, and marveled as it spun to life before her eyes. The delicate metal tines plucked themselves on the tin roller's pins, a smattering of nervous notes drifting into the still air. Eliza twirled the handle with speed and the box grew in confidence, plinking gradually into an ethereal melody that filled her heart. As she recognized the tune, the lyrics with that name she'd disdained for so many years drifted to the surface of their own accord.

> *The other night, I had a dream*
> *The funniest dream of all*
> *I dreamt that I was kissin' you*
> *Behind the garden wall*

Sometimes, when he thought she was asleep, Nemo would softly repeat the lyrics as he played with her curls. Eliza never dared let him know that she could hear every word of it. She wanted to scream. She wanted to throw the stupid trinket into the sea, to tear up every rotting floor board on this floating crime against nature. She wanted her misery to reach the very depths of the ocean and the highest mountain peaks. If she was to mourn, let the entire world know of her suffering.

But Eliza did none of these things. Instead, she went to crank the box once more to properly finish the song.

> *Little Liz, I love you, honey*
> *Little Liz, I love you*
> *I love you in the springtime and the fall*
> *Little Liz, I love you, honey*
> *Little Liz, I love you*
> *I love you best of all*

The music box left a lingering note in the air, and Eliza with renewed grief. Tears were rapidly blurring her vision, dripping down her cheeks and traveling across the curves and rigids of the instrument's gears. She could've sat like that for hours, watching her sorrow drown the mechanics until it rusted, only for a creaking gurgle outside the box's little world to snag her back to reality.

The Bastion's cap-riddled Cap'n was haunting the doorway, arm cradled around the growths at his side. If she didn't know better, and if the Feo had eyes of some description, she might've taken the globs oozing down his visor to be tears.

"That a song yer sweetheart sings fer ya?"

Eliza felt the straining at her vocal cords, realizing that her mouth had been echoing the words in her heart. She roughly wiped her face with the sleeve of her dress, refusing to give this abomination the satisfaction of seeing her at her lowest.

"Yes, my *husband!*"

She had raised her voice in anger to the Rot Admiral himself, but what did it matter? She was going to be thrown off this ship any day now. If Eliza was to walk the plank, she might as well do a flip on the way down.

"Lass, ye can drop the whole husband line at this rate," the Cap'n sighed, with the sound of damp laundry flapping in the breeze. "I've no doubt ye care for that Feo, but it be a tough story t'swallow. If he took a chance at a fresh start, that be his choice. Ye've no need to spin excuses any longer."

The fuse on Eliza's patience finally burnt down to its base.

"Why in the blinking blazes would I lie about being married to a Feo, of all things?!" she exploded, snapping the music box lid close and bearing down on the Cap'n. "The only reason I bothered to mention it was that I figured you would have some empathy for a Feo being snatched up against his will! Or did that part of you rot away too?"

Eliza heaved, pinning the festering commander to the wall with her gaze. His jaw flexed uncomfortably, until it was finally able to spit out a proper response.

"What's your name?"

Eliza wanted to spit, to curse, to rip the question right out of his sprouting mouth. But there was a new softness to his tone, the piratical accent less forced than it had been throughout her brief time aboard. He even shrank back from her glower, trying to minimize his own presence.

"Why do you care?"

"Only seems fair to trade," the Cap'n shrugged, his one arm raising defensively. "Hadn't gotten the chance for a proper introduction, m'self. My name is Barret. I came from Amrestir too, a lifetime ago."

His rotting gaze was on her expectedly. Eliza considered that under his shroud as the Rot Admiral was the frame of a simple Feo, a Feo she hadn't taken the time to learn anything about. The name did ring a bell, but it was being drowned out by the rest of the alarms echoing through her head.

121

"...Eliza."

"Mm, shoulda guessed from the song, there," the Cap'n nodded, gesturing to the device in Eliza's hands. "And yer husband, then?"

"His name is Nemo," Eliza relented. "He used to be a sailor before he came to New Amrestir. He kept coming into the coffee shop I worked at and ordered the same drink every single time just so he had an excuse to see me. First time I kissed him, I nearly burned my damn lips off... and it was worth it."

A breathless laugh at the memory turned into a hitched sob, one she barely managed to suppress before it broke free. Why was she rambling about such inane things? Try as she might, Eliza couldn't stop the words tumbling from her lips now.

"H-he always wears this... stupid hat, with this stupid feather from his friend. Even wore it to our wedding, said he wanted to look his best for me. Always thought it was just some silly fashion that he'd give up in time and I wouldn't have to look at it anymore... b-but now, I might never see—"

"Lass, it's okay. You can stop."

The palm of Barret's hand was stretched her way, a hesitancy in his frame. It reminded Eliza of how one would approach a frightened child, as though afraid she would shatter.

"I know what it's like to have someone waiting fer ye," Barret muttered, staring up at the timbers above. "I lost everything, but remained for the sake of those I've dragged down with me... Y'know, I once sailed in the name of founding a step towards the future, and ye and Nemo sound just like that sort o' step."

Eliza felt the twisted heat around Barret's frame rise, his sorely cracked visor holding a glimmer of dignity within it. She placed the precious music box at her side and rose to meet the Feo on his level.

"Does that mean—?"

"I be a romantic at heart!" the Cap'n bellowed,

contorting himself into a confident stance. "If Nemo be bound by that feeble Fríasen fleet, I'll be seein' that ye stand by his side once more! After all, it be on the way."

A new surge of hope flushed through Eliza's system, along with a new wave of nausea as her nose caught up with the rest of her senses. She moved to speak again, but an iron hand held her at bay.

"Whup, slow yer roll there! Cap'n's Rules: Ye sail with us, ye work with us. We ain't out to pile up bodies in our dealings, but ye've an obligation t'pull yer weight. Aye?"

"Yes, absolutely!" Eliza shouted, vision blurring with how quickly her head was nodding. "I've been through customer service, I can handle nasty shifts."

Barret chuckled, running a hand through his spoiled plume.

"Very well! First step's first."

With a push, the Cap'n flung back the exit to the cargo hold, revealing a clump of Stagnant crew members lurking by the doorframe. Eliza's heart jumped up into her throat, but there was enough space to cough up a response.

"Wh— Were you spying on me?"

Quartermaster Autumns shivered in his coat, a long beaten scroll draping from his grasp. He shook his head hard enough to dislodge something onto the opposite wall, fearing Eliza's wrath even in functional un-death.

"S-sorry, Cap'n, I'm j-j-just here for th-the cargo ch-check. Is… Is everyth-th-thing alright?"

"Never been better!" Cap'n Barret boomed. "Well, not never, but ye know what I be meanin'! Fellas, it be proper introduction time! This be Eliza, wife to Nemo the Feo. She be one of the crew, now!"

The excitement in Barret's voice must've been contagious, as the entire deck popped into a row of hooting and hollering. It felt wrong to just stand there and bask in the applause with less emotion to her face than the metal man, so Eliza spun her mental levers to crank up a smile.

That smile grew strained when Cap'n Barret landed

123

a hand on her shoulder and jostled her closer to him. As grateful as she was for this opportunity to find her love, it didn't mean Eliza particularly wanted to be near him any more than she'd be forced to. Still, he held her tight, a fresh rush of life radiating from his frame.

The Rot Admiral stabbed the air with a wicked digit, voice ringing loud and clear.

"Full sail ahead, lads! We got a loverboy to save!"

"Look, I don't care how it went last time, I'm not doing it again!"

"Oh c'mon, it be a classic!" Barret trilled with a burst of cheerfulness to his voice, and a pilfered noblewoman's dress in hand. "Just have to refine the act!"

The festering crew of *The Bastion* was huddled in an arc around their Cap'n, frothing with the anticipation of an eager Audience around the fashion option. It was a fancy white affair, held far enough from his body to keep it from being stained by his personal cordyceps colony, but nowhere near far enough for Eliza's comfort.

"That was an accident! I'm not playing out some 'damsel in distress' ploy like a performing puppet!"

Barret looked as though the wind had been let out of his sails, and Eliza felt a pang of guilt for making the puppet reference. She had her principles to stand on, but in this case she had to reckon with how flimsy her footing was. With a huff, she marched forward and snatched the gown from Barret's grip.

"Fine, I'll wear it. *Once.*"

Whatever noblewoman *The Bastion*'s crew had swiped the dress from certainly had fine taste in tailoring, which Eliza assumed had been the only kind of taste she allowed herself to enjoy. The fashionably wound bodice was pinching her sides, and causing the top of her chest to overflow like loaves from a bread pan. The skirts at least gave enough legroom to act without tripping over her own feet, but it had Eliza thinking back to all of Margaret's sewing circle invitations she'd gone out of her way to avoid, and all the good they could've been doing for her now.

Barret was waiting outside the impromptu changing room, along with a selection of his more aesthetically-minded crewmates. Eliza shrank under the judgemental gazes, and made a personal unspoken vow that the first one to make a snide comment about her figure would be taking a one-way trip to the sea floor.

The Cap'n rubbed at what passed for his chin, grinding his visor bars in thought before throwing up a hand.

"Aye, 'tis perfect! Like a blushing bride, right outta an ol' romantic shelling-story. Trust me, I may have more 'shrooms than sense, but I be knowin' how a sailor's gonna think seein' that whole display."

The Cap'n rose to his full height and scythed his single hand through the air, cutting the chatter of his cohorts. He puffed out his chest and whistled, rallying the whole Stagnant squad into a grotesque group gathering.

"Alrighty mates, there be a SpritFlit ship in sight due north from Aveila, laden full 'n sittin' low. If there be any catch that might be givin' ye some news of yer betrothed, lass, it be this one. Now, she be lookin' like a quick clipper, bound fer Amrestir with all manner'a packages and post. More their speed t'pick flight over fight, so we's gotta be a bit more subtle than usual here."

From out of the pirate pile peeled two aquatic-flavored figures: a fishy-stinking Ibi with a severe case of gill rot, and a dessicated Obra with a hefty reel of chain wrapped around his infected spear of a tusk. Barret beckoned them forward, inviting the wide-mouthed fish to greet Eliza with a broad grin of bristling caps. Politely, Eliza returned the greeting with a weak wave, making sure to keep her dress out of the splash zone.

"We can't be letting 'em turn tail and flee, so Bellona and Vaughn's job be tyin' a tether to the tiller. Now, Eliza, yer job be t'keep them lot nice and distracted while they make the rounds and the lads get things cookin' below. Make a big scene about yer ship bein' infected, seekin' refuge with some big strong sailor boys, all that fun

126

stuff."

"Does this mean no fake hostage ploy?" Rufus whined from the peanut gallery. "I gots me knife dulled up just for it, I did!"

Barret shook his helm, just far enough away from Eliza's dress to avoid the specular splashback.

"If we come rolling up in full regalia they'll be to the horizon in no time. No, this be a solo mission fer Eliza here, in a sense. Really sell that misery 'n despair, girlie!"

No problem there, Eliza sulked as she readjusted the dress, beyond grateful that it didn't have any buttons to worry about popping off.

Cap'n Barret pulled a flute from somewhere in his chest cavity, a sorry old instrument that looked like it had been scraped from the bottom of a wastebin. Eliza watched as he miraculously played out a jaunty little tune, doubly impressive due to the fact that the world-weary Feo currently owned neither a left hand nor lips.

"Rehearsal's over! Prep the percussion, and wait for yer cue! And get that knife re-sharpened, Rufus, this ain't a matinee!"

"*Heus,* 'Liza!" Bellona called from her spot by the starboard edge, helping Vaughn get a leg up over the railing. "Be sures to be givings us times! Let the Aves be gettings a long ganders at *mammas tua!*"

"...*Mammas?*" Eliza sighed, already regretting the question.

"*Papillae, ubera, pectora,* picks what you likes! You tries translating ons the spots!"

The damp duo launched themselves into the water with a distant *sploosh* before Eliza could make good on her earlier vow. A little disappointed, she dutifully made her way to the helm, fruitlessly tugging at her top again along the way. The rest of the crew busied themselves with their assigned roles, including a disappointed Rufus shuffling back below decks.

It wasn't long before the SpritFlit vessel was scraping within spitting distance of *The Bastion,* whose sheets were now purposely loosened to sell the helplessness of the wreck. Eliza could spot the faces and beaks of the ship's crew from her stage position, each painting a portrait of true horror. She gripped the speaking horn Quartermaster Autumns had handed her earlier, and counted down from ten.

It was showtime.

"Please, help me!" Eliza wailed in a dramatic falsetto, flailing her free arm as she did. "Oh dear Flame, I'm all alone, a-and helpless!"

The mailmen on the opposite deck were chittering amongst themselves, but Eliza didn't feel the same misplaced pity from them that she had from her first capture. Her attention was reeled away from the bickering birds by a hushed *psst*, hissed by the pile of decay and detritus that was Cap'n Barret's hiding place.

"Ey, ring-a-ding 'Lady Liz', yer doin' a lousy job. Yer face be sellin' less emotion than mine, and that be a real problem here!"

If Barret was expecting a performance out of *The Ballad of Porphiose*, he was out of luck. Still, the sight of Bellona and Vaughn's multi-hued wake cutting the distance between the ships reminded Eliza that she had no choice but to commit to the bit. She pulled her lips into a frown and blew open her eyes in what she hoped was a terror-stricken expression, channeling the wild desperation of a wounded animal or an unhappy customer.

"*Ooooh*, save me from this nightmare!"

"Good, now get some tears in those peepers."

Eliza wanted to glare daggers in Barret's direction, but the eyes of the other boat's crew were all on her.

"I don't know how to cry on demand!" Eliza muttered from the corner of her mouth. "How am I supposed to—*Yowch!*"

Something sharp had stabbed through the sole of her shoe from below. Eliza risked a peek down to spot Rufus' face through a crack in the timbers, a freshly-sharpened dagger in hand and an embarrassed smile on his face. The tears flowed as Barret had wished, and Eliza decided to shift her revenge plan to Rufus when this was all over.

"Please!" she sobbed, leaning into the pain. "I beg you!"

"What the blazes is going on here?! The *SF Rimborso* is on a tight clip, we don't have time for this!"

The Aveilan captain, a dignified rooster with a postmaster's cap atop his comb, barged across the deck in a flash of yellow and green, sounding his mighty caw across the open water.

Eliza caught a slanted thumbs-up from Barret's pile and continued.

"Please, sir, the Stagnance!" Eliza wailed, trying to sound as pathetic as she felt in the moment. "It-It sprouted from the cargo hold! The ones who weren't caught in it abandoned ship, and me with it!"

The postmaster clucked in disbelief, bobbing his head about to his crew.

"Well then! Must be the luckiest lass in the Grand Sea, happening on our little outfit all the way out here by your lonesome."

"...Pardon?"

"You think I was hatched yesterday?" cried the rooster, with none of the gentility of that Fríasen captain with the possible head injury. "Even if your story rings true, you think I'm about to risk bringing that mess on board my ship? With my men, and my mail? Sorry, doll, but something smells rotten! Besides the obvious!"

It was a special kind of humiliation Eliza felt, tears and sea salt caking her face with dozens of eyes and guns aimed at her. More than ever, she wished to be absolutely anywhere else, wearing just about anything else. The sight of two rainbow specks attacking the *SF Rimborso*'s tiller unnoticed was the only thing keeping her stable and on-script for this nightmarishly stupid plan.

"I'm a heavy sleeper! They must've thought me a goner!"

Eliza heard a din like seagulls fighting over a biscuit, and had the distinct feeling she was the butt of some cosmically unfunny joke.

"That sure is a shame! Well, if your crew considered you a lost cause, that makes a good case for us too, wouldn't you say?"

Eliza paused, genuinely stumped. Cap'n Barret may have had his share of costumes and props, but she had the feeling the Feo had spent too long leaning on his own reputation to plan this far ahead.

The rooster on the other deck sighed, waving a dismissive wing.

"This is asinine. We're on a schedule and you're not on the manifest. I'll get you and yours a nice mention in the papers for your trouble. Full sail, men, we've wasted enough time here!"

The realization that the plan was officially dead in the water hit Eliza and Barret at the same time. With a roar, the Rot Admiral and his crew erupted from their hiding spots, Eliza yanked to his side by a rough handful of her tangled hair.

"Sorry about this, lass," Barret whispered, before shouting into the speaking trumpet that Autumns had squished into the colony on his shoulder. "Avast, feathered fiends! Ye really should've taken the offer, eh? Now yer t'be privy to this little morsel's fillings spillin' on the deck, unless ye be willin' to parley!"

That got things moving on the mail ship. Feathers flew as the sailors scrambled to action, the Ave captain's comb drained white with terror. Eliza sighed wearily, resigning herself to yet another role.

This is for you, Nemo.

"Don't leave me here!" Eliza thrashed against the Cap'n's hold, wailing loud enough to bypass the horn altogether. "He told me to do this or he would kill me! Please, I want to see my husband again!"

Mother Flame help her, she was actually starting to get into this. All it took was the image of Nemo's prone body being dragged away for Eliza to tremble in desperation. She couldn't quite manage to force any more tears, but she hung her head low in wracked sobs to let the rest of her hair veil the act.

"I beg you, let me see my love again. For mercy's sake, please—"

"That be enough outta you, missy!" Cap'n Barret snarled, giving her hair another tug. "The only mercy here now be that of The Rot Admiral!"

Eliza nearly felt pity for the opposing captain as she watched him run about the deck like he'd been beheaded. The rooster's beak was flapping for a response, a fact that made her realize the boats had started to drift close enough to see it properly.

"Y-you! *Hostis humani generis!*" he cried, invoking a grave Ibian decree that marked the bearer as an enemy of all mankind. "You would stoop so low as to string along this innocent woman, and for what?! Your demented pleasure?"

131

"Now, now, sir. I may be rotten to the core, but I still got some reason rattlin' in me. I won't flick another frizzy follicle on her noggin, and let ye go about yer business, if ye give in t'my requests!"

The captain lifted his postman's cap, now near enough for Eliza to see the stress in his eyes.

"What is it you even want?"

"...About five more seconds of your attention."

"What does—"

A series of ghastly screams echoed from the bowels of the *SF Rimborso*, which meant that Bellona and Vaughn had chewed their way in and made themselves known on the gundeck. By now, the mail crew had started to chip away at the tow chain on their tiller, far too late to avoid the resounding crunch of hulls grinding side by side. Eliza watched the fast-set sails tugging desperately at the breeze, unable to escape the snare that she had lured them into.

As the sky grew thick with flying bullets and fleeing mailmen, Barret grabbed Eliza around the waist and bolted to the stairway below, trying to stain as little of the dress as he could afford. Setting her down and picking stray musketballs out of his torso, the Cap'n gave her hair a warm tussle.

"And ye say yer not a performer! I be headin' out t'make sure our fellows don't get carried away, but you stay here n' take a breather! Nothin' bad's gonna happen to you, Gilby."

The Rot Admiral charged out into the fray once more, leaving Eliza utterly baffled and alone in the foul-smelling depths. Slumping across the stairs, hearing the tail end of squishy things she was glad not to see, Eliza was left in the dark on every front.

The *SF Rimburso* had proven to be quite the profitable snag, and Eliza's new crew of colorful cohorts were indulging in the fruits of their labor with gusto. While

132

Cap'n Barret sat and stewed over the day's success, the rest of his cronies tore into the fresh plunder in search of anything worth claiming. There was a striking flavor of callousness mixed with the regular spore-scented energy of the night, a concentrated effort to ignore the price they'd exacted for their deeds. Out of the piles of loot, coveted and rationed by the Quartermaster in turn, Eliza noticed the new cases of alcohol they'd reeled in were going almost entirely unheeded amidst the celebration.

"Isn't anyone else going to break into this?" asked Eliza, swirling a bottle of gin. "Surprise I even need to ask, figured this would be the hottest commodity."

Vaughn, who up until that point had been the picture of pride for a job well done, turned up his tusk at the offering.

"That's not going to happen."

Edmund slipped behind Vaughn with a new scarf about his neck and yanked at the decaying Obra's tail.

"Smooth, blubber boy. Ignore him; bit of a touchy subject, that'un. Turns out the real curse'a all this comes out to a wicked alcohol allergy. Ain't it just the friggin' way?"

"Never one for them lick-quors, pers'nally," Rufus chimed in. "Sinful, 'n all that. Now nobody's able to have a right fun time of it... 'cept you, I reckon."

"N-not much use f-for it other than c-c-leaning, honestly," Quartermaster Autumns sighed. "Hate to s-say it, b-but it's b-barely worth r-r-rationing."

Eliza looked into the clear liquid in her bottle and tried to swallow the meaning of their words. She couldn't imagine the horror of having to go through life completely sober, let alone on a Stagnant-infected ship.

"Oh, well... sorry about that. Didn't mean to offend, at all."

"G-go ahead and t-t-take it," Autumns insisted. "Best that it d-doesn't go t-to waste."

Free booze was a gift few would reject, but the manners drilled into Eliza by her father reared its head as

133

the Quartermaster extended to her a bottle of *Bonnezeaux Pinot.*

"Thank you, but it's okay. 'To the victor go the spoils', and all th—"

A hard, wet slap on the back knocked the protests out of Eliza's mouth, and Bellona circled her like a shark.

"Downs in the Ibi Empire, we has a sayings: *veni, bibi, vici.* It means 'shuts your trap and drink!'"

Even with permission, Eliza resolved to have only a few sips of booze to take the edge off, and to celebrate another day of smelly, smelly life. While a few crew members lingered in the galley, watching with envy as she nursed their ill-gotten liquor, the majority of the pirates had taken it upon themselves to ensure Eliza's cup never ran dry. Every time she set it down, someone topped it off. Every time she hesitated, they nudged it back into her hands with encouraging grins.

However many sips later, Eliza found herself precariously perched on a barrel, cradling her mug as if it might steady her. The drinks were starting to get to her head, causing the whole room to swirl about like a full spread of old *'Ink-Credible Inks'* ads, when a whiff of something fragrant and nostalgic hit her nose. She glanced down at the barrel and realized that she was sitting on the source of all her current woes:

Bouncin', Bean

Shocked, Eliza jumped down to inspect the print closely. Gently prying the lid open, she saw that her intoxicated mind hadn't been playing tricks on her. Toni's *Tlauillibrew* blend had stayed hardy against the ambient rot surrounding it, and the rich earthy aroma rising from the beans was starting to brew an idea in Eliza's head.

"Heyyy, Autumns, are you planning on doing anything with this?" Eliza called out, patting the side of the barrel with an affectionate familiarity.

"N-not part-t-ticularly," the Quartermaster

stammered. "We d-don't have much use f-f-for them, they're a b-bit d-d-dry on their own."

Eliza rolled up her sleeves and pulled her hair into a tight tail. She'd finally landed on a task she could excel at.

"Well, I'd be happy to make a pot or two of brew if you want to try the real stuff."

Though it came from a less-than-generous viewpoint, the crew did give her a share of their spoils, and a spot aboard the only ship heading to Nemo. The least Eliza could do, from a loosening frame of mind, was to give them a token of her thanks. Toni would kill her for giving out free coffee on his shelling, but she would've paid to see him try and bring a complaint to these customers.

"Hm, w-well I d-don't see why not..." Autumns gurgled, stroking his surprisingly trim moustache. "B-but we don't have the p-p-proper eq-quipment on hand."

Eliza let out a good-natured laugh, letting the exotic cargo run through her fingers.

"Ye of little faith. I'm sure I can whip something up here."

Wandering about the ship's galley, Eliza scanned the cluttered space for anything that could serve as coffee-making equipment. Amidst battered tins and rusty utensils, she managed to scrounge up a recently pilfered bottle of 'Sister Dawn's Purified Water' and an old kettle that had seen its share of better days.

She worked under the impatient eyes of slack-jawed gawkers, many of whom she figured had probably never gotten to enjoy a cup of the stuff before. Sparking the long-unused stovetop of the galley and setting the kettle to boil was easy enough, but trying to crack the product into fine grounds without a proper mortar or pestle on hand was not a task even the water bottle's heavy bottom could fulfil. Eliza rolled over the beans in vain, until she felt a heavy flipper land on her shoulder.

"Your strength is inadequate. Watch."

Vaughn scooped a pile of the beans into a rough

iron bowl, and pressed the butt-end of a shining garden trowel lodged in his forearm into the mix. Eliza followed his advice, watching as the narwhal pulverized the beans to powder with crushing speed that could have made a crab blush. When the Obra stepped back to his appreciative Audience with coffee dusting his tusk, Eliza couldn't help but notice that the metal of the rot-caked bludgeon remained more bright and brilliant than Nemo at his cleanest.

It may not have lived up to Toni's high standards, but through her years of experience, a little ingenuity, and just a dash of luck, Eliza managed to brew a substantial pot of something that resembled the fantastic aroma that she'd experienced back in New Amrestir. The waitress-turned-pirate doled out mugs of hot bean juice to the impatient Audience and watched on as they indulged in drinks they could actually stand.

"Ahh, the t-tastes of c-c-culture," chattered Autumns.

"Makes that stuff my pa scraped up from th'mills taste like dirt!" chuckled Edmund.

"This *is* dirts! Hows can you stands this *detritus*?" spat Bellona.

"To the freshest member of *The Bastion!*" cheered a crewmate that Eliza hadn't the time, patience, or sobriety to remember the name of.

It was a toast Eliza was happy to make, and one the crew was quick to refill. With all hands on drink, it wasn't long before Eliza found herself swamped into a round of 'Slosh the Siren', a drinking game that was newly invented and severely stacked against her, given the circumstances. *The Bastion*'s ghouls took great delight in setting her up to fail, rigging calls and wagers just enough that she'd inevitably lose, ensuring her cup never stayed empty for long.

"Come now, don't make this too easy," rumbled Vaughn.

"*Egheheheh*, the blossom's already wiltin'!"

chortled Edmund, twirling his mush-stache. "Man-alive, reminds me when we snuck on into the Cap'n's quarters t'play *Here Comes The Nudibranch!*"

"And thens he founds Frankie knocked out colds under the maps table!" gurgled Bellona. "Thoughts he would slaps the ships out from us when his sheets music got rum-soaked!"

At the mention of the Cap'n, Eliza came to realize that the Rot Admiral had been an oddly quiet member of the Audience. He sat by the far end of the galley with his single hand aloft its elbow, the digits lightly twitching of their own accord. Through the bottom of her bottle, he looked almost bored and for some reason, that just rubbed Eliza's waterlogged feelings the wrong way.

With a piping-hot mug in hand, she staggered out to the Rot Admiral's seat by the back, taking care to avoid the cape of mycelium draping to the floor below him. The rancid wraith was slumped in his overgrown Cap'n's chair, idly puffing away at his flute. He showed no sign of awareness outside of his music, even as she tapped at the table with the cup.

"Heyyyyyy, Barret. Care to... wet yer whistle, there?"

"Boss got you on servin' duty tonight, eh?" Barret murmured. "Don't worry, Claude can handle the crowd."

Eliza wasn't sure if it was the drinks piling on her head, but she decided to play along.

"Ehhhh, you're the boss, here." Eliza waved the steaming mug under where his nose would be. "Boss want a beverage?"

With a second, abrupt look, Barret floated up from whatever dark water his mind was marooned in. He clicked his visor-jaw back into place, doing his best to look halfway presentable.

"Oh! Eh... *eheh,* I be more rust than iron at this age. Best not speed up the process, aye?"

Digging a canned pirate laugh out from his shell, the Rot Admiral stretched out his arm to give Eliza her second encouraging back-slap of the night.

"No worries, all's right as a raft. Ye and the lads enjoy yerselfs without ol' Barry boggin' ye down. Been ages since I's seen'em this chipper, y'know..."

Cap'n Barret sloshed back down into his cocoon of music, leaving Eliza with the rapidly cooling cup. She tapped her fingers against it, then smirked as a thought bubbled up.

"Y'know, it'sh iiiiiironic, iron-jaw," Eliza giggled, tickled at her own bit of babbled brilliance. "Heh, iron-y. But! But, but, you've been puttin' me through my paces to perform for ya, now yer gettin' it fer free! Yer the... wit 'n wind behind thish whooooole shindig, 'n ye've got nothin' t'say? Shurely you've got some bangin' songs t'bang out, Barry!"

The crew around them chimed in with a well-timed "ooooo", falling somewhere between a ghostly wail and a juvenile jeer. It was enough to pull Barret back, his visor-teeth chunking into a lopsided grin.

"Right! Ye've got some liquid courage in ye, brings ye t'thinkin' ye can twist me arm fer a song'n dance? Cuz yer right!"

Rising with a stamp that sent his Cap'n's chair toppling back, the Rot Admiral spun the ancient flute with mechanical precision. He rested the end on his left shoulder's mushroom colony, feeling for the valves with soft tendriled caps like fingertips, and breathed a hot gale through the instrument that trilled startlingly clear. Eliza joined *The Bastion*'s mates in their raucous admiration, lost in the twiddling rivers of melodies the Cap'n was getting out of the grotty old thing.

The sloshed siren swam through a sea of spirits and somehow splashed out onto the galley's table in a mad whirl. The wild hues of the curdled crew blended into a stained glass swirl, almost beautiful in their own ethereal way. She heard a wild chanting tune in the air and realized that it had been coming out of her.

So we'll ro-o-oll the ol' Bastion along!
And we'll roll the moldy Bastion along!
So we'll ro-o-oll the ol' Bastion along!
And we'll all hang on behind!

"You're spittin' right fire!" chattered Rufus from behind his coffee mug.

As the whooping abominations cheered on a bottle of the Aveilan captain's select *grappa* to her lips, Eliza allowed her cares to take a spill for a time. She wasn't dead, or part of the 'fun guys' just yet, and en route to her love in the most fearsome vessel to sail the Grand Sea. Nothing about her world seemed to make sense anymore, but what did it matter? Her life within the borders of Amrestir had been one filled with stories of high-seas peril and plunder. All things considered, she should've seen this coming.

With a new pep in her step and new booze in her

cup, Eliza rolled into the rhythm of the music with another verse. She focused on her flailing feet and imagined Nemo trying to coax her down from the table again, but none of her current companions were looking to break her stride. The odd, mottled denizens of *The Bastion* danced and sang into the night, the world's troubles set on the back burner for a little while longer.

Eliza was losing track of time as the days and the waves churned beyond *The Bastion*'s cargo hold.

She'd been having trouble judging exactly how long it had been since she'd first dangled herself out to be plundered. Without shifts at the Bouncin' Bean or Toni's faith in proper time management, it was hard to stay grounded without any solid ground below her feet. They were scorching south through the Burmagnem Stretch, an open expanse outside of Faffton's borders positively riddled with passing sloops, salesmen, and most importantly, suckers.

Cap'n Barret hadn't pressed her into the harshest labors on board, but even a mission of love couldn't get her out of having to get to work. Eliza had gone through performances from *Damsel on a Dinghy* to *The Plank Promenade*, and all other manner of schemes that'd been festering in the Cap'n's noggin for who knew how long. She'd gotten into something of a rhythm with her forsaken fellows, and appreciated having a group of co-workers that put in more effort than she did for once. Even the most grotesque of the group still had the work ethic of a proper sailor about them.

The bits of guilt that clung to Eliza through her part in the plundering were scalded away by the heat of Nemo's coal, growing warmer with each nautical mile closer to the thieving fleet. She could also see the appeal of the ideal Amrestir lifestyle as the fruits of her piratical labor filtered out from the Quartermaster's dole, including fresh vittles, a gently used coat, an engraved officer's pistol, and a full-framed bed that had nearly brought her to tears on her first official flop.

Spirits flowed and spirits rose, even as she sailed among a gang of ghosts. Idle daydreams on what she'd do with that spouse snatcher in hand were cracked by a metallic knock at her quartermaster-leased quarters.

"Oi, Eliza, are ye decent?"

Looking down at the accursed maiden's dress still stained with prismatic pain by the morning's showing of *The Shipwrecked Sadsack*, Eliza couldn't remember a time where she could be considered less decent. Luckily, nobody on the ship was in any state to be judgemental.

"Close enough, Cap'n. Come on in."

The Rot Admiral creaked in chorus with the door's hinges, a long scrap of fresh white sail wrapped about his frame. It took a bit of bending and some cut-off curses to maneuver around her temporary bedroom, but he managed to get into a lurch that kept his mushroom luggage away from their hard-fought profits.

"Didn't mean t'wake ye, if that be the case. Never got the hang of how and when folks slept, even when I knew folks who still did it."

"Don't worry about it. If I was out, I wouldn't have heard the knock. Is something wrong up top?"

Barret settled into a squat, his snaggle-tined smile and crest popping out from his sheet shawl like a garden eel.

"Got a gift for ye. But ye be keepin' it hushed, aye?"

A point of yellow poked through Barret's bundle like a crack in an egg. It expanded until the Feo's hand emerged gripping a pair of shears with the same curious shimmer that she had seen accessorizing the rest of the crew. He held them graciously, as though he were handling a holy talisman.

"These be made of *gold*, lass."

Eliza watched the edges of the blades shine, but

141

memories of her first public outing with Nemo raised both her suspicions and her brows.

"Hmph, alright. I'm not that gullible, Cap'n, I've seen this trick in the city before."

"Trick?!" Barret hushed, barely able to keep his voice down as he cradled the blades like a newborn. "This be no trick at all! We... well, ye've heard tell of the Garden of Life, aye?"

Eliza thought back on the statue of that Feo she'd met Nemo under during their first date, the legends that had preceded it. Feeling the looping clues of rigging tighten out on their pulleys, she tugged on the line.

"The basics, yeah. Far-away island, tall tales of a garden filled with treasure, got caught up in the Stagnance Plague after the Ibi had their temper tantrum? There's a spot in the city square dedicated to survivors that got back from the island."

"...Them be the broad strokes, ye," Barret admitted. "The treasure though, that be far from a tall tale. I kid ye not, that greenhouse stood gold all the way to the ground, includin' all the fiddly tool bits inside. Didn't get a chance to do the arkya-logics, but they musta known somethin'."

Eliza took up the offered shears with newfound care, admiring how the light glinted off it even in the dim candlelight. She had caught flashes of the gleaming ornaments the crew carried both on and in their person, notably free from any of the fungal pox, but never did she consider the true nature of the mythical metal.

Barret chattered his jaw, with something still gnawing away at him.

"The touch of the stuff helps the lads forget their pain. They'd hate to hear it, but it seems right t'grant ye a slim share fer all the hassle."

"This has to be..." Eliza wondered, weighing the metal in her hands. "I could buy out my apartment building with this. Oh, but who would even believe it's the real deal? All it'd be good for now is trimming this topiary up here, eh?"

She mimed at chopping through her unwashed mane like a rabid crab. Barret's laugh joined hers in the cluttered space, free from much of the manic uproar from his public appearances. With the pulsing caps kept under wraps, he almost looked like an ordinary Feo, if she was willing to match his generosity.

"Well, it be a bit of a soft metal, so best hope ye don't nick 'em on that tangle if ye try!"

Eliza's fingers went to tuck a loose strand behind her ear, wishing they were the metal ones she had grown so fond of.

"You'd best not let Nemo hear you talk like that when you meet him," she chuckled softly. "He loves my hair, believe it or not... Told me that the very first time we met."

Barret was looking down on her with the curiosity of a crow, jaw set in something of a patient grin. Eliza realized that she'd kept most of her personal woes tight to the chest after their first heart-to-heart aboard *The Bastion*, and the thrum of Nemo's surrogate heart from under her pillow helped to keep her own warm.

"You know, for our wedding, I considered going to the salon to get it straightened. He was horrified when I told him! Insisted that I keep my hair just the way it is... The sap even calls me the 'Dread Siren' sometimes, says it's my pirate nickname."

The Rot Admiral sat back, staring at the ceiling. "No kiddin'. Ye must miss him tremendously."

Eliza felt another ringlet tickle her nose and sighed. The very sight of it was a nagging reminder of Nemo's admiration and his absence. She opted to yank her hair back into a high and loose tail, out of face and out of mind.

"I really do."

Laying on the bed with the engagement coal in hand, she turned her gaze back to the Cap'n. He was quietly eyeing her from his huddle with the same distant vacancy that Eliza saw during the crew's first big celebration.

143

"Aye, I know how it be. Ye'll be with Nemo again soon. The Rot Admiral himself be seein' to that."

A thought occurred to Eliza, one she hadn't found the time nor the curiosity to ask before.

"What were you doing, floating so close to New Amrestir anyway? Anyone who'd even believe you're real would quicker light you up on sight than invite any of you in. No offense meant."

The Cap'n's head was sinking into his shawl, burrowing like a tortoise. The words that came from within sounded harrowed, almost embarrassed.

"I... I just wanted to see the lighthouse again. It's been so long and... I know I can't go back, not like this. I said my final goodbyes years ago, but..."

There was a scraping sound from below. Eliza looked down and saw that Barret was digging his fingers across the timbers.

"Just one more time. Just one..."

Barret's voice trailed away, hunched and tightly wound within his sailcloth swaddle. The most Eliza could see of the poor Cap'n was the shaking of his crest's bristles, tinged with putrid hues. She leaned forward in her bed, soothing him with the same gentility that he had shown her.

"I know what it's like, watching your old life rot away. You said you had someone waiting for you, right? Who is that?"

"I..." Barret faltered, before setting his jaw firmly. "The day I left home for the last time, I had a fight with someone very dear to me. It was on Outset Day, if ye were around t'remember that."

Eliza did remember, even if she was a child at the time. It had been a new holiday to mark Amrestir's first uneasy step to join the rest of the Grand Sea on the global stage, and turned into an absolute belly-flop of making waves. Everything had felt so dazzling, bright and filled with potential, but then so did a bomb with its fuse lit.

"I had the opportunity to make a real step towards the future for Feo. Thought I'd do what the world

144

demanded and return a hero, return with all they'd ever need... Now I'll never return again."

Eliza weighed the coal in her hand, sharing in the moment of quiet grief. The silence dragged on until her mouth couldn't hold her thoughts any longer.

"...'A step towards the future', huh? I thought that sounded familiar. I remember all the buzz going around about the first Feo captain, even Nemo ended up hearing about it way out on the open sea. Your story did make a difference for the little folk, an inspiration, even if..."

Eliza's voice faltered as she glanced over to Barret, who had slipped back into his own private world again. The silence between them was heavy, broken only by the creaking hull and the rhythmic crash of waves against *The Bastion*.

"...Please don't resent me," murmured the Cap'n.

Eliza saw Barret's jaw quivering, a tendril of a tear dripping down his grill. She stood up from the bed and placed a hand on a non-tainted patch of sail, compassion winning over ration for a moment.

"Cap'n, I don't resent you. We all make our own decisions, and what I did is on me alone. Same with you; what you've done in the past doesn't matter now."

"Doesn't matter? I abandoned ye!" Barret wailed, tearing the cloth from her grip and wringing it about himself. "I... I chose again and again t'toss ye and Claude aside, all for... for fun! For pride! How can ye just let that go, Gilby? I can't move on like that, like... him..."

There was a growing darkness about the Cap'n, the bright white of his shawl beginning to bleed through with viscous shades of rot. Eliza edged along the side of her gifted bed, eyeing the doorway behind the Feo as he festered.

"Cap'n, I don't know who—"

"What makes ye so special, Mully? Ye get yer second chance, and what be of me? Of us?! Rotten embers on a long-dead pyre, just waitin' t'be snuffed out! Leavin' all of us behind, I... you..."

145

The walls were closing in, the air growing hot and damp. As Barret wrestled against ghosts of the past that she had never seen nor known, every part of Eliza's brain was firing off signs to run, to flee, to go anywhere else. Yet the Rot Admiral dominated every inch of her vision, and only *The Bastion* waited beyond.

"Barret, I-I appreciate the gift, and everything you've done for me, but you're scaring me right now. Please, just let me go—"

"No, don't go! Please, Gilby, I never meant to hurt you! I-I was suffocating on that island, a-a-and I really did this for you! For Claude! So we could finally be in control of our own fates!"

Barret was beginning to sway like a seasick sailor, narrowly avoiding smashing supplies off their shelves in the process. He found some purchase gripping the roof beam, leering down at her with a rabid desperation. The protective sheet hung in tatters about his frame, steaming with melting mycelium.

"Look, Barry's here now! I never mean t'run off again, I swear!"

Eliza was paralyzed, unable to tear her attention from the Stagnance creeping below the Cap'n's surface. Through the delirium of his words, she could hear the echoes of her father, feel the same helplessness from all those years ago as he had struggled through the cursed fungi malady. He'd spent his last painful days calling out for people either long dead or long gone, unable to recognize her as the infection took root. Eliza could still hear his final words: a plea to let him go and pick his daughter up from her reading lessons.

Watching the body and mind of that once-robust man rot away had chewed an unfillable hole in her heart, and the Rot Admiral's despair was ripping open an old wound.

"Barret, stop! I'm not—"

Before Eliza could move, she felt a hand upon her cheek, hotly caressing the line of her jaw.

146

"I'm here, Gilby, I won't be leavin' again. I'm—"
Eliza's world exploded.

White-hot torture sparked along her face and wound its way through every fiber of her being, the hiss of searing iron drowned out by the sound of her own screams. All else faded behind the stench of scorched skin and Stagnant torment.

Eliza wrenched back from the Cap'n's caress with an excruciating rip, watching a trail of her blistered flesh and blood congeal on the sizzling palm. Dancing stars clouded her vision as she scrambled to put as much bed space between herself and the still-dripping gore, petrified and huddled before the horror of The Rot Admiral.

The Cap'n was staring at the state of his hand, pieces of skin cooking on the surface like bacon, when something seemed to slough back into place behind his visor. Desperately re-wrapping what remained of his shawl, the monstrous Feo made a vain effort to scrub the carnage from his palm.

"Eliza?! Dear Flame, I'm so sorry! Are you—?"

Any apology that Barret could try to make was muted by Eliza's agonized sobs. She let out a screech as he approached her, primal and wordless yet sending the clearest message of all. Grasping out for the first thing at hand, Eliza flung the wretched golden shears in an arc that sent both it and the Rot Admiral into a cowering clatter.

The pounding of wet metal, the slamming of a door, and confused shouts were the last things Eliza heard before being plunged into silent darkness again. She stayed balled up at the top of the pilfered bed for what felt like an eternity, crying until her eyes had no more tears to shed and gasping until her lungs had no more air to give.

The pain threatened to throw her into madness, but the rational part of Eliza's brain clawed its way to the surface, reminding her of the true danger she was in. Without immediate treatment, the burn would fester, and the spores would travel down to her lungs. She would die just as her father had.

Eliza staggered about her room, hands blindly groping around the shelves until they wrapped around the neck of a bottle. Trembling, barely able to prop herself up, her eyes scanned over a label for Faffton Gin, and tore the cork out with a savage pull of her teeth. She winced as the motion tugged at the raw flesh around her cheek, then tipped the alcohol in a stream across the left side of her face. The pain struck like a thunderclap, intense as the burn itself, and the bloodcurdling scream that followed confirmed it. Her hand spasmed, the bottle slipping free to shatter on the floor as a new wave of concerned shouts echoed through her door.

As her howls turned to whimpers and adrenaline gave way to searing pain, Eliza slowly crawled her way back to her bed and collapsed. She clawed at the burn on her face and the mattress below, each the fruits of her piratical labor, each a prospect now as spoiled as the pirate crew she served with. The thought of pulling herself together for another inane performance to raid another poor ship drove her deeper into despair.

Eliza's hand grasped to pull her pillows close, only for her fingers to brush against the core coal nestled within. Even the faint pulse against her skin was enough to send a new wave of shudders through her spine, its once soothing warmth now bringing with it a cold dread. As *The Bastion* coasted along and the coal's heat burnt on and on, the only thought on Eliza's mind was the same as that of the Cap'n.

I want to go home.

CHAPTER 9
CALLBACKS

Nemo didn't remember making it back home.

The night had grown as cold as the lingering coffee in his to-go cup, resting on the bedside table like a miniature lighthouse. Even as the Feo had stumbled his way back through the winding streets of New Amrestir, every ember of his thoughts had been dedicated to cooking on the absolutely captivating woman he'd just met. Something about her had shocked his system like an ice bath, a shiver still creeping its way up his back.

Staring up at a leaky patch on the ceiling, Nemo was motionless, save for kneading the brim of the good-fortune hat between his metallic mitts. He felt like a parched man who'd stumbled across an oasis, afraid that it could all turn out to be a mirage.

The door to the apartment burst inwards with a *thud*, and a very real Pauvus staggered right through Nemo's little fantasy.

"Nnnnnnemo!" the boozed-up bird brayed, far too loudly for this time of night. "Nemomo... mo, what'sh happening? Did'ja ack'chally get out 'n do people shtuff?"

Nemo watched his shipmate-turned-roommate nosedive straight into his own bed, neatly spearing through the mattress cover with the tip of his beak. The Feo raised his hat in salute.

"Hey Paul," Nemo hushed, the brassy tone of his voice softer than tin. "I did, actually... I think I might've fallen in love today."

"*Wfft?*"

"What?"

Pauvus plucked his face out from the muffling mattress, eyes bleary yet wild.

150

"What!? What is this, you fffffinally growin' a senshe of humor?"

Nemo rolled up into a seated position, facing the peacock head-on with the decorated cap in his lap.

"No, I'm being serious. There was this girl working at this coffee shop, the... Bouncin' Bean, I think."

The Ave chuckled and tugged himself closer to the edge of his bed, tapping the floorboards with eager talons.

"*Ooooh,* you shly rogue, you! Fallin' head o'er heels for a dame at first shight, how piratical of ya! So, what'sh this prize catch'a yours like, what'sher, *eh,* finish? Iron, copper... solid gold?"

Nemo had to think on exactly how to answer that one.

"...Skin?"

In a flurry of feathers, Pauvus was up like he had been struck by lightning. He scrambled to Nemo's side, flapping wings whipping a gale through the small space.

"Skin?! You fell in love with a flesh and blood woman?!"

"Y-Yes! Why, is that a problem?"

Pauvus unleashed a great sigh, which crescendoed into a yawn by the end. He waved his wings helplessly, trying to pick through the right words.

"I—you—well, no, there's no problem with it. I mean, I'm sure some of those preachy types might think that, but it's just— You never mentioned you were into that, is all."

"Didn't think I was," Nemo shrugged, still lost to the significance of his coffeeshop crush. "Maybe she's just that beautiful; could turn the eye of a hurricane. You should've seen her hair, Paul, those curls had a life of their own. Absolutely mesmerising..."

The Feo whistled out a wistful sigh. His visor could've traced the looping patterns of each lock for hours, if he was given such a privilege.

"Oh, she even said she liked my hat! Your feather was just the charm I needed."

151

Pride filled Pauvus' chest, as well as a barely-swallowed belch.

"Heh, more than pleased t'lend a feather of favor, can't be selfish with gifts like these. Still, looks ain't the whole story, and I know how I'm soundin' here. Could be a real bitter pit in the middle of that fruit."

"Look at me, Paul," Nemo gestured, giving his chest a quick and hollow *bonk*. "I'm in no position to judge just by someone's shell. No, she was so patient and sweet, with this zest to her just like that bean juice 'coffee'! She talked to me like I was a regular fella about town and I swear, for just a moment I was..."

The Feo felt something pop in his chest, and his shoulders sank on their hinges.

"But I'm always a spectacle. Broke the surface like a cannonball, as blunt a splash I could've managed. Even blurted out that I liked her hair! I must've made a complete stove out of myself."

Pauvus was munching on a bag of toasted seeds from the cabinet, having fully engrossed himself in the private Audience. He shrugged his wings, and picked a loose shell from his beak with a talon.

"Considerin' the options, and the local color, that's not the worst you coulda done. It was an awkward conversation; congrats, you've made it to society. Just keep that in mind and make a point to be smoother next time you give her a visit."

Now it was Nemo's turn to bolt up from the bed, nearly catching his pegged leg on a knothole in the floor.

"I... I can't! I don't think my core could take it! She's probably sitting with some suitor right now, mocking me over fancy 'coffee' drinks!"

Pauvus sighed, and swayed his way back into a proper standing position. He left the bag on the mattress and put a wing on Nemo's shoulder, partially to keep himself from toppling back over.

"Probably's are for hatchlings. I've watched you headbutt an Obra's tusk clean off, and you're afraid of being mocked over cocktails? Get in there with confidence. Say what you must, do all you can!"

Nemo felt a surge from Pauvus' pep-talk, the image of the coffee girl's face floating in his vision like the cover of a sailor's shelling-story.

"You mean I should court her?"

"Oh Flame, no," Pauvus groaned, waving a wing through Nemo's night-dream. "Might've been a bit overdramatic there. Look, you haven't gotten knocked in the drink yet, but don't start by running for the gangplank. Keep it cool, get to know her as a person, and let her have the time to do the same for you. Just act like *you*, not what others make you to be... *Heh*, well, except maybe me."

Nemo's head was buzzing with worries, confusion, and all sorts of feelings he had never bothered with before. There was a feverish warmth building up inside him at the prospect, one entirely separate from his ambient burning. From his side, Pauvus yelped, then gingerly passed a fresh feather with a tear in his eye.

"You did say she had good taste, right? Might as well try and spread the brand as much as I can, even if it doesn't simmer out."

Holding the iridescent tail feather up to his dim flame, Nemo looked back to Pauvus in a new light. He plucked the cap from the bed and carefully slipped the accessory into a loop with its twin.

"Thank you. And I truly mean those words."

Pauvus hobbled back to his side of the room, flopping back onto his bed with a scattering of seeds.

"All good, brass kettle... I'll swing by that place with you... sometime, you can... pay me back..."

The wind was falling out of his sails, and Nemo knew it was already far too late at night. It would be a new morning soon. A new day of potential, a new day of day shifts and shop queues.

"Sleep well, Paul."

"You do... you, *zzz*... Nemo..."

"...Nemo?"

"..."

"...Nemo..."

"......"

"Nemo, say something."

"...Thank you."

THWACK!

The Feo's head jolted forward with a clang. It idly looked down and saw the object of its assault was a wooden bucket, lobbed from across the deck.

"You sad sack of scraps! Do you think she'd want to see you sulking about like this?!"

The Feo glanced over to see Pauvus, the Ave looking as though he had been blown through a hurricane. The Captain and her crew had started a cruel game of sneaking behind him and plucking tail feathers at random, without any heed for his say in the matter. Soon, almost every member of the ship was sporting their own feather while the peacock who supplied them was left with a fan barely worth tucking in.

The Feo continued its mopping and its moping. "Eliza's not here. Thank you."

"Well I am!" Pauvus screeched, scrubbing his section viciously. "And I bet you she isn't sitting on her hands right now, feeling sorry for herself! If she was here, she'd sand your hide for acting so pathetic."

The air held still, save for a sea breeze whipping across the sails. The Feo returned to its work, unwilling to face anything but the task at hand.

"...Maybe she was wrong about you. Maybe Eliza did end up marrying a *DAMN FURNACE!*"

The Feo's helmet whipped about, quickly followed by the rest of it, as it blazed across the deck with no regard for assignment protocol. Pauvus could barely croak another word when a brass finger stabbed under the crook of his slender neck.

"You keep my wife's name out of your mouth!"

"Get back to work!" Remy shouted from below the mainmast, pointing accusingly at Pauvus. "And you! Shut your beak, songbird, before I cut that tongue out!"

Pauvus grudgingly and quietly returned to his duty, attacking the timbers as though they owed him money. The Feo lingered for a moment longer, daring the Ave to breathe another word. When nothing came, it returned to its task in perfect silence.

All of the Feo's attention was fixated on the tug at its core, wavering in its vision like the lure of an angler in the abyss. Every moment, the subtle shifts in its temperature drove Nemo to near madness, the prospects of his beloved waxing and waning. While the man inside the brassy shell raged against this senseless cruelty, the Feo dutifully worked the deck, as it always had.

As it was cleaning a particularly stubborn stain soaked into the wood, Antoine the coat thief scuffed a boot trail up to the Feo's space.

"Madame Vitrail wants you in her quarters! On the double!"

The Feo leaned the mop against the railing, leaving its new work to wait for now. As it trudged to the captain's quarters, it made a point to not look in Pauvus' direction as its lone act of defiance.

The captain's quarters had been designed by Madame Vitrail personally, a fact that was obvious even at a glance. Records of past maritime conquests hung in sheets across the walls in a patchwork of wallpaper, illuminated in a garden of colors by a series of stained-glass deck prisms. The gaudy admiral herself sat behind a grand oak desk, her impressive boots resting atop a map as she idly read through a recent plunder manifest. Her eyes shot up when she heard the door creak open, a shark-like grin spreading across her face as she spotted the Feo standing in her doorway.

"Ah, *ma petite bouilloire!*" Vitrail called, swinging her feet to the ground with a flutter of papers. "I must say,

I'm impressed with how well you adjusted to life on *La Fille Patronne*. And in your uniform and all, *bon goût*[19]!"

The Feo looked down to its simple white shirt and brown pants, a forest green sash wrapped around the waist. The patriotic pop of color was joined by a generously re-gifted Pauvus feather in its cap, practically an official crew accessory in its own right.

"...Thank you."

"Ahh, music to my ears! This has been a long time coming for me, *bouilloire,* you're living up to expectations. I know it's been a change of pace, and change of management, but you have been a model tool for Fríasa, and for myself. As such, I have a very important job you can do for me. Would you be so kind?"

"Yes. Thank you."

"Mmm, *très bien*," breathed Vitrail, strapping her ceremonial chestplate on in a sparkling display of self-confidence. "Now, I've a word to be had with some fellows aboard *Le S'envoler*; some white wine, some light flogging. I plan to make a fun night of it, truly. In the meantime, you handle any clever swine looking to take advantage of my good spirits to rifle through my room... including that shifty *salaud*[20] Antoine. I am positive that man was sneaking through my things during our little excursion, and I don't intend to let down my guard twice. Understood?"

"...Understood. Thank you."

Madame Vitrail coasted past the motionless Feo, a lingering hand held to the helmet's cheek. She checked her teeth in the muddled reflection, then gave the brass a trio of taps.

"Fantastic. Be good, keep to yourself, maybe tidy up the place if you get bored. Now, *au revoir!*"

The Feo didn't turn as it was left alone, listening to the bootfalls disappear behind the slam of a door and the click of a lock. It stood and considered its well-decorated

---

[19] good taste
[20] bastard

156

cell, scanning across the commands and executions framing the private quarters in a collage of unabashed pride. With little else to occupy its time, the Feo paid attention to the dense swathes of text, thoughts of recent lessons in letters bubbling to the surface. It scanned through frustrating mixtures of strange, unknown jumbles of characters in a vain hope to find the word 'Marigold', and maybe a petal of news about its fate.

Carefully picking under the wall pins to check for partially-covered contracts, the Feo nearly jumped as something slipped from the trophy board and fluttered to the embroidered rug below. It was a discolored sheet of poor-quality paper, with a charcoal sketch in the center that nearly cut the Feo's core cold then and there.

Rough black curls framed the roughly-hewn face of a young girl, shaded but faded from years without proper framing. The Feo turned the picture in its hands to find a letter scrawled in easy-to-read letters, even if the meaning in some of the words went over its head.

Dear [......],

I hope this letter finds you in good health. If you read nothing else but the next few [.........], please let me tell you how our [.....] is doing.

She learned to walk the other day. Her first word was 'Dada', much to my [........]. At night, she still cries out for her mother. I cannot sing 'Little Liz' as well as you do, and I cannot tame her hair to look as [.........] as yours. I drew a picture of her on the back of this letter so you can see how much she has grown.

There are sleepless nights, days when the world feels too [.....] to bear at times. But her tiny hands gripping mine, the smell of her forehead, and the sound of her [.....] calling for me, I find a [........] I never knew I had. I have [........] with what you have done, the pain you brought on me and your [........]. I want to hate you, but I cannot find it in my heart to. You gave me Eliza, and she is the greatest gift I have ever [........]. No [.........] or [........] across the ocean can ever replace her.

The [......] part of me still holds out hope that you will come back to us one day, but you always did say I was a romantic fool. On the first day we met, you told me that I was the sort of [.........] that writes legends, and you were the sort that lives them. Perhaps I should have known you would run back to the sea. You do have the soul of a [......]. I only wish you would have waited to see the woman Eliza will grow up to be.

Farewell,

[........] [......]

If Nemo could weep, the tears would have flooded the hull.

Eliza often brushed off questions that pried too deeply into details about her father, framing it as not wanting to single Nemo out for his lack of personal experience, but he could always sense the sadness surrounding his legacy. Now, he had the words of that

158

elusive man in his hand, a one-way conversation with the dearly departed.

'Little Liz'

Nemo clamped his gaze upon the lovingly-drawn doodle, his anchorline in a world that was wavering beneath his feet. It was the closest that he had felt to Eliza in weeks, the sight of her face filling his chest even through the filters of charcoal and time.

Something flared inside him. Was it fury? The dangerous beauty of hope? Longing, even? Trying to pick out the spikes of passion in his core was hard enough normally, and now his chest felt like a stewpot about to bubble over. Fate was a notion that always rubbed Nemo the wrong way, especially with how some tended to use it as an excuse. Now, taking in the sheer scope of the words before him, and the gravity of exactly whose ship he was property of, had him staggered with genuine seasickness.

He'd been lost amidst a mire of memories since losing his love, but in this lost message Nemo could see a guiding star, connecting the past to a future that he could claim for himself. Letting the letter hang loosely, the Feo allowed himself to drift far beyond the floating walls around him, buoyed in the profound silence of his revelation.

A metallic jingling shattered the moment like glass. The Captain was always the sort to make her imminent arrival to anyone and everyone as blatant as possible, which made the sight of Antoine squatting in the doorframe all the more appalling. The silence had returned, and neither man moved a muscle nor hinge.

"...Can I help you? Thank you."

Antoine's fingers moved faster than his brain, shoving what was clearly a brass set of picks and pins into pockets that didn't belong to him. He made a broad show of jiggling the handle, inspecting the rivets with one squinted eye.

"Told 'er these were lousy quality, and no, you can't help. I'm handling security, checkin' these cheap locks t'make sure nobody gets any bright—"

The shorter sailor leveled his eyeline to Nemo, and the paper he was still clutching. Within a wink, the letter was in the First Mate's hands, its heartfelt message crinkling in his grip.

"...Ideas," Antoine muttered, his square jaw tightening with tooth-straining effort. "*Mh*, actin' up wise even without a brain, are ya? Y'know, if the boss heard how little her favorite toy thinks of her trust... She'd be crushed. And you'd be next."

Nemo glared down to the man's stony visage, indignant fury raging in a single pupil. A pulsing shame threatened to drag the Feo back down to his servile roots, but the sight of Eliza's family history being handled like a piece of litter sparked a fresh fury of his own.

"If she hears anything, it would be the exact same story for you. The Captain told me that she doesn't appreciate you 'handling security' without her."

Antoine's sneer faltered for just a moment, shifting his stance far enough that Nemo could hear his pockets jingle guiltily.

"And she'd take the word of the walking merchandise over her own blasted First Mate?"

"She'd take the word of her favorite toy," Nemo boomed. "The key difference is that I know how to keep to myself."

Nemo watched as Antoine's eye began to water, the man beginning to feel the heat. That flash of mortal fear was a sight Nemo had grown to hate bringing out in people, even on the face of someone like Antoine. The Feo thought of the lad Twitch; another uninvited memory of past barbarities washing through his mind, fighting to avoid being the first to boil ov—

—*His punishment endured, the limp rigsman squelched back down to the*—

"Argh, fine!" Antoine relented, so steamed up that his hair was frizzing. "Yer point's been heard. Dig through whatever gets you goin', rusty, I know how to *keep to*

160

myself too."

Nemo found the letter pressed into his hands once more, firmly enough to nearly knock him off-balance. Flicking the collar of Nemo's honeymooning jacket defiantly, Antoine turned and sulked back down into the dead night air. The Feo kept watch until he was sure that no other soul was watching, diligently locking himself inside the belly of the beast once more.

"...Thank you."

With a twist and a *chunk*, Nemo popped his peg leg from its stump and prodded the rolled-up note deep inside. It would only be a matter of time until his new owner would return and press him into obedient service once more, but holding onto the forgotten relic of Eliza's past kept his feet firmly grounded. For now, the Feo could swallow his shame and soldier on, with the comforting thought of who truly owned his heart.

A fresh dawn reeled the sun just over the waterline, bleeding shades of orange and pink into the boundless horizon.

Nemo watched the natural miracle apathetically from his post at *La Fille Patronne*'s portside shrouds. Countless skies and horizons had painted themselves for the Feo in his time sailing the Grand Sea, but it was Eliza's reactions to the world's masterpieces that he had been looking forward to seeing. He imagined her experiencing the rolling vineyards of Gémissant, catching dazzling salt-cliffs off Lunemar Skerry's coast, trekking the frost-rimed climbs of the Frigid Gardens for her first glimpse of snow.

Lost in his thoughts of what he had missed out on, Nemo pointedly ignored the snickering of his fellow sailors as he worked out tangles in the rigging. There was no accounting for taste among a crew like this, no matter how much they tried to snatch Pauvus' fashionable valor.

"Oi, *poêle*[21], come over here and light m'pipe!"

If Nemo had lungs, he would have been tempted to treat the man to a drawn-out sigh. As it was, he still had to put up a good show of being a model Feo, even as the refreshed fire in his core railed against another stint of servitude. Pivoting on his peg, the brass man prepared to settle into an attitude of gratitude when a speck above the man's upraised pipe caught his attention.

"What is that behind you? Thank you."

"Are ya tryin' to pull one over on me? That is the dumbest—"

"What's that? Jean, stop wastin' time over there, look!"

The brute named Jean bitterly replaced his unsparked pipe with a spyglass, now focused in the opposite direction of the morning's glory. Nemo may not have had one for himself, but even in the rising light the mystery object was clearly growing larger.

No, not larger. Closer.

The speck turned into a dash, which turned into two flapping wings on the breeze. It scraped closer and lower until the green and yellow uniform of a SpritFlit courier could be made out against the waves, along with a white flag of peace dangling from their undercarriage. *La Fille Patronne* buzzed with excitement, half of the crew fretting over possible political spying with the other half eagerly anticipating a chance for airborne target practice.

Nemo kept his gaze on the approaching Ave while the officers did their due diligence in keeping the deckhands under control. He could make out two orange eyes bulging from a head of grey feathers, and a flight pattern that looked just about ready to drop into the drink. Enough organization had been beaten into the crew for them to stretch out a large net lattice and brace for impact, giving the carrier pigeon a dragnet for their crash-landing.

Rocketing onto the deck mere feet from Nemo's post, panting and gasping on comparatively solid ground,

---

[21] stove

the courier cooed in breathless terror. Within seconds, the crew was swarming them with questions and sabers, cutting right to the point.

"What's yer business here?"

"You some kind of spy?"

"Got any Press comics in that sack?"

The passenger pigeon locked eyes on the Feo just long enough for Madame Vitrail's door to bust open under the force of a freshly-polished boot heel. First Mate Antoine, who between the old coat and feather had practically stolen Nemo's entire style, cleared a path for the Captain with a four-bored blunderbuss at the ready. Vitrail clomped to the center of attention and regarded the Ave with a cold nod, brushing her fellows aside with a flick of the hand.

"What is your designation, *facteur*[22]?"

The courier had barely managed to get a word in edgewise since their landing, but it gave them enough time to catch their breath. They jerked to attention with a skybound salute, wincing as their wings hit full extension.

"*Hooh, huff*... Mailmaiden Martha of the *SF Rimborso*, ma'am! Apologies for the unannounced visit, but I—"

"You're excused. You're also distracting my crew, so *arrête*[23]. They've a busy schedule for the day and I'm sure you must too, so let's make this visit brief and private. Antoine, handle things out here. *Oui?*"

"*Oui, madame!*"

"Marvelous. *Bouilloire, venez ici*[24]!"

Nemo's Fríasen was rougher than his literacy, but he knew when the Captain was looking for a chance to flaunt her fancy Feo. He abandoned his knotwork by the railing and trudged to Madame Vitrail's side, shooting Antoine a glare that could've blown the gun right out of his hands.

---

[22] postman

[23] stop

[24] Kettle, come here

163

Vitrail's quarters were the same as when he last left it, luxurious and cold like its designer. The captain pointed Martha to a chair that looked to be stuffed with the feathers of her kin, and waited for the courier to settle in before they could get to business.

"*Bouilloire*, get out the *givré blanc* for our guest."

Nemo fetched two stained glass cups and the wine while the Captain made her pleasantries, doing his best not to heat up the frosted bottle as he poured. The mailmaiden didn't look very comfortable, even in a chair with a fancy drink, but Nemo couldn't blame her. Vitrail had a way of pinning you to the floor with her gaze, picking through every gnarled root and bud of thought as she searched for fresh dirt to work with.

"We haven't caught sight of another ship in days, that's quite a solo flight to make right into the middle of an active fleet. You must be simply exhausted."

"Er, well, yes," Martha stammered, doing her best to balance a filled drink on the tips of her pinion feathers. "Apologies again, but I had no other choice. Our vessel was ambushed, and well, so was about every other ship I tried to hail. Figured strength in numbers might help."

Vitrail watched intently from above the lip of her glass, passing lingering looks between the Ave and Nemo. She swirled her rimmed refreshment dramatically for the sake of the two-person Audience, allowing Martha's silence to marinate in the air.

"Mm, take a moment to appreciate that. Nothing like frosted grape for a warm welcome, straight from Lady Pontaine's estate. Now, I hear your story, and think that the common ingredient in those follies would be... you. Wouldn't you agree?"

Nemo knew that the Madame was looking for a reaction more than a response, and the mailmaiden was struggling over how to deliver either.

"Wh–no!" Martha croaked, nearly choking on her *givré blanc*. "We were on our way to New Amrestir on standard delivery, when we came upon a ship infested with that horrid Stagnance! There was a girl aboard, some damsel in a dress and hair like a two-family nest. She was wailing up and down about being abandoned, begging for aid... but they weren't the ones that needed help."

"They?" Vitrail mused, a well-threaded brow rising on her forehead.

"Well, she claimed to be alone, but our Captain wasn't having it. We're just trying to move along to keep our schedule, you know how it is, and suddenly the blasted Rot Admiral of all things pops out like a stuffed tick! I'm ashamed to admit that I've abandoned my post, but frankly I'm getting too old to risk my tail for some rotten old letters. See, what I'd really love is to get into the printing business, and..."

The mailmaiden's retirement plans bounced right off of Nemo's head, too densely packed with her informational letterbomb.

No, it couldn't be...

"...couldn't get the shading just right, but here! Trying to get a spot in the funny papers after all this, what do you think?"

Nemo leaned in along with Madame Vitrail to gawk at what the Ave was unrolling onto the Captain's table. For someone without thumbs, Martha really could've earned a spot in a Press desk job as she revealed a stylized doodle of a ship bloated with puffy mushrooms in sharply inked detail. In the midst of the mayhem, though exaggerated by someone who clearly needed some practice with drawing human faces, Nemo had no question who the 'damsel' staring back at him was.

Eliza.

Nemo's brass fingers twitched. It took every ounce of his willpower to not snatch the drawing from right under Vitrail's nose while she chuckled away.

"Wow, get a load of that one. I know I'd pick up a copy of this at a Press stand. So then, too busy thinking up comic ideas to bother just... sailing away?"

165

"It's not like we didn't try!" Martha cried out. "They'd snared our hull and rudder while she wasted everyone's time! A-And we weren't the only ones! Came across a rowboat packed with scrap tradesmen not long ago with the same story to tell! They called her The Rot Admiral's Siren... Makes a good headline, right?"

The pigeon was gesticulating wildly now, wasting some of her wine in the process. To the Captain's credit, she was taking the whole affair with a stunning amount of self-control, considering the parties at play.

"It all starts out the same! Some lads too long out on the sea catch a glimpse of this lady all by her lonesome, whether it be on a ship, raft, or dinghy. She begs them to save her, they get too close and *wham!* The Rot Admiral and his crew jump 'em! Leave 'em with nothing but their lives and lifeboats, snatch the rest and keep heading south... Eh, about the same route as you lot, actually. I was just hoping to pass along the news for the sake of safe passage, there's not much life left in these wings."

Nemo stepped up to take the empty glass being handed to him, feeling his core ache as Madame Vitrail casually cast the illustration back onto her table and folded her hands. The Captain sighed, rose to her boots, and stepped around the perimeter of her desk to squeeze a nervous *coo* from the mailmaiden's shoulder.

"The spirit of Fríasa is grateful for your due diligence and speedy delivery. I'll be crunching the crew's shifts as we near the Twin Isles and keep close watch for... them. In appreciation, *factrice*[25], my Feo will take you to the galley for some much needed food and rest."

On cue, Nemo gestured for the Ave to follow, an offer she couldn't exactly refuse in her state. He half-dragged her up from the comfortable guest's seat and led her to the exit, blinded by his own smokey thoughts.

"Wait, what about my drawi—?"

The door slammed behind Martha, but not Nemo. He turned to meet Madame Vitrail's appalled face, and gave the newly-reinforced door's lock a defiant click.

"*Abruti*[26]! You're supposed to leave before locking the—"

"Is that anyway to speak to your son-in-law?"

That was enough to leave the Captain speechless for once. Nemo took the opportunity to pull off his false leg, balancing on one foot while carefully peeling the precious letter from its hollow hidey-hole.

"What are you, broken?! What is this?"

"Does the name 'Eliza' ring a bell?"

Madame Vitrail's steely expression softened for a moment as her voice took on an unexpectedly wistful tone.

"Aye, she was the first ship I ever served aboard. Finest clipper in the sea, but how would—?"

"No, not the ship!" Nemo groaned, waving his nicked note. "*This!* Do you recognize this letter?"

The mirth in Vitrail's face drained out onto the floor like Martha's drink. She aimed her judgemental glare at the

---

[25] postwoman
[26] Stupid

167

stolen letter, then tracked squarely to Nemo's visor. She had a rage in her eyes that went beyond irritation at a malfunctioning tool. It was the most human reaction she had given him during his entire stint aboard her crew, and it felt immensely satisfying.

"...*Oui*."

"Well then, we're going to wait for the Rot Admiral's ship. That woman, that 'siren', is your daughter... and my wife."

The Captain's eyes darted from the young child's portrait to the amateur cartoon, taking in the connections before her and attempting to piece together the whole story. In a flash, she snorted, then laughed, then cackled to the sky with the tone of the truly mad. Nemo waited patiently for Vitrail to work the humor out of her system, and for her to stop slamming on her desktop.

"Hah, *hooooooh*. Wow, that is rich! You really must be cracked to think that sorry display would mean anything here. Even on the slimmest of chances you could make an assumption like that, why would it mean anything to me? Least of all enough to drift ourselves right into that floating oubliette?"

Nemo sputtered, trying to grasp the extent of the woman's sheer apathy.

"Wh— If Eliza truly means nothing to you, then why keep her father's letter after all these years?"

"Because look at it!" Vitrail snapped, snatching the letter right from his stunned grasp. "This drawing is hilarious! Ugh, look how creepy it turned out! And that hair of hers, what in the—"

Nemo returned the favor and re-snatched the letter from Vitrail's distracted hands. The Captain was fuming hard enough to match his own flame, making a concentrated effort to force feigned indifference.

"You want to know the real reason I bothered keeping it around? It's a reminder. A true sailor never lets anything tie them down, and family trees have anchors for roots."

Vitrail leaned forward, bracing her elbows on the desk as she rubbed her temples. "Alastair was always such a sentimental sap. I—*rrgh!*—It was cute when I was a girl, I guess, but sweet talk can only tide you over for so long. He was content living out his days in that little hovel, believing that little life was greater than the Grand Sea itself."

"...Greater than your own daughter?"

"I think—" Vitrail sputtered, "I've had enough of your ramblings, *ferraille*[27]! It doesn't matter because it doesn't make sense, because it's not happening! We're not stopping for some *chaudière*[28] and its so-called wife, even if there wasn't a blasted specter of death nipping at our heels!"

Nemo caught the wayward glance a second too late. In one fluid motion, Madame Vitrail gripped the delicate letter in a crushing grip and stormed over to her personal porthole.

"This is nothing to me!"

Before Nemo could follow, or even secure his leg back into place, she had tossed the antique letter out into the squall of the uncaring Grand Sea.

"NO!"

With a mighty chain of hops, Nemo cleared the distance to the window and shoved her away, staring as the paper and charcoal melted into a saltwater slurry. Reaching out in a desperate grab at nothing, Nemo felt a sharp stamp right to the side of his good knee. The sea fell away from his sight as he clattered in a heap to the timbers, the cherry-red face of Madame Vitrail consuming his world.

"Such a shame. I really thought you'd put all that silliness behind you and settled into your proper place, but I suppose that's my idealism talking again. Well, even the best mates on board need an attitude adjustment from time to time. We'll see how long that little spark holds out."

Prone on the ground, heat rising, Nemo fought to

---

[27] scrap
[28] boiler

keep himself moving. The door was locked by his own hand, his façade in tatters, but he would not allow himself to give in again. The gleam of Vitrail's great snuffer bell was approaching, and he had just enough time for one final slight against the deceitful deadbeat.

Little Liz, I love y—

CLANG!

Nemo sat on the floor beside *La Fille Patronne*'s oven, both stewing in shared silence.

He was right back where he'd started, when that vile Captain had first brought him aboard and broken him down. He'd held his cards close to his chest for so long, played the game even as his patience boiled away inside, all to lay out a handful of nothing. Madame Vitrail still ran the house, swiping the very clothes off his back as back payment and even confiscating his precious cap. The only thing Nemo had left to hold onto was the unseen thread tugging him on and on towards Eliza, clinging to it for purchase above a bottomless despair.

Sister Ann kneaded the tinder within the Feo's immobile twin stove, the cleric now acting as Nemo's new roommate and warden since the loss of his working privileges. They hadn't shared a word in however long he had been shuttered up inside her candle-strewn quarters, but he didn't have to listen to know exactly what the old holy woman would have to say about him.

The walls groaned, Nemo having to grip the side of the oven to keep from clattering over. Scattered Fríasen shouts and screams sifted in from somewhere above, but it didn't matter to him at all. So long as the boat stayed afloat, the whole loathsome fleet could be battling a cornucopia of nudibranchs without the Feo missing much, aside from the chance at seeing that miserable excuse for a mother become seafood.

One voice in particular was getting louder, and now seemed to be right outside Sister Ann's room. From his corner, Nemo could hear the scratching of talons on wood from the other side.

"I'm gonna die, I'm gonna die. I'm going to *die!*"

Sister Ann billowed to her feet, leaving Nemo to sit by what would soon become tonight's supper. She took a creaky yet authoritative step over to the entrance and laid a hand over the singed teak door, in place of where Nemo assumed a peephole should have been.

"You are not going to die yet. Please stop shouting."

"Well fine, give me one last chat with my friend before whenever that is, then!"

Nemo was shocked to see the door actually opening behind Sister Ann's hand. In an instant, the blue flash of Pauvus was standing in the roasting quarters, out of breath and unprepared for the sudden steaming.

"*Whew*, that's toasty," he remarked, before the sight of the Feo had him fluttering over with manic abandon. "Nemo! Thank Flame you're alright, half-expected they'd have scooped you out after that whole scene. Savor it for now, neither of us has got much time left!"

The sight of Pauvus in such a state of genuine terror was enough to drag Nemo out from the sargassum of his sorrows.

"What are you talking about, Paul? Just calm down, what's going on up there?"

"Calm down? *Hah!*" Pauvus spat, fidgeting with a bundle of cloth in his wings. "That Martha lady told us all about the nightmare on our tails right now, and it just popped its ugly bow over the horizon! Of course, she's in no shape to fly, so who's the Captain's pick for suicide by scouting? That's right, good ol' Paul! I'll be stone-cold dead on the water by the time I'm halfway along, if that abomination doesn't get me first!"

Nemo glanced over to Sister Ann, who of course didn't return the favor. He felt the unseen rigging between

171

himself and Eliza tightening while Pauvus loosened the drawstrings from his bundle, pulling out an embarrassing costume with his beak. It was the sort of skeleton suit tailored for young boys, a one-piece affair plastered with patriotic Fríasen hues.

"Look at this travesty! Of all things, *this* has to be my funeral formalwear?"

Nemo hesitated at confiding in Pauvus with his holy jailer standing right beside them, until he remembered that it was she who had given him the inside scoop on their situation in the first place. Tugging along a wall beam to his feet, the Feo rose to meet the Ave eye-to-eye.

"Paul, Eliza's out on that ship! 'Atop a floating abomination'!"

"What? Where did you—" Pauvus started, before catching another glance at the unimpressed Sister Ann. "...Ah. Fair enough. Well, that doesn't change the fact that I'm not built for this kind of trip! Mom was right, I don't have the pinions to make for a proper postman. I'll never make it!"

Nemo reached out, gripping his friend firmly by the shoulders. "Your feathers were able to help a simple Feo find love, against all odds. Who's to say this is any more far-fetched?"

Pauvus gave him a long stare before he sighed, then wriggled his way into the back of his new fashion statement. Had the circumstances been different, Nemo might've found the sight of the dignified Ave wrapped up like a gaudy present hilarious. As things currently stood, he felt nothing but a yawning chill in his core.

A faint, trembling smile crept across the bird's beak as he gave the costume a pathetic show-off turn.

"On a scale from one to ten, how stupid is Eliza going to think this looks?"

Nemo gave the frilled collar a quick straightening and a brush of the hand. "I'd guess a six. Maybe a seven for the team colors, but at least you pull it off well."

"*Peh heh,* that's fair." Pauvus trailed off, trying and

failing to puff himself up again. "I... I'll do all I can, for both of us. Stay cooking, alright?"

Nemo knew he'd never be able to repay this debt to his friend, not with all the coffees or clams across the Grand Sea. Pulling him into a tight embrace, the Feo could hear the peacock choking back his sobs.

"W-Well, best head off before Vitrail makes a full hat outta me. I'll... seeya soon, y-you—*hic*—damn furnace."

"I love you too, Paul. Thank you."

Pulling back and giving one more glance in the reflection of Nemo's chassis, Pauvus reluctantly clacked along the timbers to his fate up above. His last look back was cut off by Sister Ann sealing the door shut.

The Feo was once again alone with the cleric and her supper. He stood silently in the wake of what may well have been his last moments with his best friend, when a thought drifted to mind.

"You let him in to see me. Why?"

"I am not blind to the bond you share," Sister Ann shrugged, stirring at a large cauldron of something or other. "I am no more heartless than you yourself, 'Nemo'. In any case, it would be remiss of me to not allow you a farewell for his final flight."

No more words were spoken that night. Nemo huddled beside the great oven, shivering in the glow of its radiant heat. Now he was truly alone, the infinite possibilities that he had pictured through Eliza's locks tangling him in a net of despair. With no solace but the faith in the bonds he had forged, Nemo followed in Sister Ann's example and turned to prayer in what had to be for the first time in his life.

Mother Flame, keep them safe. If nothing else, keep them safe.

CHAPTER 10
UNDERSTUDY

"Mother Flame, please, melt away the corruption of the soul, embolden the blaze of Life within..."

Eliza had no idea how long she had been sailing atop the fetid *Bastion*. Without the rhythm of raids or windows to speak of, the only things she had to keep the time came from counting restless sleeps and the throbbing heartbeats radiating through her wound.

But now, there was someone else in the cargo hold with her. Eliza opened one eye to spot Rufus poring over a small rotten book at her bedside, a collection of empty liquor bottles resting on the crate beside him. When the Saumondt-bred lad caught sight of her, he shrugged with a wobbling of caps and offered a docile smile.

"Heard you wasn't feelin' well. Me ol' Ma use'ta read this to me when I was goin' through it, wondered if'n it'd do more fer yer soul than mine. Lads joke it's gots to be some sorta sin fer me to even holds it. Wonder if that's the case, sometimes..."

Rufus lapsed into an almost thoughtful silence. Eliza was just about ready to sleep him away until the sailor's soft voice filled the air again.

"The world's a right cruel place, fer truth. I mean, you's seen all'a us. We's all decidin' to go honest for a change, and this is how it fetters out... But the world's bad enough, eh? I mean, we's all in the same boat n'all, but sometimes things gets a bit... Just passin' along apologies, is all."

Eliza shot Rufus a withering look that shriveled his stalks, then swiped a half-empty bottle from the table. By the time she finished, he'd gotten the smart idea to head on out, and her mind wasn't too far behind.

The only other visits Eliza received beyond that were the scheduled check-ins from Quartermaster Autumns. He carried himself with a level of professionalism and brevity that she appreciated, especially considering she was technically squatting in his workplace.

"W-we're still on course for the Fríasen f-f-fleet," he had chattered to her over a bowl of his mystery stew. "Shouldn't b-be long til we're at-t-top them. D-don't worry about the sh-shif-f-fts, you will still get your share. If anyone has a pr-problem with that, or wants to p-poke their noses about my c-c-cargo, th-then they'll have to deal with me."

A few sips of the surprisingly decent broth was enough to ease Eliza's thirst and help her settle into bed more comfortably. Maybe, just maybe, it would be enough for her to finally get a clear and restful—

"Ahoy-hoy, Liz. Still stinkin' up the joint?"

The eye above Eliza's burn twitched. She dragged herself back into consciousness only to spy the spindly, garish form of Edmund, arms too far crossed and body leaning far too casually against the wall.

Great security, Autumns.

Eliza gave the sailor her best silent treatment, but it didn't seem to pierce through the caps clouding his skull. He had a sneer tweaking the peaks of his mycelial mustache, and a devious twinkle in one of his eyes.

"Heard you got an infection problem," he sniffed, examining the edge of his scythe-like cordycep claw. "Don't have a cure fer that, would've used it on m'self ages ago. So, I got ya the second best thing."

Edmund slid a fresh crate of bottles in from the doorway, and shoved it with a leg in sore need of a proper foot. Doing her best to ignore the spectrum of filth caked on the edges, Eliza quickly tucked into a new bedtime bottle.

"Ey, good to see yer in the mood fer good spirits. Maybe the rest'a ya will catch up soon. Enjoy it; once yer this far along, booze can't do much more than bring ya

175

pain."

It was about time for Eliza to fall back into sickly misery, but the rotten rigsman wasn't following along with the script. He kept staring around at things that only he seemed to see, chattering to a Audience that only he seemed to think cared.

"But pain's just part of livin'. It's a choice ya either make, or get made on ya. How ya know yer still alive, y'know? Like that SpritFlit ship! I'll tell ya, from experience, them mailmen and corp'rate types're worse than any pirate. Life only gives what ya take, so if a bird gets a pluckin' that's their choice! Not yer fault, that one."

Eliza had been feeling plenty wretched already, but Edmund's yammering about her role in their performances brought her mood down to a new bottom. The bottle dropped from her lips to her lap as she managed to claw herself to something approaching sitting.

"...Of course it wasn't my fault," Eliza rasped, trying to scratch her voice together again after the extended silent treatment. "I didn't have a choice. Being Barret's puppet is the only reason I'm still on board now."

"Oh, izzat right?" hissed Edmund. "So sorry, 'Lady Liz', forgot yer little love quest cleared ya of all 'sponsibility! Ain't any less selfish than our raids just cause it got a sappy coat'a paint on it!"

A flash of heat, unrelated to the fever, surged through Eliza as she dug her nails into her comforter.

"When you love someone, you'd do anything for them... Not like you'd understand."

Edmund pushed off from his spot on the wall, taking a step towards what might end up being her deathbed.

"Oi, I care 'bout my mates! Done enough for 'em to make Mother Flame blush. Folks on them boats got people who care about 'em, too. Prolly left another 'Liz out there without her Nemo, but what do you care?"

Something inside Eliza cracked. The bottle was in her fist, moments away from hurtling right into what remained of the sailor's skull, but a shout from the timbers above made her flinch.

"What we got....Ye truly think...Kill ye..."

"Reel it back...Madame...Is there..."

Based on how Edmund's facial fungus was twitching, he knew just as much as she did about what was going on outside. Eliza could pick up on three things: There was a new arrival on *The Bastion*, Cap'n Barret was making far too much noise, and she was too sick to tolerate any of it right now. With a groan, she propped herself further up on the bed, trying her best to ignore how the room was swirling about like a whirlpool.

"Edmund, grab my coat."

To the surprise of both of them, he did. Keeping his head down from any follow-up bottles and passing along the navy-blue Amrestirian coat, Edmund gave her the space to drape it atop the maiden's dress that practically hung off her frame now. She took a moment to tuck Nemo's core coal in her breast pocket, only to find an unfamiliar mass already filling the space.

The shears. Eliza couldn't remember if she had pocketed them through her delirium or if someone had rifled through her belongings, but the way Edmund was lingering by the door convinced her to save that mystery for another time.

Shooing away an ill-conceived helping hand, Eliza staggered up from the bed and felt to make sure her other pocket was still properly loaded. Taking a moment to get feeling in her feet, and feet in her boots, she thundered up to the upper-deck with storm clouds on the mind.

"Ye picked the wrong pirates to perch with, matey! We ain't expecting any mail, and we don't tolerate spies here!"

"How many... *ack*, times do I have to... tell you?! I'm... *hoogh*, not a spy, or a blasted mailman!"

Too many bodies were in the way for Eliza to get a proper look through the squabble, and too many voices crowded the air to get a proper word in.

She stepped up to the top of the deck landing, slipped the engraved pistol from her pocket, and raised it skyward.

BLAM!

In one shot, Eliza had drawn the Audience's eye. She leaned against the entranceway frame, her gun barrel still trailing a line of smoke.

"...Barry, *dear*, if you're going to kill someone, do it *quietly*."

Eliza lurched forward, the capped crew parting the way for her. She might as well see who the soon-to-be dead bastard was if she wasn't going to get any peace today.

Cap'n Barret stood in the middle of the deck, his one hand tight around the long, blue neck of a frazzle-feathered Ave. Eliza's vision tracked down to see that the rest of him was just as colorful, clad in an ill-fitting Fríasen tunic with an all-too-familiar fan tail tucked underneath.

"Paul?"

Even through the chokehold, Pauvus' face bloomed in relief.

"Eliza!"

That was enough for Barret to finally relent, dropping the peacock unceremoniously to the deck. Both Ave and girl cleared the rest of the distance to each other, colliding and babbling every scattered thought that burst to mind.

"–Paul, you featherbrain, what are you doing here? Flame, but I'm so happy to see you. How did you–"

"–Oh, Eliza, thank goodness you're okay. Nemo and I were so—"

Eliza pulled back from the winged embrace. "Nemo?!"

Too many thoughts were swirling in Eliza's head for her to spit out a coherent question. Luckily, Pauvus was able to catch his breath long enough to choke out the answer she was looking for.

"Look, Nemo's alright! I... *phew*, just came in from *La Fille Patronne*, they sent me along to 'scout things out'. He's hanging in there, holding out hope that he'll see you ag—"

Pauvus' beak dropped, hanging wide open. It took Eliza a moment to realize he was staring in horror not at the faces of the ghosts behind her, but at her own. He brushed away a dangling clump of hair to fully reveal the damage, both of them hissing in shock.

"What is that?! Oh my— W-What in blazes happened? Those colors, you're infected!"

Eliza tried to protest, insist that she was fine, but Pauvus had already gone into full mother hen mode.

"You poor thing, you're burning up something fierce! Wha—" Pauvus halted, taking the time to peer into the shape of the lingering burn. "Hold on a tick. This isn't an ordinary burn... Who did this?"

Pauvus rose to his full height, wings protectively cradling her, his meager tailfan held tall. The abject terror from before was gone, replaced by a fury Eliza never

179

thought him capable of.

"Who did this?!"

When his query was met with silence, the bird continued his wrathful questioning, stamping down the line of Stagnant sailors with the authority of a schoolmaster.

"Well? Are any of you cowards going to confess?"

The words hung in the air, dangling like a sword above each suspect's head. It was an unfortunate moment for Edmund's to pop out from behind the door frame, trailing a safe distance behind Eliza since exiting her quarters. In a moment, Paul was upon him, tossing wild feet and puffing himself up enough to spook even one of *The Bastion*'s ghouls.

"You better fess up, stretch! What I'll do to you will be nothing compared to—"

"H-hey, claws off!" Edmund wailed, trying to defend himself from the Aveilan onslaught. "I didn't do nuthin'! She was like that when I—"

"The fault be mine."

One second, Pauvus had been standing at Eliza's side with a twitch tugging at his beak. The next, he was on top of the Rot Admiral, laying a levy of kicks and pecks into the least grotty spots of his shell in a mess of flying feathers.

"You foul, loathsome, eye-searing savage!" cawed the peacock as Barret tried to carefully peel him away. "Better hope those ghost stories about you are true, 'matey', 'cuz I'll find a way to make that death stick one way or another!"

None of *The Bastion*'s sailors moved to intervene. They knew anyone foolish enough to try and throw down with the Rot Admiral hand-to-hand would, at best, be completely wasting their time, and at worst a new addition to the corrupted crew.

"Oi, ye think I was in me right mind when I did that?!" Barret defended, gently swatting a leg away from his battered cuirass. "Us Feo get hot when things be heated! Me brain be rotted, what can I say?"

180

"Oh, you just wait 'til her husband gets here! He'll turn you to mulch then use your chest as a cooking pot!"

Against her better judgment, Eliza wobbled into the middle of the fray to pull the irate bird down by the talons, more for the sake of his safety than that of the Cap'n. She held Pauvus' gaze intently, even as he kept eyes locked on the baffled Rot Admiral.

"Paul, cut it out! I'll explain everything, but I need to know about Nemo!"

"...Fine," Pauvus muttered, shutting the rest of the crew out with an upraised wing. "Come on then, let's get that burn looked at proper. Is there anywhere on this putrid raft we can do that without squishin' in something?"

"The cargo hold," Eliza croaked, her burst of adrenaline spent. "Probably the cleanest place on this whole ship, thanks to the good Quartermaster."

Eliza caught a brief thumbs-up from Autumns before Pauvus ushered them back below decks, leaving the rest of the crew to glower in the terrified Edmund's direction. She tried to avoid leaning on the Ave as much as she could manage, but the exhausted peacock was determined to support her in any way he could.

The two friends hobbled along together, gratefully clinging to each other as calm ports amid a raging storm.

Back in the dingy cargo hold, Pauvus eased Eliza into her burgled bed. He had the good sense to leave her question-free for the time being, taking the moment instead to scavenge *The Bastion*'s plunder for available supplies.

"We've got to disinfect that, heard the spores can be a nightmare for your throat. You got any— hm, looks like you're covered for alcohol, there. See you've been self-medicating."

"The booze's the only reason why I'm alive and sane... Mostly sane," Eliza amended, taking a quick swig of her Vorvaň Vodka before the Ave swiped it away.

"Surprised you even know about that, Paul."

"Huge fungal explosion devastating an entire country thanks to some colored ink?" Pauvus pointed out as he soaked a torn strip of fresh sailcloth from the spare sheets. "I have a hard time believing someone wouldn't know. Now hold still, this is going to sting a bit."

A long hiss escaped gritted teeth as the peacock tried to clean her burn as gently as possible. The fresh wave of pain brought her back fully to the waking world, to the point where Eliza could finally get a good look at the state of her husband's friend.

Aside from the fresh marks about his neck, the Ave looked as though he'd been tossed around a hurricane, drained and deprived of the bulk of his prized feathers. The rest of him had been packed into a ridiculous little Fríasen suit, buttoned across the back and hemmed with tattered frills.

"I'll throw your question back, Paul. What—*tssss*—happened to you?"

"Ugh, it's a travesty," Pauvus groaned, setting the cloth in place and digging for more clean stocks to work with. "Everyone on that bootlicker's ship's been plucking me balder than Nemo ever was! Really diluting the brand, but I suppose those ugly bastards need all the help they can get."

As he tended to the burn, Pauvus had to constantly brush aside strands of Eliza's wild hair that stubbornly made their way back into his workspace. The salt of the sea, exposure to countless fungal spores, and simple neglect brought on by her illness turned the usual rat's nest into an untamable beast that the bird had trouble maneuvering around. When she heard one too many sighs of frustration, Eliza reached into the breast pocket of her coat.

Pauvus froze as he spotted the glint of metal in her hand. "What the– Did you steal that from one of the—?"

Before he could finish, Eliza grabbed a handful of her curls and, with a decisive snip, sheared them off.

Clumps of thick black locks fell to the floor and mattress as Pauvus squawked his protests.

"You're mad! I didn't tell you to hack it all off!"

"Calm down," Eliza said curtly, cutting through another section with ruthless efficiency. "It was in the way, so, problem solved."

With her business done, Eliza ran her fingers through what was left, noting how the ringlets barely grazed the bottom of her ears. She couldn't see the final result, but Pauvus' grimace said it all.

"That bad, huh?"

"It looks like you glued two puffs of cotton to the side of your head," Pauvus said solemnly. "You better hope it grows back quick, Nemo's gonna be devastated when he sees that whole display."

Nemo was the only reason she held onto keeping her hair as long as it was, despite her stretch of time at sea. Soon, Eliza had told herself, she would feel his brass fingers running through her knots and tangles once more.

Not soon enough.

"How is Nemo?" she ventured, weighing up the coal in her pocket.

Pauvus went back to dabbing at her cheek, sighing as he worked to stretch a spare eyepatch string across the homemade bandage.

"I won't mince words Eliza, he's practically a shell of himself without you. You know how he can get, flipping full 'thank you' mode without someone to keep his spirits up. Got a bit of his fire back when he heard you and your 'friends' were hot on our tails. Really making a name for yourself, eh 'Siren'?"

Eliza managed the strength to chuckle at the title as Pauvus finished securing the wrap to her jawline. It stung with the cool touch of a caring hand, and finally allowed her a moment's peace amid the confines of her cargo cell.

"There, that should do it for now. Lie down and get some rest, you're gonna need it."

Rest. Though she yearned for it, Eliza found it impossible to drift off now that she had Pauvus by her side and Nemo on her mind. The aches and pains coursing throughout her body begged to differ.

"How can I sleep at a time like this?" Eliza mumbled. "You look even more wiped than me right now."

Pauvus tugged the sheets over her with a talon. The bird smiled down at her, a tinge of melancholy tweaking the edges of his beak.

"*Shhhh,* just calm that botched plumage of yours and let me tell you a bedtime story. Hey, did Nemo ever mention the first time we met?"

Eliza thought back on their coffee shop chats, realizing that the topic of how their unlikely friendship formed was never brought up.

"Nnnno, I don't think he mentioned it before. I know it was on a ship, and that you slept down in the cargo hold with him sometimes."

Pauvus popped a cork off his own bottle, and flopped down next to her.

184

"Yeaaaahh, before that. It was a few days after I'd hopped on board the *SF Rapaci*, barely out of Aveila. Bunch of pirates rolled up and blindsided us, swinging right down the blocks like all the stories said. A hulking Bulwark bodybuilder had me dead-to-rights on the deck, and this Feo dives right in to take the blow for me. No hesitation, no expectation of a reward at all. Figured that was just standard procedure for Feo, but even getting to know him... that's just the sort of man Nemo is."

Eliza settled in while the peacock took a long, deliberate swig, as if hoping the liquor would blur the edges of his memories.

"...You know, it's funny, not even my parents gave me squat without expecting it paid back. Everyone I ever knew was playing some massive competition, trying to ride each other's currents and peck at anyone who couldn't keep up."

There was something to Pauvus' tone, like a champagne flute moments away from cracking. Eliza scooched up on the bed and thought she could see his eye wetly shimmering in the dim light.

"I've lived my whole life thinking people only stayed if they had something to gain from me, but Nemo never asked for anything in return... I owe Nemo, and you, more than I could ever afford."

Eliza let out a chuckle, wincing as the motion tugged at her wound. "Why do you owe me?"

"Because you like me," was Pauvus' simple reply, the peacock already half-asleep. "You and Nemo... remind me that not everyone... is keeping score..."

The two passengers of *The Bastion* sat in the silence of her hold, letting Pauvus' words and consciousness drift along. Eliza was thinking of the right thing to say to her friend when she felt his weight sag into the pillows at her side, the breath from his beak softening to a snore. The Ave had been burning the midnight oil since he'd arrived, practically cooking in his battered suit. Frankly, Eliza was amazed that he'd managed to make the journey at all, considering how he had complained in the past about his lack of proper training.

That meant Nemo was close. Close enough to the scumbags they'd been chasing all the way across the whole rotten sea. She was still aching, tired, and frightened, but Eliza knew there was nothing more terrifying on the whole sea than the ship she was on. It was enough to lull her into the same doze that had caught Pauvus.

She needed to be well-rested and ready for a proper raid.

Out across the Grand Sea, distanced by years and the yaw of the open ocean, Vivian prepared to leave home for the last time.

A full moon was dangling low over the yet-young town of Amrestir, slicing through the half-drawn curtains of her meager hovel by the shore. The sailor knew that she had only a few hours until she was to depart on *Le Foudroyant* under cover of darkness, but the pale silver glow would not allow her to turn a blind eye to the faces of those she would be leaving behind.

I'm not a coward. This is for the best.

It was a lie, yet Vivian clung to it all the same. She'd been living a life of self-delusion for over a year, filling her near to bursting with each concession and compromise. This was simply one more drop in the bucket, one more piece of kindling stacked onto her own pyre.

Vivian listened to Alastair's snore rattle the ink bottles above his little desk, the gentle coo-ing of their infant snuggled into a small crib by the bed. The two rested peacefully, ignorant of the empty space they would awaken to for a little while longer. Even for someone in the privateering business, it felt wrong to Vivian to steal one more peaceful night away from them.

One thing she didn't mind stealing was a fresh sheet of paper and quill from Alastair's supply. The man's silver tongue and honeyed words had been responsible for ensnaring her like a fly, and Vivian found it only fitting to take a page out of his book for her final message.

Staring at the empty space, Vivian struggled to distill her deluge of thoughts into ink. She reminisced on her first encounter with the bright-eyed Press man, mutually charmed through daggers and drinks by the dockside.

My dear Alastair,

How to describe the pains she'd gone through to change, to try and build something real atop an island of shipwrecks and sand? There was a wide world of beauty beyond Amrestir's titchy boundaries, countless sights to devour and treasures to grasp. Vivian couldn't help her heart from briefly drifting through the rolling greenery of her distant home, as lush and vibrant as the curls atop Eliza's noggin.

~~*My dear*~~ *Alastair,*

A teardrop smudged the scribblings beneath Vivian's hand. She'd often mocked Alastair's penchant with a pen, but fighting to find the right words stung deeper than any blade. There was nothing that she could say that either of them would understand. Alastair had sent countless schmucks out to sea, but he'd never heard the ineffable siren song of adventure, or been entranced by grand wooden hulls and fluttering sails. As much as she tried to bundle herself in the love of her little family, Vivian knew deep-down that she could never stop the sea from tugging at the threads.

Sometimes, on quiet afternoons with Eliza on her hip, Vivian would find herself walking down to the docks. She'd stand at the water's edge, watching the sailors prepare for departure with a longing gaze, only to be pulled back to reality by her daughter's cheerful squeals. As they sailed away, a pang of jealousy would twist inside of her. The ships called to her, reminding Vivian of the adventure she had sacrificed in the name of this little life.

Still, she stayed. Until she couldn't.

~~*My dear*~~ *Alastair,*

Vivian held herself back from ripping the letter to noisy shreds, grasping for the ivory comb in her pocket for support. It was a trinket that Alastair had scrimped and sacrificed to buy despite barely being able to afford a proper roof over their heads, advertised as being carved from a Bulwark guru's tusk.

The overpriced gift was left on the desktop with a click. Vivian snatched up the failed note and stood back, the comb her final message and as her test: If the man had the strength, he would sell the thing and move onto the next stage of his life to help their daughter bloom. If he was too trapped within his own sentimentality to part with it, then she had been right about him all along.

It was time to go. The floorboards, usually groaning with age, were strangely silent as she crept across them. If she stuck around a moment longer, her nerve would crack, and she would never be able to—

A faint wail broke the silence, and nearly took Vivian's heart with it. She crept back towards Eliza's cries, footsteps softened under cheap boot treads peeling at the edges, and gripped the crib's edge desperately. The top of the woman's head brushed against the homemade mobile hanging above, a glass collage of rainbow refuse, as she leaned down.

"Eliza, shush! Don't cry, please..."

Her words were as useless as the ones she had written. Eliza kicked and flailed in distress, begging to be comforted with arms wide.

Relenting under the pressure, Vivian scooped up the infant and pressed her close. The delicate tufts of Eliza's downy hair were beginning to grow out into small dark curls. Alastair would go on and on about watching it grow out in full, chattering about his hopes that it would match her mother's mane.

This would be the last time she would hold her, breathe in her familiar scent, feel the warmth of the tiny body squirming against her chest. As if sensing her mother's impending departure, Eliza flailed harder, babbling in protest.

So fussy, Vivian thought. So willful, Alastair would've said. He could never speak ill of Eliza, not even when her cries threatened to collapse the ceiling. In times like this, the mother knew what would settle her daughter down.

Little Liz, I love you, honey...
Little Liz, I... I...

How she wanted to sing, to soothe their shared woes with the lyrics that inspired her tender love, but her words once again faltered. Vivian simply held Eliza, swaying her gently, stealing anxious glances at Alastair's undisturbed form as her daughter's whimpers faded into restful breaths.

The room became quiet again, the silence heavy in its finality. Vivian laid her daughter out into her crib once more, hardly able to bring herself to watch Eliza's chubby cheeks glisten under the moon's stare. A perfect moment, frozen in silver light.

Vivian had never asked for pity in her life, and never deserved any. She would miss them, if nothing else, but time and travel would wear down the sharp edges of her pain like tides crashing over glass. If she stayed any longer, she would only grow softer herself.

Slipping out the door with but a click of the latch, Vivian burst along Amrestir's slapdash docks as hard and as fast as her legs could take her. Every footfall brought her further away from her past, and onwards towards a future that was yet to be told. In the wake of her flight, the ink-stained note fluttered on the breeze, and melted into the dusk-blanketed sea.

There was nothing left to say.

The Bastion rocked along with its crew in full form, but the ship's sway was anything but soothing. All Eliza wanted was to settle back into one of her famously deep slumbers, but the dull throbbing of her cheek kept her drifting between waking and resting dreams.

Pauvus didn't seem to have the same hang-ups, quietly snoring away atop a bundle of pillows at her side. The Ave had worked his wings to the bone on keeping her comfortable, despite Eliza's best protests. He was practically a parrot on her shoulder in their impromptu infirmary, hovering over her every waking moment save for food runs. It was bad enough having to show her seared mug off, even to an Audience of one, without feeling completely helpless in the process. She didn't talk much during their time together, allowing the bird to spin out whatever wild yarns came to his mind while she focused on rest and recuperation.

But sleep was just not coming to Eliza, and she was sick of feeling sick. Silently slipping from the depression she'd left in the mattress, she stretched her sea-legs and tightened the sash around her waist. She casted a lingering look at the music box gathering dust in the corner, and left it all below her.

The topside of *The Bastion* was still scattered with sailors even under a high-strung moon, but none dared to bother Eliza as she trod across the deck to the railing. She knew they were close, but being able to see the faint shape of ships against the pitch of the sky had her guts feeling like they were tied up in fishing line. It had taken who knew how long, traveling across who knew how much of the Grand Sea, but Nemo was practically within spitting

192

distance now.

Watching the distant fleet intently, Eliza reeled the coal out from her sash, wincing at the touch of its ever-growing burn. Clutching it to her chest, she fought against the signals in her brain and listened instead with her heart.

"Heh, so that be why Nate added 'Clumps o' Hair' to the manifest."

Cap'n Barret's voice rattled from behind Eliza's ear, setting her nerves rattling in turn. That brief moment of shock was enough to pop the coal out from her grip, her mad clawing swipe knocking the thing directly into the hungry mouth of the waves below. A sizzle on the sea was all that remained now, quickly swallowed in a careless spray.

Eliza's fingers twitched. She was left empty-handed yet again, her truest reminder of Nemo snatched away as abruptly as the Feo himself. Like the turning of an anchor's capstan, she speechlessly creaked around to face the Rot Admiral.

"Er, sorry lass, didn't mean t'startle ye. This be a bad time?"

A silent fury burnt inside, threatening to engulf her entirely. Eliza felt like screaming, tearing away at the Cap'n's caps until he was nothing but a pile of mushroom mush. Yet in the midst of her anger, she noticed a thick leather glove shielding the hand that had caused her such pain, now recoiling against the Siren's icy glare.

She paused. With Nemo in arm's reach, it wouldn't pay to spoil her one advantage heading into the fray. Eliza sucked in a chilled breath, gritting her teeth and forced herself to embody the customer service spirit once more.

"It's... nothing. Give my apologies to Autumns for leaving a mess down there."

Barret ran the glove through his crest, doing a remarkable job of looking uncomfortable for someone without muscles or a proper face.

"Ah, well, it be no worry at all. Best ye and yer... buddy have a space to be safe. But the end of yer journey rests close at hand now. We'll be out of yer hair soon... Seems ye've already started on that yerself."

Both looked out to the dotted fleet in the distance, faint lights dancing in the dark. Eliza gripped the railing, trying to ground herself in some small way.

"Doesn't pay to have it getting in the way when I'm rending that Feo filcher limb from limb. After all, it's not like I'm in a state to keep up the whole 'damsel in distress' gambit anymore."

"Ye say that as though yer average sailor wouldn't wanna rub shoulders with a girl who's got some grit t'her."

The stare Eliza shot the Cap'n would've been able to crack a mountain in half. He coughed on a stray piece of lichen and softened again.

"I be sorry fer that, and fer everything, really. I know we've been no worthy hosts... downright barbarous, on me end... Yer friend's a right medic though, yer lookin' fresh as a marigold. Comf'terble too. That dress was no rag to relax in, and none of the crew be willin' to fill that bodice. Tried to pour Edmund into it on a lark, and... well, ye can imagine how that went along."

Eliza continued to stare as Barret nervously chuckled. She couldn't bring herself to go as far as to join in, only half-present for the conversation at hand. Looking down into the inky black below, she couldn't bring herself to exchange any sort of humor with the Rot Admiral.

"...Maybe you should've worn it yourself, then."

"Hoh-hoh!" chortled the Cap'n, not reading the deadly aura radiating off Eliza. "There be that salt again. I may be an ol' shamblin' shipwreck now, but I been told I cut quite the figure back in me days at ol' Ogden's! Shoulda seen some'a the performances back then, I be all washed up now."

From her bitter depths, something familiar glinted like a hook, and Eliza was compelled to bite.

"Wait, Ogden's? Those hokey performing Feo, that was *you?*"

Barret pulled off as smug a look as he was able, the meager iron peeking out from his mycelial shell shining with pride.

"Yes indeed! Mr. Ogden weren't a perfect man, but he was business-savvy. Gave us lot the first taste of identity a Feo could ask fer, 'hokey' as it may've been... though don't let Claude hear ye spit that, if'n ye ever come to cross paths."

"That's that tiny one, right?" Eliza wondered aloud, caught in a syrupy nostalgia sticky enough to trap her for now. "My dad took me there as a kid, remember I got freaked out by him. He was... a lot. Hurt my little ears."

The laugh that Barret unleashed sounded genuine, but the way his gnarled visor-teeth gnashed against the moonlight put Eliza on edge once again. She tried to

195

remember back to that day, to line up the simple Feo flutist she'd seen with the beast before her now, but the connection was as rotten as he was.

"Yep, that be he! Always a little firecracker. Let me guess, Ol' Gilby was yer favori... favor... Oh, Gilby..."

The Cap'n was starting to get that far-away look again, and Eliza could already see a line of smoke seeping from his glove cuff. She had the instinct to yell out, to flee, but to where? To what end? There was no world beyond the railings of *The Bastion*, and she was more sick of being pushed around than she was of her own infection.

With steely resolve, Eliza planted her feet firm, and shot out her hand to halt the one venturing towards her.

"Barret, no thank you!"

The gloved hand froze in the air, a brief flicker of reality flashing across the Barret's visage. She clutched her chest, breathing hard yet standing tall in the path of the stunned Rot Admiral.

"You are not doing this! You are not going to unload your blasted damage on me again, alright? Get any closer and I'm dropping you right down in the drink there, just like you made me drop my coal!"

The Rot Admiral writhed, and with a tug of effort, managed to pull himself together. He looked down into the waters below, her words crashing over him like a breaking wave.

"O-oh, I'm... sorry, Eliza. About the coal, about the burn, about everything. All I bring to ye is pain... all I bring to everyone, really. Treatin' ye just as I did me siblings, and none of ye deserve dealin' with my mess... Maybe ye'd be doin' the whole sea a favor, there."

A crackle of lightning flashed behind her eyelids. Eliza rubbed at her eyes, trying to fight back a thunderstorm of swirling emotions.

"Just stop, alright?" she sighed. "You screwed up. Apologize if you want, but not for your sake. I'm not going to pretend that what you did was fine, or that I'll go on like nothing happened... but you've helped me this far, and I know you still are. I can't forgive you, but you clearly haven't forgiven yourself either."

The deck behind Eliza was silent. She turned to see the hanging head of a poor Feo with no piratical nonsense left to spew. Letting *The Bastion* follow her quarry for a time, Eliza faced down the Rot Admiral on her own terms.

"Barret, I know you've got a heart in there, however much mold's growing on it. Just— You can't just wallow in your problems until you forget them again. You're in charge of a whole crew here, take charge of yourself already."

The Cap'n's crest bounced with a shake of his malformed shoulders, somewhere between a snicker and a sob.

"I hate t'say it, but ye really do have some of Gilbetrine's spark."

It was the first time Barret had spoken the name in full, no nickname or spiraling away by the end. Eliza let out a breath she'd been clinging to, and ran a hand through what remained of her hair. For all his missteps, the decaying Feo before her was guilty of carelessness and madness over anything else. With the whole context in mind, another bit of Amrestir trivia bloomed in her head.

"...Gilbetrine. Your sister, I'm guessing? I've seen flyers for a 'General Gilbetrine' all across the Press boards lately, apparently there's a big diplomatic mission to the north. Supposed to be the Governor's right hand, but I wouldn't be surprised if she's the whole arm behind it too."

There were those prismatic dribbles running down Barret's visor again, viscous in the light of his core.

"Heh. Always knew Claude would dazzle no matter what he did; picked up some promotional performance posters from a schooner a ways back with his ugly mug plastered all across it. Brilliant as ever. But Gilbetrine..." Barret's head drooped, the corners of his maw leaking. "...She always had a hard time finding a path in life that could fit her. A full-blown General, I'm... I'm so proud of her."

197

Eliza waited for the Cap'n to utterly drench his glove with treacly tears, and managed to dig up a faint smile from somewhere inside.

"Sounds like the whole Feo family has a thing for big world tours, right, Mr. Rot Admiral? But there's still work to be done, and you've got a reputation to maintain."

Barret's head rose, his chassis crackling and squishing to full attention under his crest. She felt a fresh heat filling the empty space, a tempered respect bridging the distance he didn't dare breach.

"You be right, Eliza. We're nigh on the tail of those wretches now, and yer beau... Ye know, the lads're gonna be missin' ye once yer off with Nemo again. Heard 'em jawing about them raids bein' the most alive they've felt in ages, and I'd have'ta agree there, so... thank you."

As the two stood aboard the festering *Bastion*, watching the long-pursued Fríasen fleet creep nearer with each moment, Eliza allowed the "thank you" to ring out over the water. The coal may have been lost to the Grand Sea, but she felt the warmth blooming in her chest all the same.

In the depths of *La Fille Patronne*, Nemo was alone.

Sister Ann had been called for a rare visit to the upper decks some time ago, leaving him to sulk in his stillness. The crew had figured the sorry Feo had no more fight in him, and they weren't far off the mark.

With no word of his friend's fate and a tugging at the core to remind him of his love, Nemo could do nothing but sit, wait, and carry hope within him. He'd never been one to turn to faith, considering how often faith had turned on him, but there seemed no more fitting place to pray than the Sister's personal sanctuary.

"Mother Flame, I don't know if you care for the words of a simple Feo, but if your love embraces all, please, *please*, let Eliza and Pauvus be safe."

And Mother Flame answered.

A cold sizzle sparked through Nemo's chest like permafrost. He clutched at the bare brass of his cuirass, desperately trying to delude himself from the horrible dread that pierced his thoughts like the lighthouse over New Amrestir's skyline.

She's gone.

It was as though a winter gale had blown through his head, snuffing out his core until nothing but a dim ember remained. Nemo looked about Sister Ann's quarters lovingly emblazoned with veneration of the Flame's mercy and the countless unlit candles framing the walls.

*She's **gone**.*

Nemo finally broke.

He clutched one candle and hurled it against the wall, shattering on impact. The Feo scooped his hands in a wide sweep across the collection, melting through fury-fueled fingers. A flurry of wax sprayed in jagged streaks over Smoulder tapestries, dripping down the embroideries like spilled blood. There was a *crack* underfoot where Sister Ann's little desk now lay in pieces, an accidental casualty of the Feo's rampage. He stomped again and again, until the prophetess' table scattered the floor in splinters. Not a single sound escaped Nemo's visor as he whirled about the quarters like an inferno, the flames of the great oven roaring in sympathetic rage over Nemo's despair, casting monstrous shapes upon his storm of broken hopes.

Then, silence. Nemo found himself standing in the aftermath of his own personal cataclysm, crimsoned debris splattering a room in ruins. The weight of his solitude crushed his chest like the pressure of the sea floor, heavier than any load he'd ever hauled. He collapsed to the floor in a pile of fresh woodchips, the fire in his vision sputtering away.

Pauvus had gone on his final flight, as the holy woman had foretold, and Eliza no longer held a piece of

199

Nemo's heart. The uncertainty crushed at his core, now little more than a dying flame burning within a useless metal chassis.

...Maybe not useless.

A new lick of determination sparked inside, fed not by hot grief, but something cold and sharp. Brass hands scooped scraps of table to Nemo's face, devouring shards of hickory like a starving man.

His plans for the future had been stolen, but he could still choose how his story would end.

His movements were mechanical, deliberate, as he stormed across the room. Without slowing, Nemo raised his foot and drove it into the wooden frame of his flimsy prison. The door gave way with a splintering crack, fragments scattering into the hallway.

First Mate Antoine was already at the door, unarmed save for a murderous look in his uncovered eye.

"C'est quoi ce bordel[29]! What'dya think yer doin', Feo?"

The Feo's visor locked on Antoine's singular eye, then drifted to the man's coat. *His* coat. If Nemo was going to go out in a blaze of glory, he was going to do it in style.

Brass fist met fleshy stomach. Antoine doubled over with a wheeze that was music to Nemo's ears, who then put a coda to the piece with a knee to the man's temple. The Feo twisted and pulled the crumpled man's frame until the maroon coat was free in his grip once more. It was stained, and in dire need of some proper care, but he had worn far worse.

Triumphantly draping the coat over his steaming shoulders, Nemo gave the collar a dramatic flick.

"Thank you... asshole."

Nemo stepped over Antoine's prone and groaning body, continuing on a warpath scorching to the world above. Busting out through the main deck door and into the coat-flapping open air, he found the breadth of the horizon dominated by a crime against nature.

---

[29] What's this mess

A hulking atrocity floated just out of firing range, crowned with blistering fungal caps that stung the eye, even to someone who didn't have any. Nemo's bloodlust froze, the Sister's words returning to mind.

A floating abomination.

Madame Vitrail was up at the forecastle deck, with the crew of *La Fille Patronne* crowding about below. Nemo spotted Sister Ann doling out mugs of loin-girding hot cocoa throughout the congregation to placate them, ignorant to the state of her room.

"Avast, you bastards!" the Captain boomed, calling into a stained-glass vase of a speaking trumpet. "So, these are the legendary wraiths of the sea? *Pitoyable.*"

"Ahoy there, Vivi, ye old crone! Long time no see!"

Nemo watched the Fríasen sailors exchange puzzled glances and confused whispers. The attention of the rising Audience was being far too well-fed to pay the Feo's dramatic entrance any mind, torn between a free show and a potential slaughter. All eyes turned to Madame Vitrail, whose expression was a rattling cycle of disbelief, outrage, and a fleeting glimpse of sheer horror. Finally, the roulette settled on anger, tight and unyielding.

"*Qu'est*— Nobody calls me... Barret?!"

"Aye, 'tis I!" he boomed. "Goin' by The Rot Admiral these days, got a bit more sting to it."

Nemo may not have been able to rush up and strangle that foul woman, but it was enough for now to watch her choke on her own bewilderment.

"B–wh–I don't care what you go by now, *pot de chambre!* You and that atrocity you call a ship best float on by, lest our Sister on board call down the wrath of Mother Flame to torch your whole miserable troupe!"

"Aw, ye still carryin' a torch fer me?"

A sole chuckle escaped from the cocoa circle, gutted sharply by a harsh jab to the ribs. For the second time since Nemo had been captured by the Captain, he had the immense satisfaction of seeing Vitrail lose her composure. She sputtered, jaw flapping like a fish out of its depth.

"You are worthless, Feo, if I can even call you that now! This is an expedition of the Fríasen government, under official letter of marque, to the shores of Faffton for legal trade. You attack us, and there will be no quarter for you in any contemptible corner of the sea!"

The Rot Admiral laughed, a bizarre mixture of malice and absurdity that sent a shiver through Nemo's brass.

"What else be new? Yer country o' dirt diggers don't scare me half as much as the freshest terror on the Grand Sea, and she be standin' right next t'me! Ye managed t'peeve off none other than the Dread Sire– Hey, come on—!"

"WHERE IS MY HUSBAND?!"

That voice, the most beautiful melody he had ever heard, wrapped around the Feo's chest like a lifeline. A wild hope wrenched at Nemo's heart, jerking him through the fresh spray of righteous fury and back into the land of the living.

"Eliza!"

He had called out to her despite himself, but the Audience was deaf to all but the main event. The lot of them reminded Nemo more of the gossips from the Bouncin' Bean than hardened sailors, drowning out the barbs between the captains with their speculation.

"Which one of you scoundrels left a lady at the altar?"

"Say, didn't you tie the knot a while back, Jean?"

"You was there at me and Henri's matelotage two years ago, Hugo!"

A new voice cut through the commotion from over the water, clear and unmistakable.

"Oi, Nemo! I told you I would find her! And in near mint condition!"

If Nemo could weep, he would've drowned himself out. Not only was Eliza alive, but right alongside Pauvus, in what sounded to be high spirits. Relief surged through him like a tidal wave, joining in with the chaos across the deck.

Madame Vitrail's icy composure dripped down her face. A harsh whistle from her lips killed the crew's chatter, narrowed eyes pinning each frightened face to the spot. Those eyes scanned over and finally snapped straight back onto Nemo's dome, now wide as wine glasses.

"I've had just about enough of Feo woes for one day! *Capturez-le*[30]*!*"

Nemo spun about the encroaching wave of sailors, downing their drinks reluctantly and cracking their knuckles. But the Feo had no flesh to cut, and a good foot on most of them. For once, he had no qualms showing these sailors who The Brass Brute truly was.

Jean caught a handful of hot brass and an elbow to the schnozz, while his mate Hugo took a head-first trip into the timbers. Nemo whirled about with a savage sweep in the direction of the steaming cocoa cauldron, when

[30] Capture it

203

something knocked him right off his feet from behind.

Antoine stood upside-down in Nemo's vision, a heavy length of chain in one hand and his throbbing head in the other. More loops of anchorline draped over the Feo's frame as the Fríasen meatheads found a new burst of confidence. He writhed under a hail of boots and blows, and the *clang* of what sounded like Sister Ann's ladle. The cackle of the Captain rang out, followed by a horrible roar from The Rot Admiral's deck.

"Well now, seems we have a bargaining chip!" Vitrail declared, smugness seeping back into her tone. "I commend your efforts, *fillette*[31], but you may be just as brainless as your '*amour*' here! Chasing a crippled Feo on a floating timebomb, thinking you have any authority to make demands of me?"

"You mother—! I'll feed you that stupid vase, shard by shard!"

Nemo clawed to look out towards Eliza's voice, but the railing was too high to see over. He pulled in vain against the heavy chains binding him, only able to see the bottoms of the Captain's boots as she spoke out.

"My word, it's a wonder how you managed to lure any sailors with a mouth like that. You catch more flies with honey than vinegar, *sirène*, but I'm sure you've already got plenty of those circling you over there. Now, let's say we act like civilized people and chat this over on shore? One rowboat each, bring the, *ugh*, couple along. Settle things like proper mariners once that's out of the way, eh Barret?"

"We be agreein' to yer terms of parley," gurgled the Rot Admiral again after a suspiciously long pause. "No funny business on me end or yers; the lot of us be keepin' the peace until there be no peace left to hold."

Nemo strained to hear the rest of the shouted conversation, but the jangling of his chains overpowered everything around him. *La Fille Patronne*'s crew had broken from the Audience mindset for the moment,

---

[31] little girl

scrambling to prepare for the Captain's departure. The Feo found himself being dragged like a broken toy to the portside launch boat, the sneer of Madame Vitrail hovering over him.

"What a bundle of trouble you've turned out to be, *amoureux*[32]."

"Id's scum, is whad id is!" groaned Antoine, still nursing his wounded pride and busted nose. "Jusd snuff id 'n be done wid' id already!"

"Quiet, Antoine! We've lugged along the brass scrap this far, and I'm not letting it go because some *lavette*[33] demands it."

"Captain, please, heed my warning: you do not want to do this," whispered Sister Ann, keeping an unseeing eye trained on Nemo. "You seek to bargain with an emissary of evil intent, the act will surely defile us all."

"Who commands this fleet?" barked Madame Vitrail. The captain was breathing hard, chest heaving under her dazzling breastplate. "By whose grace do you owe your sorry lives? I have had quite enough insubordination from cowards and enough riddles from you, *musaraigne*[34]! I will not stain my name with cowardice, even in the face of Stagnant death!"

Her crew stood as speechless as Nemo himself, all stunned by their new peek behind the curtain of 'Vivi'. She dragged a hand through hair that was beginning to fray at the edges, and shoved her prismatic speaking trumpet into Antoine's hands.

"Once we depart, send word to the fleet. Tell them to coast around the western edge of the isle and to wait for the flare that Sister Ann here will personally be taking care of. I've no intention to give these morons anything, save for a certain demise."

Leaning against the dinghy's resting place in a fresh jacket of chains, Nemo coughed up the ashes of the good

---

[32] lover
[33] mop
[34] shrew

Sister's table.

"Hope you're a better negotiator than a mother, Vivi."

Madame Vitrail, ranting off sabotage plans to her bosun Remy, froze in her tracks. In an instant, her face dominated Nemo's entire vision, close enough for her breath to puff through his visor in a whisper.

"Feo are meant to be seen, and not heard. One more sound that doesn't begin with 'thank' and end with 'you', I murder you the second that twit wife of yours washes ashore, Rot Admiral or no. Have anything to say to that?"

Nemo didn't. He stood defiantly silent as Vitrail stormed away to her scheming, listening to the rowboat's lines run taut. No pyromantic coal was needed to feel the surge of life in his core, thrumming hot enough to warm the chains binding him.

I'm coming home to you, Eliza.

"Well, I be thinkin' that went well, all things considered!"

Cap'n Barret turned from *La Fille Patronne*, passing the speaking trumpet back around to Quartermaster Autumns. *The Bastion*'s fetid crew was a blur of activity, each working away according to some unspoken line of command. While Eliza watched *La Fille Patronne* bobbing in the open water, glaring at it as though she could light the mainmast ablaze with enough concentration, Pauvus nervously flitted between the mushroom mates he dearly hoped not to die alongside.

"Uh, Barret," Pauvus piped up. "This is a terrible idea. However well you know, um, 'Vivi', I spent enough time over there to know that there is no chance she is going to keep her word."

"Take me own word fer it then, Pauly, I be trustin' that hag as far as I could shoot her. Nope, ol' Vivi's a sharp n' twisty hook for certain, and I be lookin' to turn two wrongs into a right. When them lot float on into shore with them schemes all tucked away, me aquatic squad are already gonna be settled in with a nice lil' surprise for that privateering prat."

Bellona and Vaughn were already lowering themselves down into the water by Eliza's side, lugging along a heavy-looking barrel. There was no reaction from the siren but a short-haired nod. The end of her journey was floating close at hand, and the end of her patience wasn't far behind.

"Do *not* call me 'Pauly'," Pauvus cawed. "And what's your whole deal with Miss Madame, anyways? Sounded like she was about to blow a gasket when she saw you."

"Ah, heh, that do be quite the yarn! Y'see, a long ways back, out on me first—"

Pauvus didn't get a chance to hear the juicy details. Eliza's hand was around the ridiculous frilled collar of the Ave's messenger suit, dragging him away from both the Cap'n and his conversation.

"*Ack!* Hey, what's with the rough play?"

"Argh, are ye ever gonna let me finish a speech, Eliza?"

Eliza continued stomping across the deck with the bird in tow, checking her pistol and tightening her coat's belt.

"I'm getting Nemo."

"Now hoist yer sails, there!" called Barret, smartly holding back from holding her back. "This be parley! We've prep'rations t'make, there be rules we gotta at least pretend to be followin'!"

Eliza glanced over her shoulder to the Cap'n, trimmed hair falling behind the bandage across her cheek. There was fury in the eyes of Lil' Liz that burnt bright enough to rival any Feo.

"Then get moving, Rot Admiral. I'm not letting that woman lay another finger on my husband, and I'm not wasting any more time."

Barret ran a hand through his crest, watching the rest of his crew go out of their way to get out of Eliza's.

"Ye be— Paul, give 'er some sense!"

Pauvus wriggled under Eliza's grip, talons clattering backwards to keep up.

"Don't call me that, either! Friends-only privilege, 'matey'. Besides, do I look like I'm in a position to argue here?"

They were already at *The Bastion*'s embarking dinghy, a recent addition courtesy of *The Merry Bower*. Pauvus fluttered around to properly stand beside Eliza as she worked the boat's releases, wings jittering with nervous energy. Eliza had barely swung her leg over the boat's edge before being nearly bowled over, turning to see the Cap'n's gloved hand braking the drop-lines.

"Look, I... I know ye've got the fire in yer belly, but ye've got to heed a bit of caution, fer all our sakes. We do all be in the same boat here."

"Not for long," muttered Eliza, fetching the oars from under the boat's bench. "I know how to handle myself, I've dealt with plenty of bad customers. Do what you need here, I can buy some time."

Something like a chuckle echoed from Barret's visor. "Fair enough, lass. Just don't be sparkin' the mayhem without us, aye?"

With Eliza and Pauvus about as comfortable as they could get in the small outset boat, Barret allowed the lines to scorch across his hand down to the water below. A spray of sea salt drenched the both of them on impact with the water, Eliza's first moment away from *The Bastion* in what felt like ages. Pauvus shook out his feathers, still barely at grips with what he was being thrown into.

"Eliza, do you know what you're doing? I don't think—"

"Don't think, just man the tiller. I've got this."

Feeling for the comforting weights in her jacket pockets, Eliza took up the oars in a white-knuckled grip. She pivoted the bow towards the blurred shore on the horizon and rowed, working her arms like the crank on her gifted music box. *The Bastion*'s rotting hull drifted off behind Pauvus' fantail, backing closer and closer towards whatever ending fate would have in store for them.

For all his years of sailing the Grand Sea, Nemo rarely got the unique experience of staring across a stretch of beach he had never seen before.

Faffton, as much as Nemo had gathered, was never the sort of country to openly welcome uninvited guests. They'd been one of the few western powers to refuse any involvement with the affairs of Amrestir back when it had been up for grabs, and the fallout of the whole Stagnance mess had made a strong argument against getting any friendlier.

Two barrier islands, one long and one short, sat beyond the mainland in open defiance of interlopers and would-be salesmen. The fact that the gathered parley team from *La Fille Patronne* had been able to land at the western shore of Short Island, without being bombed to oblivion, spoke to Madame Vitrail's impressive political sway even outside of her home turf.

Nemo had been left to rust by the neighboring treeline while Sister Ann tended to an early-morning bonfire, with nothing but time to think. Looking down at his own shell, the Feo stewed over the piles of highly-polished brass that had been left behind in the ship's cargo hold. He considered how similar it had appeared to the fake gold that shop keeper had been hocking back on Amrestir, how easily they'd managed to slip into sovereign waters, but it was impossible for Nemo to wrap his head around the whole scope of the Fríasen plot.

It would've been easier to do so, if the island's strange, native creatures would leave him be. Long of tail and pointy-eared, the little beasts kept climbing and lazing about the warm blanket of chains weighing the Feo to the ground. They didn't seem to mean him any harm, but the fur shedding into Nemo's visor kept sparking fits of ragged bursts that sent stars across his vision. Squirming and sputtering, Nemo's discomfort garnered him no attention from what he worried might end up being his final crew.

"Shib inbound!" called Antoine with some difficulty, sniffling through a still-bloodied nose. "Loogs like a small pardy, thad girl, and... oh gread, and the bird."

"Bring the leverage over!" Madame Vitrail barked. "I want it on full display for her arrival."

Nemo heard the crunching of sand underbrush, then the *mrow*-ing of upset animals being shooed off from his torso. His view of the unknown beach was replaced by four wicked blunderbuss barrels, black holes with no sympathy to be found within. Looking up to the impression he'd left on Antoine's face, Nemo had no sympathy to return either.

"Hurts, doesn't it?"

"You don'd know pain yed," the Fríasen First Mate spat. "Ye'd besd ged walkin' if you've god any sense, I'm nod lugging you oud there."

Nemo struggled to his foot and peg with a huff, straining to keep balance beneath his chained burden. Keeping his un-hatted head high, the Feo clomped down the beach under watch of the gun's vacant gaze, back to the impromptu meeting space on shore. Madame Vitrail gave Nemo only a brief look of acknowledgement, watching the incoming dinghy along with her crew.

"Who said you could play with those nasty little things?" Vitrail murmured, attention still locked on the furious rowers scorching across the water. "Prisoners don't get to have... fun..."

The rowboat didn't slow down. All present winced at the sound of a keel digging into shore, spraying sand and saltwater across the beach, along with the flailing feathers of an unprepared peacock. Nemo was about to rush forward when a shape launched up from the boat's bench, silhouetted against the rising sun.

The Feo's fire roared. He heaved at his chains, the

210

iron links glowing from within.

"Eliza!"

Eliza had reached dry land once more, with too much hatred in her eyes and too little hair on her head. Those same eyes softened the moment they landed on his tied-up form, her boots soon beating across the wet sand.

"Nemo!"

"Vitrail!" Madame Vitrail called, leveling a pistol directly at Eliza's chest. "Honestly, you've got no sense of manners, you… *Et merde, tu as vraiment les yeux de ton père[35].*"

Eliza stepped forward and scooped Pauvus to his feet, defiant in the face of the fearsome firearm. She was close enough for Nemo to fully take in the state of her, from the chop job that had been made of her hair to the tattered state of her classic dress, and the bandage wrapped around her jaw. Despite his flame, the Feo felt cold, aghast at the terrors his love must have endured all for the sake of his sorry shell.

"Stop talking nonsense!" Eliza snapped, any sense of pain or doubt absent from her voice. "What do you care for manners? Robbing our cruise blind, stealing my husband, and for what?! A trophy? Just another piece of plunder?"

"She's a loon, this one!" Pauvus chimed in, wildly gesticulating in Vitrail's direction. "I'll tell you, she had all these little outfits, just at the ready for—*ack!*"

Pauvus found Hugo's hand around his throat, and a dagger pressed to his ribs. Madame Vitrail's gun was now mere inches from Eliza, and Nemo could do nothing but rock in his chained cocoon and watch.

"Such assumptions you have, while you use this… thing to fill some sad hole in your life. Well-adjusted people don't let talking furnaces melt their brains to sludge."

"Yer one t'talk, Vivi!"

Every head in the Audience whipped to the water. A

---

[35] Damn, you really have your father's eyes

211

new dinghy crunched into the coast alongside Eliza's, packed to the brim with a sight even Sister Ann's warnings hadn't prepared Nemo for.

The Stagnant crew was composed of flesh from all walks of life, woven together through a rainbow splash of fungus. They bristled with weaponry and gardening tools of a material that Nemo could tell at a glance were no mere bronze. Rumors and gossip on the high seas brought together bits of the full picture for him, but seeing its full shape put a quiver in his rivets.

A nightmarish thing of metal and mushroom pulled itself from the throng with a savage squelch, looming before Nemo and the collected crews. Its form was a horrifying mockery of a Feo, a shambling colossus draped in fungal growths that pulsed and oozed with squirming tendrils. If there was anything across the Grand Sea that could be branded a Rot Admiral, it was this monster.

"Reel in them trigger fingers, thar, else ye do somethin' ye'll regret," it growled, rising behind Eliza as the other horrors stood to match the Fríasen band. "Why must ye all be so overdramatic? Honestly, it'd be nice t'enjoy one soddin' second on solid ground without everyone immediately jumpin' at each other's throats!"

"Took you long enough, Cap'n," Eliza muttered, halfway through pulling a gun from her own coat pocket. "I have had it with this so-called 'Madame'."

"Calm that fire, Eliza, it be parley time." The Rot Admiral stepped past Eliza casually, waving with his one hand for her to simmer down. "Ahoy again, Vivi, yer lookin' dreadful."

Madame Vitrail was reeling back with Antoine and the rest of her crew. From the sight of their disgusted faces, Nemo was grateful to not own a nose. The rival crews shuffled into mirrored firing lines, while the Fríasen captain raised her long gun to what counted as the other Cap'n's head.

"*Toute charmante*[36], Barret," she hissed, waving a

---

[36] How charming

cloud of spores from her face. "How long's it been since that tour on *The Mallory?* Figured you'd learn something since then about tact... or subtlety."

"*Argh,* me heart!" The Rot Admiral leaned back, clutching at his subsumed core dramatically. "Figured ye were fond o' me jokes, seemed to leave quite the impression on ye, after all. What, now yer trying to rekindle old flames through that sorry sap?"

The Fríasen crew watched their Captain sweat in her boots, and Nemo noticed that more than a few were enjoying the show.

"Wh—You've been trailing our sails all this way, and I'm the one that can't let go?!"

"Don't flatter yerself, a plunder's a plunder! We was just givin' this lass a ride fer a time, wasn't till the plucked parrot there spilled 'bout the Captain's name that I got the hint." The monster chuckled. "Miss 'Stained Glass', eh? Ye still breakin' bottles and hangin' them up by portholes? 'Cuz we heard ye've been in the market fer somethin' much more valuable, as of late."

"I don't care!" shouted Eliza. "Get some counseling on your own—"

"Shut up," spat the Rot Admiral, "let me handle this."

"HEY!" Nemo roared. "You don't talk to my—!"

"You shut up too, Mully. The Rot Admiral be talkin' now, and we be wantin' that gold from yer hold!"

"And you believed that?" Vitrail scoffed. "Our cargo has no more gold in it than the Feo here. It's called a con, any self-respecting pirate should know what that means. Not that you'd know anything about that, 'Rot Admiral'."

A smug grin spread across Vitrail's lips. "An admiral, with naught but one ship? If anyone deserves claim to that title here, it is *moi.*"

Nemo's righteous fury fizzled into confusion, watching the faces of the collective Audience twist in madness and despair. Eliza and Pauvus were the only ones unmoved by the drama before them, staring daggers across the divided beach at the dueling captains, as the Rot Admiral drooped his head down to Vitrail's level.

"Ah, it would fit ye, tryin' to take me name. To be true, it be more fer marketing's sake than anythin', though *The Bastion* do be a beast of many decks. But, ye be right, even if ye be swindlers. Yer lookin' to be a genuine Admiral yerself, and with a right neat fleet to yer name…"

The implication hung in the air between parley parties like a storm cloud. Realization fell upon the Fríasen crew in a cold shower, quite a few of whom were looking back out to their parked ships on the water.

"You wouldn't dare," choked Vitrail, trying not to breathe too close to the fetid Cap'n. "I do not care what the stories have said, *homme fantôme*[37], we'll see how long you last baking in sacred fire!"

Sister Ann aimed a glowing hand towards the cursed crew, but her blank stare was aimed squarely upon Nemo. However much she was truly seeing, the cleric kept her cool for the moment, even in the presence of the Stagnant terror.

The Rot Admiral smiled in the face of the flame, a grotesque thing to see a Feo accomplish, and casually squatted onto a stool that one of the grotesqueries had slid beneath him.

"Well now, them be the cards laid bare, aye? Good chance t'back off 'n put things to perspective. How's about everyone practices a bit o' patience, cools off fer a— For pity's sake, Eliza!"

Eliza, who up until this point had fallen into the background of the parley's attention, was now waving a very fancy gun in a sweep across the gathered Audience.

"I'm sick of being patient! Get to business or get it over with! I've had it with your pirate insanity!"

Madame Vitrail snorted, an act she clearly regretted considering how close her nose was to the Rot Admiral.

---

[37] phantom

214

"Very professional, *coquine*[38]. Sadly, there is no business to be had here for you. You have as little to offer us as your putrid pal, and you'll meet your end just as quickly on this beach."

Nemo spotted a twitch in Eliza's eye, and braced himself for whatever she was cooking up.

"Oh, so you want a ransom for him?! Fine! I'll give you a ransom to end all ransoms!"

Eliza's hand slipped to her jacket pocket again, every trigger finger tightening at the prospect of sparking a showdown at dawn. Instead, her arm rose to the sky with an oddly bladed object in her grip, glinting with the same light as the Stagnant crew's accessories in the creeping sun. Nemo caught a stifled, nervous hiss from the direction of the Rot Admiral and upon closer inspection of the tool, he knew why.

"Oh, as if I'm the one in need of a trim, you..." Vitrail trailed off, her brain catching up with her eyes. "*Quoi?* That's... No, those couldn't be—"

"Yep. Real, genuine gold, straight out of the legends. You can choke on it!"

Nemo watched Eliza toss the priceless artifact at the Captain's feet like a littered to-go cup from the Bouncin' Bean. A collective gasp rippled through both crews as the blades struck sand, voices from all descending into a cacophony of greed and disbelief. Madame Vitrail held enough sway to haul her men back, but the Rot Admiral's crew was practically frothing at his heels.

"W-wha–where did y-you... Th-those are p-p-property of *The Bastion*, by right!"

"Eliza, why? We really need them things, they're medicinal-like!"

"You greedy, little sneak! We tool all over the damn sea for that metal mate of yours, and this is how you repay us?!"

Pauvus and Eliza backed away from the swell of their fetid fellows' angry shouts. Nemo was about ready to

---

[38] stupid girl

215

step in, chains or no, until the Rot Admiral halted them in a one-handed sweep.

"Fellas, fellas! Eliza be no thief, those be my gift t'her! I'd say she's earnt it, aye?"

Silence dropped across the crew like an anchor. One of the ghouls was rolling out a long scroll from a sleeve, muttering and gurgling in disbelief at the list.

"W-why would you n-n-not r-report it? G-g-gifting is m-my authorit-t-ty! After all th-these years, you disrespec-ec-ect me, and *The Bastion*'s m-manifest?"

"Some crew loyalty you've got—" started Vitrail.

"She ain't even been here that long! Not only do we not get fresh gold, we gotta give up what we already got?"

"Maybe we could just burn your whole sorry—" attempted Vitrail.

"Hey, I've done a lot more for you people than just parade around in a dress!"

"*J'hallucine, allô?*[39] Parley time? What is—" deflated Vitrail.

"Everyone, get a hold of yourselves! We've got to—"

Pauvus' plea was smacked out of his beak by the butt of a pistol, sending the Ave wheeling into the ground. Before he could get his bearings, Madame Vitrail descended on him, fury radiating off her in scorching waves. She raised her heavy heel high and brought it down.

"Stop!"

CRUNCH!

"Interrupting!"

SNAP!

"Me!"

KRRAK!

Her voice rose with each blow, sharp and unrelenting as her boot slammed into the delicate joint of Pauvus' right wing. The impact echoed, a dreadful mix of splintering bone and piercing screams, slicing through the Stagnant crew's discord.

---

[39] Am I hallucinating, hello?

Nemo could only watch helplessly as his friend twisted in the sand, agony written across every twitch of his broken form. The weight of injustice pressed against the Feo's chest, the heat inside him growing like a brass kettle left to boil—

—busted and alone in the cargo hold, he felt a feathered form settle into his side. Together in the dark, Ave sat with Feo, and Paul offered a wing of friendship to—

The crushing weight of Nemo's helplessness dissolved into fury. It threatened to overflow, and he had no intention to stop it this time.

Vitrail's flimsy lock glowed to its breaking point, shattering with a final heave. The Feo was on top of Antoine before he had a chance to raise his blunderbuss, rolling straight over the man in a clatter of unraveling chains, spinning out into a ragged sprint. The Fríasen captain raised her bloody boot heel for another blow, and pivoted just in time to catch a fist of brass directly to the sternum.

In an instant, Vitrail's stained glass breastplate fractured, along with any chance at peace on the island.

For her first attempt at making parley, Eliza had thought things were going pretty well. With the most feared band of ghouls known to pirate-dom at her back and a legendary bounty to offer, who could refuse the Dread Siren?

Evidently, the Fríasen captain could. Sparked by shattering glass, the beach was now in the midst of an outright war. Shots and smoke choked the morning air as men, women, and mushrooms raged in battle, their voices rising and falling like the tide. Eliza watched Cap'n Barret sweep across the battlefield like water through musket fire in a blur of colors, his laugh ringing clear in a cold gurgle that held no fear and gave no quarter.

Eliza's heart pounded in her chest. The pistol in her grip weighed heavy and clumsy in her hand now that she was facing down a genuine gunfight. She swiveled around, trying to find Pauvus in the mayhem, in time to catch a cluster of Vitrail's men emerging from the treeline for a surprise burst. Just as the cavalry rolled in with guns blazing, Eliza heard a low whistle that grew louder and louder by the second.

They never knew what hit them, but Eliza did. A heavy, familiar-looking barrel slammed directly into the squad, bursting on impact in a sickly-sweet spray. The gunners writhed in pain and panic, caked in fresh Stagnance blooms and shards of Bouncin' Bean branded wood. She looked up to spot Bellona and Vaughn, perched like painted coconuts in the tree boughs, cackling away like young pranksters.

"Gweh-heh-hah! *Macte virtute, amice!*[40]"

"Hail, siren. Watch your stern."

Eliza tore her vision from the moaning mass before her to squint through the growing gunsmoke. One of the battling silhouettes had broken away from the fray, barreling towards her like a cannonball and slamming into her chest. Eliza felt both wind and sense get knocked out of her, but she hadn't stopped moving. The figure scooped her up before she could get her bearings, and she watched the chaos of the failed parley shrinking towards shore in a blur of flashes and bodies.

Landing on the sand with a *thud*, the sordid scene fell away behind the hull of Cap'n Barret's rowboat. Digging in the folds of her pocket for her pistol, Eliza finally got a chance to whip about on her snatcher.

"Hope you're hungry for gunpowder, you—"

Brass shone down on her, tarnished yet gleaming from behind their barricade. The coat he'd been wearing on their ill-fated cruise hung in tatters over his shoulders, sizzling at the fringes. Nemo was cooking as hot as a forge, searing an odd blend of fear and nostalgia through Eliza at his touch. The Feo pulled away at her recoil, cast behind the ambient gunpowder fog in a silhouetted halo of light.

"...Eliza."

The battle fell to silence, as did the world. All that existed in this moment was the two of them, linked across thousands of miles and countless wasted days. Eliza's lungs heaved in her chest as she reached out, half-worried he was just some dying delusion. When her hand brushed against solid metal, the scorch across her fingertips brought an overwhelming relief to her heart, and a fragile smile to her lips.

"There be my First Mate."

They pressed into a burning embrace against a backdrop of distant explosions. The Feo remained kneeling even after she pulled away, shoulders trembling from the intensity of their reunion.

---

[40] Be brave, my friend!

"Eliza, I-I..." Nemo sucked a sharp breath of air, and certainly would've been sobbing had he the eyes for it. "I can't believe you came all this way... for me. I'm sorry, this is not how I wanted your first trip abroad to go."

Eliza let out a soft laugh, feeling the string of her makeshift bandage shift with the motion.

"We did say in our vows that we'd stand by each other's side. I'm not letting you go that easy."

Nemo's crackling chuckle was a sweeter sound than any 'Little Liz' performance.

"Thank Mother Flame you're safe. I kept thinking something dreadful had—"

Eliza watched Nemo freeze, in more ways than one. She felt the sticky pull at her bandage and braced for the reaction she knew would be brewing.

"Wh-what is that? That's... What did those fiends do to you?!"

"Nemo, it's fine," Eliza lied. "We've got bigger things to—"

CLONK!

Something had bounced in behind their shipwreck shelter, causing Nemo to reflexively swing in as Eliza's shield. She peeked under his outstretched arms to see a very familiar head sink in the sand, amazingly still alive judging by its muffled swears.

"Edmund?"

The head pulled itself up on two tendrils of a mycelial mustache, eyes flashing at the sight of the couple.

"You cowards! We're busy bustin' heads out there, and you decide to sneak off for a snogging session?"

A new wave of fire surged through Nemo, as he lunged to clutch what remained of the sailor in a brass vise.

"What happened to my wife?!" Nemo hissed, flickering dangerously close to Edmund's face. "Was it you who hurt her?!"

Edmund scoffed in the face of the very real threat of being pulped to pirate paste, defiantly crossing the tendrils of his mustache in place of his absent arms.

221

"Here we go again! Blame ol' Eddy for maiming Liz when I didn't do nothin'! You can thank our fearless Cap'n for that lil' beauty mark, bud."

"...What?"

Eliza couldn't say that Edmund was anywhere nearing a friend, but that didn't mean she wanted to watch his skull crack like a crab shell. She frantically waved her hands from behind Nemo's back, silently pleading for the sailor to shut his trap, but Edmund had never quite learned the ropes on that skill.

"Don't know the full details, but yea, apparently Cap'n Barret had a bit of a meltdown 'n melted half her pretty face off. Ey, still got the other side though!"

Nemo dropped Edmund to the sand with a *thud*. Eliza braced for whatever was to come, whether it be Nemo going full inferno or their dinghy getting perforated to splinters. Time itself held its breath in anticipation, but no great outburst was to arrive. Eliza and the head of Edmund watched the Feo peer out to the beach, following his stare to the whirling rampage that was the unleashed Rot Admiral.

"...Yep, I can kill that."

Eliza rose to meet Nemo, grasping for the Feo's shoulder before he could rush out into chaos on his own.

"Nemo, we can deal with him later. One fight at a time, Madame 'Vitriol' is first up on the chopping block."

Another shape was pounding over through the smoke, lugging two slumped masses in its wake. Rufus dove in towards the edge of the beach, Edmund's decapitated body in one hand and a limp Pauvus shivering in the other.

"Hoy-hoy, Ed! Saw you head-ing over here, *peh-heh*. Pull yerself together, dem Fríasens ain't got any quit to 'em!"

Edmund's head squirmed out of its crater, grateful for an exit from the conversation. Eliza averted her gaze, as he crunched and squished himself back into shape.

222

Eventually, she opened her eyes to the sight of Edmund leaping back out into the open, and Rufus resting the prone form of Pauvus on a pillow of sand. The Ave was still breathing, chest and wing shuddering with effort, but he was barely clinging to consciousness.

"Stay here, Eliza. I'm going for the captain."

Eliza turned to face Nemo, noting his proper 'Captain' pronunciation. A rush of fear filled her once more, and she roughly tugged at the foolhardy Feo's collar.

"No, I'm not leaving you to fight her alone again! This is my score to settle too."

"Well, I'm not letting you get hurt again!"

"You're not indestructible, Nemo!"

"You're not made of metal, Eliza!"

A groan of pain from beside them broke the stalemate.

"Can't you two just... go dancin' downstairs or som'thing? 'm trying t'sleep here..."

Both turned to face Pauvus, half-delirious and

223

half-winged. They looked between their friend and Rufus, who was carefully digging through the boat's bench for spare supplies.

"Don't be frettin'. Ol' Rufus can handle the birdy boy. You do what you's gots t'do, yea?"

Nemo turned to face Eliza, and she matched his gaze. Somewhere in the back of her mind, Eliza thought she heard the wild twiddles of The Sick Fiddle. She smiled, and felt for the loaded pistol in her pocket.

"May I have this dance?"

Behind Nemo's visor, Eliza saw a flicker of a smile. "I'd be honored."

For the first time in a long while, Cap'n Barret felt truly alive. The solid beach beneath his feet, the breeze through the trees, the mewling of little Twin Isle beasts looking to lick up the leftovers, all worked to help him feel more grounded than he'd been since he last left home.

His crew had forgotten their fear of danger a long time ago, most taking the opportunity to have a raucous time of the whole farce. There was no greater curse than boredom, and rollocking away on a quest for true love certainly put a fire in everyone's chests. They took swords and bullets to those same chests like sponges, and the only one among their ranks who could really cook them away was busy firing into the treeline.

"*Conne*[41]! What are you—*wheeze*—doing, Ann?" Vivi panted, clutching her shattered chest with one hand.

"I can't be expected to aim myself, can I?" the Smoulder priestess called out, letting loose another volley in exactly the wrong direction.

Barret backed across the shoreline with four sabers flailing in his face, and another four lining his extended arm to clash against them. He heard a fresh war cry, and

_____

[41] Idiot

224

turned to let his duelists wear themselves out attacking his back for a bit. Edmund had gotten himself back into fighting shape, just in time to stamp out Bert's bonfire-burnt body, but it hadn't been either of them doing the shouting.

Eliza and Nemo burst out from behind their beached dinghy, reeling through a river of angry soldiers and brawling to a rhythm all of their own. They ducked and weaved around wild and exhausted attacks, the Feo pivoting on his peg to take the swings and swing his wife in turn.

The Fríasen privateers were wholly unprepared, their attention torn between a two-pronged assault of the cursed and cavorting. As an arm of their countries military force, the soldiers present had been prepared for conventional warfare, but no amount of training could have prepared them for the mad jig sweeping through their ranks.

It was hard for Barret to keep track of the brass flurry of blows that was Nemo. With a brutal headbutt, he sent one man stumbling back, dazed and disoriented, before grabbing him by the collar and hurling him back into the throng of his fellows. Meanwhile, Eliza cracked the skull of a following sailor with a wicked pistol-whip, firing hot even while unloaded. She ducked behind Nemo, her hands a blur as they brought her gun back to life under the Feo's protective stance. When Eliza managed to twirl a low sweep into a teeth-cracking high-kick, even Autumns cheered her on.

Tearing himself from the Audience's pull, Barret's neck snapped back to Vivi. She was crawling to her feet with her First Mate's overcompensation gun for support, the wind taken out of her sails. Barret clicked his tined visor into a smile, appreciating that he even could, and crouched for a deadly leap.

"*Tu dois te*—[42] Ann, blast those two! They're right there!"

---

[42] You must be—

225

The Sister of the Smoulder, who'd been casually blind-firing for most of the engagement, suddenly whipped about on the Cap'n. He nearly stumbled at the sight of her trembling fingers, bloodlust faltering when she threw her hands to the sky in frustration.

"I cannot do this anymore, Vivian," Sister Ann groaned, clutching at her hood. "I have remained patient, lent you the guidance of Mother Flame, but have you heeded it? No, you had to water your pride. Had to steal away with that poor Feo, had to provoke his love, and simply had to throw yourself right to these living sins. You've lit your own pyre, and I'm not jumping in behind you."

The flames flickering across the red-robe's palms sizzled in the faces of both Barret and Vivian. The two captains watched the Sister back out from the camp towards the yawning forest, until her light was swallowed by the trees.

'Madame Vitrail' looked about ready to shatter for a

second time, but a bayonet to his shoulder ruined Barret's opportunity to revel at her misery. He spun about, whipping the thing out of the dim soldier's hand.

"Ye wait yer turn! I be tryin' to enjoy the show!"

More than a few of the Fríasen landing crew were starting to lose their fighting spirit in the wake of Sister Ann's strategic retreat. The ones not littering the sand or fleeing to the water were still forced to contend with the overwhelming force that was a happily reunited couple.

Nemo spun Eliza about by the wrist in a dramatic sweep, under the shadow of a bosun with a wicked two-handed blade. She whirled with coat and skirts flying, carrying along his momentum to slide below a flying slice. The Feo's shoulder took the brunt of a follow-up chop in a spray of sparks. Any chance at a third attack was interrupted when an engraved barrel popped out from under his armpit.

BANG!

Barret whooped and cheered with his crew as the pathetic privateer lost his mind, all over the sand.

"Now that be a tango o' terror!"

Barret saw Nemo's head snap around, staring him visor-to-visor.

"You're next."

BOOOOOM!

The Rot Admiral watched Nemo's wooden leg explode, sending Eliza tumbling from the blastback. While the spouses finished their dance with a splash into the surf, Barret swiveled to spot Vivian stomping out to the clearing. Chest held high and cleared of loose shrapnel, she aimed her borrowed blunderbuss directly at Eliza's head, one of its four barrels still smoking.

"I'm going to make a widower of you, *bouilloire*."

Vitrail's eyes glittered like broken glass over the water.

Nemo staggered through the shallows, barely managing to keep his brassy shell dry. Eliza was fighting to keep her face above the surf, struggling under the Madame's heavy bootheel. With a fresh flame of rage, Nemo dug through the sand for the discarded pistol, only to watch saltwater pour out from the barrel.

"I've still got three rounds, soggy. *Bien tenté*[43]," Vitrail spat before turning back to Eliza. "So much trouble, so much chaos, all over some sad excuse for a life. Life is suffering, little siren. Let's help the Feo feel alive, as a final wedding present."

Gunpowder or no, Nemo was ready to explode. He tried to stand, sinking under his own weight in the sand, but something caught his coat by the collar.

"Steady on, lover-boy!" Cap'n Barret called, reeling the other Feo back. "Gonna tip the candle when yer so far down the wick?"

---

[43] Nice try

Nemo clawed against the Rot Admiral's grip, wild and desperate. Madame Vitrail, or 'Vivi', or whoever she was stood mere feet away, but there may as well have been an entire ocean between them. Every rivet in his body strained near to bursting against the injustice that had been pressing down on him, from as far back as he could remember. He remembered the depths he'd stooped to under so many corrupt captains, that helpless resignation he vowed to never feel again.

"Be reason'ble now, Vivian," the Rot Admiral bartered, his hold on Nemo firm as iron. "Ye pull that trigger, ye know two more rounds won't be enough t'put us lot down."

"Looking to test that?" Madame Vitrail scoffed, plucking a canister of Red-Hot Fiery Plasmotic Grapeshot from her coat sling. "Courtesy of the cleric. I'd be delighted to give you a taste of cleansing fire before I'm gone."

Nemo dropped the useless pistol with a splash. "Vitrail, don't do this. Best case scenario, even if we all end up in pieces, those pieces won't go away. Your bosses back home will be stuck explaining to the Faffton government that you brought them nothing but piles of rot, and proof of how worthless those piles of gold in the hold really are."

"Aye, that be true," followed Barret, beginning to catch Nemo's line of reasoning. "All the world'll remember 'bout the great Madame Vitrail will be a blight on Fríasa's reputation, a legend not worth 'er spit. That how ye'd like yer story to end?"

Barret's voice was still tinged with piratical bravado, but Nemo could see the Rot Admiral was starting to unravel just as much as Vitrail. He wondered at the consuming pride of a captain, and where it had brought the two of them. With his wife so close yet so far, Nemo was struck with the gravity of how far it had taken them as well.

Struggling under Vitrail's shaky footing, Eliza defiantly pushed the barrels of the blunderbuss back with her forehead.

"Couldn't just grab the gold and scram, could you?"

she snarled. "Have to ruin one more thing before you die? At least I'll have someone I love to remember me. Not even your crew's sticking around, who'll be left to care once you're dead on the sand?"

There was a quiver to the gun's stock, a falter in the captain's step. Nemo thought of the lonely letter tucked away in Vitrail's cabin, the words of Eliza's father still ringing through his head.

"Captain, please," Nemo called, holding his hands up to the woman pleadingly. "You left home for freedom, fought to claim your own happiness. Eliza struggled and suffered for hers, and so much more. She's forging her own legend, on her own terms."

Like you.

Vitrail's gaze darted between Nemo and the Rot Admiral before falling upon Eliza once more, a new shard of light breaking through the darkness in her eyes. Whether it was out of fear of death, rage of defeat, or some buried sorrow at a life left behind, they wavered all the same.

"Please..." Nemo begged. "Eliza is the greatest gift I was ever given."

The captain's eyes squeezed shut, along with her trigger finger. A blast rang out over the beach.

Nemo finally pried his gaze up from the surf when the gun echoed out its last note, unable to bear what he thought he was about to see. What he did see was Eliza shivering in the shallows, alive and as unharmed as she could hope to be. The end of the wicked rifle was pointed to the sky, smoking with reconsidered malice.

"Plunder earned by right of might, *oui?*" Vivian pondered out loud. "Those are terms I suppose I ought to respect. Sounds familiar, doesn't it Barry?"

Her crew was retreating with all the treasure and animals they could carry, preferring to fight another day than keep up the current one. Madame Vitrail rested the heavy gun over her shoulder and gazed across the beach, squinting into the sun. With a sigh, the Captain stepped back from her slippery slope and off of Eliza's chest.

"Take what's yours then, siren, and clutch it tight... Do not disappoint me, Liz."

Nemo had been struggling to fight the moment Vitrail had let up her guard, but Barret held firm. Even the lingering wretches of *The Bastion* allowed her to sulk away without another blow, as though called by an unspoken command.

The woman staggered away of her own accord into the hull of an overpacked dinghy, casting one last glance to what she would be leaving behind. She fled to another dawn that Nemo believed she didn't deserve to see.

Only after the Fríasen forces had officially left the coast did Barret loose his grip, freeing the beach of the whole rotten parley. Nemo broke into a mad hopping sprint the very same moment as Eliza finally clambered to her feet, just in time for the flailing Feo to nearly topple her right into the drink again. Together they stumbled, and steadied, and held each other once more.

Eliza gazed into Nemo's fiery glow as he steamed in the cool sea air, her eyes a sight he had feared he would never experience again.

"Nemo, I... thank—"

"No 'thank you's are necessary."

Nemo held Eliza close, afraid she'd vanish the second he let go. There was something distant in her stare, left behind miles and miles ago. She wrapped her arm around the Feo's waist, leaning in to help lead him back along to dry land.

Nemo scooped up a scattered oar as a crutch, limping over the bodies that fell somewhere between unmoving and running out of juice. Aside from Barret's celebrating crew, the only Fríasen stragglers were those in no state to flee. The one Eliza had called Edmund was picking through the leftovers with morbid curiosity, while Rufus emerged from the dinghy defense with a freshly bundled Pauvus in tow.

"Aeeyyyye, Nemoooo!" the Ave swayed, "You... won the day! Good on ya*aaaAAAH*!"

231

Nemo spun in the direction of Pauvus' thrashing to catch Sister Ann snuffing out the fire she had set on the sand. She was unarmed, save for three of the native furred creatures purring along her back. If the cleric had any burning emotions at being left behind, she was doing a very good job at hiding it.

"Ey, beat it red-robe!" snarled Edmund. "What'dja miss the boat?"

Nemo hobbled his way to the Sister with Eliza at his arm. As her face came into focus, Nemo thought he saw the hint of a smile tugging the corners of her milky eyes.

"You... why did you disobey the Captain?"

"You're one to ask," Sister Ann chuckled, scratching the base of a local beast's tail. "Vitrail never respected the wreckage she left in her wake. I felt the force of your bond, the calamity its shattering would bring."

Looking across at the monsters still littering the beach, she waved dismissively in their direction.

"Now, begone from this place. You've little to gain from staying here long, aside from Faffton questioning. Leave me to my peace."

Nemo heard another groan from Pauvus, with Rufus balancing the bird's slumped form like a fragile hatchling.

"Er, Sister, are you sure on that?" asked the Stagnant sailor. "I mean, considerin' the whole—"

"You may have strayed from Mother Flame's path, poor soul, but I have not. Whatever is to come, I will face it bravely. Call it divine inspiration."

Rufus flinched in heretical shame as she approached to hold a warm hand against Pauvus' side.

"I hope you made the most of your final flight. I look forward to hearing all about it, one day."

Sister Ann shot the confused couple a warm smile, and trudged down the beach once more. As she disappeared into the green, Nemo spotted a brief flash of the gold shears being pocketed by one of the Rot Admiral's cronies.

"Hmmm, w-would be a sh-shame t-t-to leave empty-handed... Lots of fresh invent-tory wasted on th-these little b-b-beasts."

"On it!" whooped Edmund, already beginning to scrape the flattened torso of Antoine up on a crate lid. "Finally, spare parts! I'm gettin' me a new foot! Ey, Bert, need a hand?"

Nemo felt Eliza's body fall limp in his arms, her body finally catching up with her exhausted brain. He eased her down onto the trunk of a fallen tree while their extraordinary cohorts picked up the pieces.

"She called me 'Liz'... The way she said it..."

Nemo felt the tang of a rivet in his chest. It was a name that had no right being on Vitrail's lips. He stewed on exactly what he learned about his mother-in-law, but the faraway glaze of Eliza's eyes made him swallow his words.

Eliza deserved the truth, but she deserved peace even more.

"...She'd heard me going on about you," Nemo stated gently, as if one wrong word could pull back the curtain on his lie. "Wanted to stick the knife in one more time, I suppose."

Whether it be she was too exhausted to question him further or that she was content with his answer, Eliza didn't press him on the matter. The couple sat in perfect silence for a time, watching a little black fuzzball paw at the peacock feather dangling from Vitrail's discarded hat.

"So," sighed Eliza, ruffling the sand out of her hair, "does this mean we've got the church's blessing?"

"I'm blessed she won't see what I did to her room."

That was enough to bring a smile to Eliza's face, however faint.

"Would've loved to see it. What I'll love even more is the chance to finally get back to New Amrestir, as crazy as I feel saying that. How about you, Nemo? Ready to go home?"

"...Just about ready."

The Feo had been watching the Rot Admiral direct the supply piles, the war drums in his head beating louder and louder by the moment. Pushing up on his oar, Nemo left Eliza to rest as he launched himself in Barret's direction at a wild half-gallop.

"I'm going to rip that smile off your jaw!"

"Nemo, stop! I don't want you to—!"

"Don't listen t'her, Nemoooo!" cheered Pauvus woozily. "Show him... like y'showed that... walrus, back in*nnhhznnsf*..."

The Bastion's crew continued their work while their Cap'n backed into the surf, casually outstepping Nemo's shambles.

"Wait, hold on, let me— Lad! Hold yer hoppin', there! See them grey sails? Faffton welcome wagon, means it's time t'be off. Temper them tantrums fer the time bein'."

Nemo managed to wrench his gaze from the Rot Admiral to the horizon. A flotilla of Faffton vessels were incoming, and he knew the isolationists wouldn't be happy to find a mess on their sovereign property. Glancing back ahead, the Feo wished that he could give Barret a proper evil eye.

"I can't forgive you for what you've done."

The two Feo stood at an impasse in the morning light against a hostile horizon. Barret's gaze flickered between Nemo and Eliza, a new spark of life dancing under his visor.

"That be fair... but maybe I can be doin' somethin', t'help make amends."

The Bastion sailed until all signs of land and ships were but a memory, and the empty stretch of the Grand Sea dominated the landscape.

Eliza sucked in a deep breath, instantly regretting it. She was happy to be back aboard the rancid ship, if only because it meant they were finally making it back home. She'd be even happier when she could step off the rotten thing for the last time.

For the first time since their honeymoon, she truly gazed at the stars painted across the night sky. They twinkled like shards of glass, hung with care into the constellations that Nemo had spun stories about. While the Feo tended to Pauvus below deck, Eliza could feel the expanse of night staring back at her, the empty spaces between the lights prodding at something deep inside of her. There was that nameless, gnawing dread still clinging, the kind that she had hoped she'd be able to shake by now.

"Ho-oh! There's the Dread Siren!"

Eliza's head whipped around. Bellona and Vaughn were traipsing up from the lower decks, shutting the door on the commotion below. The Ibi flashed her a shaggy-capped grin, elbowing the long-toothed Obra with a fin.

"I thoughts that *probrum*[44] 'peaceful parley' was goings to be such a slog, but look at yous! Didn't knows you hads the nerve for righteous brutalities like thats! And in such style!"

"Burst that bosun's dome like a sea cabbage," Vaughn grunted. "Solid work, there."

---

[44] stupid

The face of that man still clung to Eliza's eyelids, along with the aftermath of it. She swallowed a shiver and slapped a brave face over her scars.

"What can I say? I got swept up in the heat of the moment."

"Mmhmhm, wondersful," chortled Bellona wetly. "Wells, they's broken the seal ons a fresh cask downs in the galley. Indulges yourself!"

"Not like anyone but you or the bird can enjoy it."

"I'll pass on a toast for now," Eliza snorted, a swiftly realized mistake. "With you two around, I'm not taking the gamble on waking up in a floating dinghy... again."

"Fair 'nuff," Vaughn admitted.

As the aquatic pair turned to leave, they crossed Nemo's path, stepping out onto the deck with a fresh mahogany peg. Bellona nudged at his shoulder as they passed him, waving a fin along to Eliza with a wink.

"Oi, *debellator*[45], *tua puella*[46] is up theres!"

They left Nemo to join Eliza once more, finally allowing them a moment in peace. The Feo was still wearing the maroon coat he'd been sporting when she last saw him aboard the *Marigold*, now soiled, scorched, and tattered with misfortune. It had been pressed through the filter of time and hardship as cruelly as themselves, yet still clinging to some sense of shape.

Eliza's brain was flooding with things she wished to say, but her tongue couldn't keep up with the current.

"Nemo..."

What happened to us?

"...How's Paul holding up?"

Nemo glanced back to where Bellona and Vaughn had disappeared to, faint sounds of celebration muffled behind the door.

"He's doing fine. That Rufus fellow managed to set his wing in place and wrap it up proper. Don't know if he'll

---

[45] champion
[46] your girl

236

ever fly again, but Paul handled it like a champ... Then again, we did liquor him up pretty good."

"Hey, if there's anyone here tonight that deserves to get roaring drunk, it's him. Can't believe that's the same Ave we'd left whining about new clothes back in town."

"He really changed," Nemo chuckled, "and he's not the only one. The Rot A— *Barret,* was telling me all about your adventures as the 'Dread Siren', you know."

Eliza imagined she looked about as miserable as the nickname made her feel, judging by the extinguished look behind Nemo's visor. She forced a wry smile for his sake, and felt another chew at her chest.

"Can't really call myself a siren anymore, now that I've got a face only a mother could love."

That struck Nemo even more rigid than before. Whatever he'd been thinking of, the Feo thrust forward to grip her in a tight hug. Eliza felt her heart race at the touch, the memory of the Cap'n's grip still seared in her mind and body. In the dark of *The Bastion*'s sails, all she could smell was burning skin.

"Does... Does it still hurt?"

Eliza blinked back to the present. The bandage had fallen away at some point during their *danse macabre,* leaving newly-formed skin exposed to the night air. She'd been making an active effort to bury the memories of those fevered nights and stinging disinfectants, all bearable once blanketed with the thought of Nemo's safety.

But for how long?

Eliza pulled back from Nemo's embrace, and scratched at her cheek.

"Eh, not much worse than a coffee spill. I'll manage."

Nemo orbited around to stand beside her, both willfully ignoring the true gravity of the situation. Eliza leaned into him, pushing down her fears and grounding herself in his presence, as he ran a hand through her short hair.

"So, how do you feel about the Rot Admiral's

offer?" the Feo asked, doing his best to brighten the mood. "It wouldn't be my first choice by any means to share our day with that blackguard, but I'll stomach it to make this official. Captain's binding signature doesn't have an expiration date, even if the Cap'n himself did."

From the depths of her mind, Eliza tried to fish up the same giddiness she'd felt back on their private dock, but all she could catch were glimpses of *The Bastion*'s atrocities. The skyline was littered with ghostly silhouettes of the ships she'd helped raid, haunting her vision like specters. For a fleeting moment, she could see the crews from those same ships on their lifeboats, fragile vessels adrift somewhere in the unknowable ocean.

"...Sorry," Nemo fretted, leaning by the railing. "We don't need some piece of paper to tell us we're married, especially if *he's* the one officiating it. I'm— I'm just tired of having to prove ourselves; I won't stand for anyone else across this Grand Sea denying us being together ever again."

Eliza had hoped she could keep her discomfort under wraps, but she'd never been much of an actor, no matter what Barret claimed. She sighed, and leaned onto the railing with Nemo.

"No, it's not that. It's just... this whole, stupid 'Dread Siren' thing. I don't regret what I've done to find you, but I can't say I'm proud of it, either."

The constellation of Lophina glittered overhead, surfacing to her brilliant end. In the darkness between the stars above, Eliza hoped that the Dread Siren's story wouldn't be remembered alongside hers.

"I just... don't like the person I had to be."

From beside her, Eliza felt the hands of the Feo on her shoulders.

"Eliza, you didn't do the Rot Admiral's dirty work because you wanted to."

"So what?" Eliza snapped, squirming under a grip that burnt her memory. "I was still down there, celebrating right alongside them after each raid. I did things I never thought I would stoop to... things that made the world just a bit more rotten."

A new round of cheers echoed up from below, where Eliza had to assume that they were still egging Pauvus on in drowning his woes. The couple allowed the moment to drift on the air, listening to the fun roll on without them for a little while longer.

Nemo tugged at the frayed hems of his coat, having to resist reaching out to hold her again.

"...I think I understand, more than you can imagine. I've had many owners with many orders in mind for something they saw as heartless. And I followed them all because I didn't know that there was any other way to live. They even had a nickname for me, 'The Brass Brute'."

Eliza flicked back through the stories that the Feo had spun of his time at sea. Dear, sweet Nemo being aimed like a weapon of war didn't fit right in her image of the man, but she had seen what he'd been like out on the beach. The same frame that was unflinchingly supportive could

239

make for just as terrifying an enemy as Barret, given the right motivation.

"You always seemed so happy, talking about your time as a sailor," Eliza said softly. "Why chase a world that was nothing but cruel to you?"

A low puff of steam escaped Nemo's visor as he placed the hat that Vitrail had abandoned on the beach on his head, joining Eliza in watching the stars.

"It helps to put things into perspective. Even when I grew to understand the horrors I was forced to partake in, it made each spot of light shine all the more brighter. The sights I've seen, the wonders I've experienced... the people I love."

Nemo's words took root in her mind. Even when the whole world proved itself to be terrible, it amazed her that the Feo managed to find the wonder in it and its people.

Flame, I love this man.

The water over the railing was an inky abyss, misting over Eliza in cold sprays, the light from Nemo's visor joining the moonlight in dancing off the waves. She thought, if she stared deeply enough, that she could see the core coal still burning below.

"I wish I had the same optimism as you, Nemo," Eliza admitted. "If there's one lesson that growing up in Amrestir has taught me, it's that life, especially people, tends to disappoint you... Can't say I've exactly been proven wrong on that count, either."

The sound of a flute filled the empty space around them, and sent a shiver down Eliza's spine. She clutched the railing tight, doing everything she could to avoid thinking about the man behind the music.

"Did it ever get easier for you? Dealing with all... that?"

The glow of Nemo's visor flicked back to face Eliza again, an unspoken, shared understanding in its flames.

"It did," Nemo rumbled. "With time, and with people that help make life worth living. I promise."

Eliza wrestled with the concept, unable to tell

whether his words were a sincere truth or a comforting lie. The touch of brass digits upon her own pulled her back from a tidepool of distress, to a face with no judgement in its stare.

"Do you want to know what I love about you?"

"My hair?" Eliza chuckled weakly. "Guess I'm in trouble, now that most of it is gone."

Nemo ran a hand through her trimmed locks again, ruffling the cropped cut lovingly.

"Granted, that's what first caught my eye, but no. I've seen more than my share of selfishness and cruelty, Eliza. You didn't choose to hop aboard a ship for riches or glory. You slogged across half the ocean for an old brass Feo, out of the love in your heart."

"Of course I did," Eliza murmured, leaning into Nemo's touch. "I'd be a lousy wife if I didn't."

"The world can be a rotten place, true," Nemo continued, "but the little kindnesses make it worth sticking around. We both had to stand on our own two feet alone for so long… we don't have to do that anymore."

The glassy gloom surrounding Eliza was beginning to crack. She spun to face him, faint tears trickling around the corners of her smile. Wrapping her arms around his ratty coat, Eliza sunk into his grip as though she hadn't rested in years.

Perhaps she hadn't. Not until she'd met Nemo.

"You are— How'd a Feo get to be so soft?" Eliza laughed breathlessly. "Let's give the pity party a rest, we've got a second wedding to plan!"

Nemo's flame flared up with freshly fueled excitement. "Oh, yes! I know we've done it before, and the venue's not as scenic this time, but now I can do this properly!"

With a rusty creak, Nemo kneeled down onto his fresh leg, visor sparkling in the dark. He held her hand gently, and this time, the warmth coming from it was a genuine comfort.

"I don't have a new coal to give, but… Eliza, will

you marr—?"

Eliza didn't let him finish. She threw herself into Nemo's arms with unrestrained joy, sinking down until they were on even, uneven footing.

"Yes!"

They held each other tight, embracing under a sea of countless stars. It was hard to tell the constellations from where they laid, but the shapes of the legends were written in the spaces between the lights, bound by unseen stories no matter the distance.

"...*in solemnizing the rites of matelotage between Eliza Preston and Nemo*—hm—*Nemo Preston, under the auspices of the law, as ordained by Cap'n Barret of* The Bastion, *and witneffed by...*"

The Bastion was the cleanest it had been in years, sailing on towards the faint silhouette of New Amrestir's skyline. The crew had taken pains to cull as much of the fungus away from the quarterdeck as they could, arranging benches, barrels and chairs in full-bodied attendance. Cap'n Barret stood at the stern of the ship with Quartermaster Autumns, scribbling to legitimize the last bits of legal documentation on a desk dragged up from the galley.

"...you lot, I s'pose. Anyways, *in accordance with maritime charter, do you agree to take each other as mates, and affume relation and obligations thereto pertaining*— Nate, what does this even be meanin'?"

"It's t-the entire p-point of the b-b-blasted ceremony!" barked Autumns. "R-Respect the p-p-paperwork!"

"Argh, fine! *Pertaining to the responsibilities granted therein*—yatta datta datta—The two of ye, do ye accept these terms of matelotage?"

Nemo looked to Eliza, standing by his side at the helm. She shone radiant in a strip of clean sailcloth, hastily sewn by the Quartermaster into a dress. Her hair had grown back a little over the course of their journey home, much to Nemo's joy, and now framed her face in soft but wild waves. There was a quiet beauty to her presence, a shock of purity against the rainbow of rot surrounding them.

"Absolutely, Cap'n."

Barret turned to face Nemo, a hint of a smile on his metallic jaw. "And ye, Nemo?"

From under the brim of Vitrail's stolen hat, Nemo stared into Eliza's eyes. He felt a tug at the sleeve of Eliza's hand-me-down navy coat, and heard a familiar ruffling of feathers.

"Hey, tin-man, it's your turn!"

Pauvus was at his place by Nemo's side, wrapped in bandages and a scavenged dress coat that he deemed clean enough. The Feo flickered back to business, and nodded up to the cap-packed Cap'n.

"I do."

"Brilliant!" Barret called, scrawling the last of his signature and slapping his quill to the desktop. "Well, now be the fun bit. Lad, ye said ye had vows in mind, aye? Speak yer truth freely, 'pon the open air."

The flame in Nemo's head swirled in elation. He'd practiced what he meant to say to Eliza countless times since the ceremony had first been planned, even though they changed little since he'd first said them back on their boardwalk.

"Eliza, I promise to provide and care for you, to stand by your side through every storm that comes our way. Whether the world will have us or not, I swear we will always have each other."

"*Ach*, what a smooth sailor ye be! Anything ye want t'add, Eliza?"

Eliza smiled, and squeezed Nemo's hands tight. "I promise to stand, *and fight*, by your side, *on equal footing*, through every storm that comes our way. Right, Nemo?"

"Ah, right, right. Sorry, thank y—"

Nemo didn't finish, as Eliza had pulled him into a deep kiss on the visor. The crew of *The Bastion* burst into cheers, and from somewhere in the mix a rifle shot burst into the sky. Pauvus clacked his talons in celebration, Barret wiped something from the side of his visor, and Autumns gave a polite cough.

"Y-yes, that was b-beautiful. You still n-n-need to sign, though."

Eliza snatched up the quill with a decisive wink at the Quartermaster and scribbled out the looping path of her signature. When she was finished, she passed it to Nemo with a reassuring pat of confidence. With an unshaking hand, the Feo etched the letters Eliza had taught him onto the paper with pride, taking in the sight of their names printed side by side.

Cap'n Barret plucked up the freshly inked document, raising it to the sky. "Here be to the good fortune of the Prestons! Oughtta be properly binding fer any across this Grand Sea, 'n if any be havin' qualms about that, they'd best take it up with the Rot Admiral!"

The license passed from one Feo's hand to the other, and Nemo clutched the proof of his love tight. Him and Eliza embraced once more to a chorus of applause from the Audience. Cap'n Barret capped off their celebration with a quick pipe from his flute, stepping around to signal the end of their business.

"Right then! Love to be keepin' ye around fer the afterparty, but we be comin' in hot on Amrestir, 'ere. Best to keep the welcome party small, else you be wantin' to see some real fireworks from shore. But before that…"

The Rot Admiral handed a neatly folded bundle to Eliza. She unfurled the wrappings to find a stack of letters, scrawled in varying levels of literacy.

"Been many a year since the lads've heard from home," Barret sighed, running a hand through his crest in a spray of spores. "It'd mean the world to 'em, havin' some link back to the land o' the living… meself included."

Nemo watched the Cap'n point out a particular letter to Eliza, the two of them sharing a moment of silence. Whatever the contents could be, he felt it wasn't his position to pry.

"Hey, Nemo, I've got somethin' for you, too."

Pauvus re-emerged onto the deck, carrying a suspiciously familiar carved box under his one good wing.

"Is that… Eliza's music box?" Nemo marveled. "How did you get your feathers on this?"

"Found it in the hold!" the Ave cooed, passing it into the Feo's hands. "Played with the key, figured it must've been hers when I heard the melody. How much of your pension did you blow on this thing?"

"Hoy, happy couple! And wingman! Yer ride awaits, matrimon'yal-like!"

Rufus was by the starboard-side rowboats, stringing up the last of the supplies and decorations. He gave a solid pat to the hull and a warm smile.

Nemo ran his hands along the smooth sides of the music box, and looked over to Eliza. She re-folded the bundle of homesick letters, eyes glittering against the growing backdrop of New Amrestir on the horizon.

"Shall we be off, Mr. Preston?"

The trio stepped off the rotting decks of *The Bastion* for what they dearly hoped would be the last time. Guiding Eliza to her seat in their spousal setoff ship, Nemo realized that he finally had a home to feel homesick for.

"...a timekeeping spout, a stuffed Lefanti toy, a ceramic crab pen holder, a Smoulder— Wait, is this a shopping list?! I thought these were letters!"

"Why are you reading through other people's mail?" Eliza questioned. "Isn't that supposed to be a federal offense in Aveila?"

Pauvus tossed the letter back into her lap, wincing slightly at the strain of his bandaged wing.

"I am no longer beholden to bird law. Besides, I'm not respecting anyone who asks for a penholder of all things after a decade of rotting at sea."

Eliza wrapped up the request bundle again, eyes rolling over a playful smile. It didn't feel right to deprive those poor sods of their privacy, even if the letter tantalizingly labeled 'Gilbetrine' was making it an ordeal to resist.

"Look, I'm in no position to judge what a dead man walking would ask for. They're not exactly in the best state of mind."

"Ceramic... crab?" asked Nemo, words stalling with each pull of the oars. "That sounds... familiar..."

The sea was marvelously still, even as they inched ever closer to New Amrestir. *The Bastion* had fled to the horizon the instant their little boat had touched water, and the bustle of the city's maritime traffic was quickly filling in the space. Eliza clutched the sides of the dinghy tight each time a full-size vessel scraped by, still getting used to not being part of the most threatening ship on the sea.

New Amrestir's tall lighthouse towered in the

distance, orbited by flocks of couriers and balloons. Each pull of the oars from Nemo dragged them back towards civilization, and all the things that Eliza had up until then let drift past her notice. She thought about Toni, Margaret, the countless citizens she'd never considered that she would miss seeing. Thinking about the messes the three of them had left in their wake, Eliza also couldn't help but wonder who exactly might be waiting for them in turn.

"*Oughhh*, Nemo!" Pauvus groaned dramatically. "What're you, getting tired? I want to sleep in my own bed tonight!"

Eliza turned to give Pauvus a sharp scolding, before she noticed the peacock longingly watching a mailman soar overhead. She let him rest his head on her shoulder, taking in a deep breath that was gloriously clean.

"He's rude, but he's right. There's a second set of oars here, Nemo, do you want a hand?"

Nemo shook his head, causing Vitrail's hat to swivel on his noggin.

"You've been… through enough… Eliza… I've got this… Just a lil'… longer, Paul… 'til we're back…"

"If you say so," Eliza relented, swapping the letters in her hand for the old music box. "Can't say I'm in a massive rush to get back, anyways. Toni's going to flay me for wasting that bean shipment of his."

The docks of the island town were nearly in view, as bright and vibrant as Eliza had seen in her restless dreams. Catching the wake of a fishmonger's ship, Nemo paused a moment to scrape his oar clear of a loose net.

"I'm sure he'll understand, once we get a chance to tell our story. Who knows, maybe we could be an inspiration for the folks on shore, another shot at a fresh start."

"I can already imagine the kind of frenzy the Press would get into over a headline about the 'First Metal Marriage'." Eliza shrugged. "I just hope we can get back home without being the talk of the whole town."

"I'm hoping we can get back home without being

arrested," Pauvus squawked. "Feel like they might still be a bit sore about me steering that coast guard ship into a disaster like that, don't need to add another international incident to our tally. And to think, all that without a speck of treasure!"

"I hate to... say it, but... Barret was right. You deserved that... gold as much as... any of those... pirate pests... Eliza."

As he tugged and toiled away, Eliza spotted the bulk weighing down Nemo's borrowed coat. She leaned back in her bench seat, feigning ignorance.

"You know Nemo, I absolutely agree. Unrelated, but check your inner pocket."

Letting them coast on their momentum, Nemo dropped one oar to fish into his pocket, and nearly dropped the other in surprise.

"*Bwuh?!* No, aren't these—?"

Nemo held up one half of the golden shears to the light. Both he and Pauvus inspected the gift in disbelief, giving the bladed edge a slight bend to test its legitimacy.

"Eliza, how'd you get that?" Pauvus chirped. "I thought those Stagnant saps were going mental over you having it. Don't tell me you out-plundered the pirates!"

With a grin, Eliza plucked up the treasure, feeling its surprising weight in her hand again.

"That'd make a great boast, but I'm not a thief at heart. On the ride back, Barret and Autumns told me they owed me back wages for the 'Dread Siren' position, and a wedding gift."

"More like a shopping budget," Pauvus grunted, getting comfortable again. "Must've been what those coordinates at the end of the list were for."

Nemo leaned forward to hold Eliza's hands in his, visor flaring with excitement.

"That'll barely make a dent in what this could be worth! Everything we could ever want or need, right at our fingertips. Like a golden ring! Freshly forged, just for you!"

"You're sweet as always, Nemo," Eliza laughed. "But you know I don't want anything like that. Gold is fine, but… I like brass much better."

She leaned in to give Nemo a peck. His metal was hot to the touch, but she no longer minded.

The welcoming ports of New Amrestir laid dead ahead, open with the possibility of a proper ending to this chapter of their story and a fresh beginning ahead. Nemo turned towards the shore, and called with the pride of a true sailor.

"Land ho!"

FIN.

ABOUT THE AUTHORS

Greg Lucci is an author, digital artist, marketer and general beach bum living in Long Beach, NY. An experienced writer and former Editor in Chief for Stony Brook University's literary magazine, Greg loves to amble and ramble down the beach talking shop with Kristina about all sorts of nonsense.

Kristina Shevlin is a born and raised Long Islander, a fact that she complains about frequently. After graduating from the College of Saint Rose with an MSED in Educational Psychology, she moved back home where she likes to take long walks on the boardwalk with her boyfriend/co-writer.

www.ingramcontent.com/pod-product-compliance
Lightning Source LLC
Chambersburg PA
CBHW011512100726
47899CB00010BD/3332